I, ALIEN HUNTER

A <u>LIQUID COOL</u> CYBERPUNK DETECTIVE NOVEL

Book Five

AUSTIN DRAGON

Published by Well-Tailored Books, California

I, Alien Hunter
(Liquid Cool, Book 5)

978-1-946590-58-9 (paperback)
978-1-946590-52-7 (ebook)

http://www.austindragon.com

Book cover design by Leslie K.

Printed in the United States of America

CONTENTS

Introduction

"I had never, ever dealt with—extraterrestrials." That was what I said in my last major case, *The Electric Sheep Massacre*.

I was a detective. Detectives are supposed to detect, and do detective things like surveillance, missing persons, routine investigations. I was still relatively new to the private eye biz in Metropolis, but already had dealt with government conspiracies, super assassins, secret megacorps, killer robots, killer cyborgs, and even killer clients. However, I was married now and had a kid. Those big "saving the world" cases had to become a thing of the past. I couldn't be doing that kind of craziness anymore. To quote my posthumous mentor, Wilford G., "For the street detective, boring is good. Boring keeps you out of the hospital and the morgue. Say 'Hallelujah, I love you boredom.' Curse the action, no matter how fancy your gun or how quick you are on the draw."

Then how did I find myself in it again?

Like any supercity on the planet or Up-Top, there were many sub-cultures in Metropolis. There were the standard fare—tattoos, sports, gaming, drugs, sex, virtual life cyberpunkers; the suave—cigar aficionados, classic hovercars, retro hat collecting; the brainiac—build-your-own-robots club, tri-dimensional chess, IQ 160 and beyond associations; and the more exotic like Jules Verne steampunkers, neon claw manicuring, competitive beard-growing, cybernetic parts-swapping, and toad licking (don't ask).

There were also Alienists—extraterrestrial watchers, I called them. I wanted nothing to do with any of it. There was a saying that even a broken clock was right twice a day. Well sometimes, the borderline mental patient did see what they said they saw. Not every fable was fiction or a daydream. Sometimes the myth, the urban legend, was based on something real—something tangible that could reach out and hurt you. Being a street detective that intended to live a very long life was all about realizing when something could reach out and hurt you. It didn't matter where it came from or what it was.

I found myself in a case where I wasn't just a private detective on the ever-rainy, gritty streets of Metropolis fighting "grime and crime." I became *I, Alien Hunter.*

PART ONE

The Thing From Above

CHAPTER 1

Oh, Baby!

Metropolis was the premiere supercity on the planet. Everything here was bigger—the mega-skyscrapers, the neon digital signs, the hovertraffic congestion, the pedestrian traffic below, the government bureaucracies, the megacity corporations, and so too the criminals. Liquid Cool had staked out its own tiny corner of the supercity for the last couple of years—and everyone noticed.

Rare was the day when it wasn't raining in Metropolis—today, it was especially fierce, so much so that it looked like night rather than noon, which it was. A yellow hovertaxi descended from the busy, but slow, sky traffic with white landing lights blinking.

"This is Circuit Circle?" the burly man in the back passenger seats asked.

"Yeah, this is Buzz Town," the taxi driver responded.

"That was fast. I mean with all this rain and traffic. I don't know how you guys can even see zipping up, down and around other hovercars like you do."

"I'm a professional." The driver smiled as he looked at the man in his rear view mirror.

"Is that your way of asking for a bigger tip?" the man's wife asked. The only expression on her face was a stern frown. The driver maintained his smile.

"Why shouldn't he want a bigger tip?" the man asked his wife. "We're here. And faster than we thought."

She ignored him. "This is the building?" she asked the driver.

"Main entrance right there." He pointed. "Watch how you walk though. I've seen people slip, fall and get washed away in flash floods on these streets."

"I don't why this city doesn't invest in hoverwalkways. The technology has been around for decades, but they won't do it," the wife said.

"You know why," the husband answered, though she was not at all interested when he started talking. "It's cheaper for them to pay the lawsuits than do so. That's how it always works."

"Well, I better not slip and fall and get washed away." She reached for the door, as her husband tapped on his mobile phone.

"Thank you, sir," the driver said.

"My wife doesn't, but I believe in tipping."

The driver handed him a business card he pulled from his breast pocket. "Call me anytime."

The husband took it.

"Come on, let's go," the wife nagged as she stepped out of the hovertaxi; her foot sloshed into the standing water. "It's a full-blown lake out here!"

The husband glanced at her and immediately turned back to stifle a laugh. His eyes caught sight of the driver in the rearview mirror, smiling again.

"I know you're laughing!" she yelled. "Get out of the taxi so I can kick some water on you and see if you find that funny." She continued with a stream of cursing under her breath, as she completely stepped out of the hovertaxi. "I'm standing in a damn lake! I'm in the middle of the city on a city street and I'm standing in a damn lake! Look at this! No wonder people get swept away in flash floods here! Look at this!" Her stream of cursing began again.

The husband was no longer smiling and shook the driver's hand. "If you keep her with you, I'll give you the biggest tip you've ever seen in your life."

The driver vigorously shook his head. "No thanks. In fact, can I have my business card back?"

Thirty-seven minutes later.

"You can go right in and have a seat," the cyborg secretary's voice said. "He'll see you right away; his 2 o'clock client is running late."

The husband and wife were in a much better mood, thanks to her attention. The wife walked into the detective's open private office first; her husband followed with their coats draped over one arm. Both of them stopped dead in their tracks. Standing in the middle of the office was a toddler with a menacing gun in one of his tiny hands. He looked up at them and aimed!

The couple stood in place not knowing what to do. The baby's eyes were locked on them. He wore a purple sweater and standard diapers, but the gun—it looked real, and he held it with ease.

"What's wrong?" They heard the secretary's voice ask. There was some kind of noise behind them—desk drawers closing, chair rolling; she appeared behind them. "Cruz! I'm gonna tell your wife on you! Your son is 'gun-baby' again."

I had noticed a scratch near the bottom drawer of my desk and was trying to rub it out with a cloth. I jumped up fast from behind my desk, seeing Cruz, Jr. "Oh, snaps!" I yelled out.

CHAPTER 2

Punch Judy

My Liquid Cool Detective Agency office was on the 100th floor of one of the many commercial mega-towers on Circuit Circle in Buzz Town. As my supposed "fame" grew, I received unsolicited landlord offers all the time to move to upper-level, "premium" offices. There was nothing premium about them. I didn't need a bigger office—at least not now—and nothing could beat the price of free. I still didn't know who my secret benefactor was who paid for the office, and probably never would. That was all fine with me; the office had become my home away from home.

Late in the morning, I strolled through the office door with Cruz, Jr. I knew what was about to happen. He was bundled up like an Eskimo, and since his mother had dressed him—my wife being one of Metropolis's ultimate fashionistas—that meant that ever piece of clothing on his little body was some major, high-end fashion statement. He had his skullcap, his coat—collar-up—down to his knees, his leggings, his little frubber booties. She even put a tie on him. The boy didn't know what had hit him. When I dressed him, he was smiling and giggling. When she dressed him, the boy was in a daze for hours afterward.

Then the coochie-cooing began. Children, grown adults, even seniors, who should know better, all turned into babbling monkeys when a baby came into their line of sight. I came into my office with Cruz Jr. in his hoverstroller and my cyborg secretary PJ—full name Punch Judy—who could punch a 300-pound, seven-foot male cyborg through a steel wall (and had) became a giggling mess—tickling my baby, making baby sounds, laughing.

PJ had short, dark crimson hair, a simulated mole—a dot, just above her lips—and her lipstick of the day was dark red. Nowadays, she dressed professionally—corporate skirts, but she kept her trademark sleeveless tops—to show off her bionic arms—and her heeled boots.

"I don't want your bionic paws all over my baby." I tried to shoo her away, but PJ kept coming, and now Cruz Jr. was giggling like a maniac so that meant the battle for me was lost. Who knew how long the coochie-cooing and baby-talking would last. "Here, you watch him then."

"Hello, Cruz Jr.," she said to him with her French accent, as she wiggled her bionic fingers at light speed. Cruz Jr. laughed and clapped his hands.

PJ took control of that hoverstroller, as if she owned the place. PJ was my secretary, at least that's the job I hired her for, but now she was office manager, video surveillance display watcher, bouncer (if needed), whatever. The receptionist-waiting area was her domain; my private office was mine. The door was open, and I walked right in. However, I stopped at the threshold and looked around.

I wanted to see what she changed. My wife was the ultimate stylist when it came to people. PJ was the equivalent when it came to interior design. In the main waiting area that seated up to eight people comfortably—two each on the couches, one each in the single lounge chairs—all geometric and purple in style around a glass table on a shimmering, neon powder blue rug. The reception table had her French fashion magazines—lots of pictures, few words. On the walls were pictures of my previous cases from the media. There was me with clients, megacorp CEOs, politicians like the mayor, shaking hands, major headlines: "Cruz Gets the Blade Gunner!" Yeah, PJ had it covered and had the wall covered too.

Her personal haute-couture workstation looked the same. There were her psychedelic posters on the wall, her fancy "modern" glass desk with see-through glass drawers, and both her boombox with her French language music playing low in the background on an infinite loop and her mobile computer. I stepped forward to see the metal barrier protecting it all with its decorations—pictures of Neo-France and more French words.

I looked at the LIQUID COOL DETECTIVE AGENCY neon sign right on the wall outside of my private office, which was the first thing to catch the eye for any new client. Something was different with the office, but I couldn't figure it out.

"You are useless, Cruz! You're supposed to be a detective," she snapped at me.

"What did you change?"

She stood there grinning, rocking a giggling mess, formerly known as my son, in his hoverstroller back and forth. He loved to laugh and clap at the same time.

I snapped my fingers. "The paint."

"Wow, Cruz. I'm glad no clients were waiting. Look how long it took you to realize that. The colors look nothing alike. You should have noticed as soon as you walked in."

"I was focused on the baby."

"What kind of detective are you? Where are your powers of observation?"

I shook my head. "I'm the detective who can pay your salary. Why again did we need to repaint the office?"

"We have to change up the office every so often, so it doesn't become stale in here. We need to maintain a good ambiance to attract the high-level, paying clients."

I laughed to myself. '*Paying*' was the key word, but I was no different. I had no patience for the non-paying client-set that were, unfortunately, very plentiful in this business. "How much did this cost me?"

She looked at my son. "Watch me prove your father has very poor observation skills for a detective." She looked up at me with a grin. "Why don't you tell me what color it was before I had it repainted?"

"It was blue before, and you changed it to one of your many favorite shades of purple."

"It's true. We have to match walls, furniture and carpet."

"And!" I raised my finger. "The original wall color was that blue-green sick mess."

"Impressive." She turned to look at my son again. "Your daddy does pay attention. He just plays the fool."

"You do know that paint needs to be changed every few years. All that bacteria, germs and grime gets into it—"

"Yeah. It called washing. Wash the walls, please, not replace them. One's cheap and effective. One's not—"

"Effective! Ha!" She turned to my son. "Isn't that right, Cruz, Jr.? Auntie PJ knows these things."

"Auntie PJ?!"

It was time for me to take back charge of my son!

Cruz Jr. was safely back in the hands of *moi* away from her—to use one of the only six French words I knew. One of the many things you wished for as a parent was the ability to grow a third or even a fourth arm, because you needed it. I passed my new coat rack near the door, but without that third arm, my tan coat had to stay put.

I moved to my new main desk, past the two chairs in front of it. The desk was bigger and badder than the last. It had to be bigger because I created a type of on-desk baby pen for Cruz Jr. so I could set him in his corner right in direct sight of me at all times. Both Dot and I learned the hard way that Cruz Jr. apparently possessed the ability to teleport himself across the room to be able to do things he shouldn't be doing, like trying to turn on the stove (was my son a latent pyro?) or get at the big, shiny cutlery that Dot's parents gave us for a wedding gift. Maybe he was a secret ninja in training too.

I set him down in his desk playpen on my super-desk. He had gotten to expect to be placed in his place—it was his designated workstation. He had his little toys scattered around, the six-inch railing around it to keep him from falling to the floor on his head; I flipped on the anti-bacterial light I had secretly installed in the ceiling above it. The last one was much better but it emitted a red light and, unfortunately, Dot walked in unexpectedly and thought I was microwaving our son. No amount of pleading that the first few years of a child was critical to keeping all the germs, bacteria and nastiness from him. She was unconvinced; my anti-bacterial light was snatched down from the ceiling and thrown down the trash chute. So, I secretly had this one installed with its invisible light. Some protection was always better than none, though he didn't seem to share my concern for his biological well-being. He was already putting toys in his mouth.

I walked to my coffeemaker to get my first cup of silk coffee. Then I whirled around to catch Cruz Jr. about to do something. He stared back at me with a deer-in-the-headlights expression.

"What was I about to catch you doing?" He smiled, then started his laughing and clapping. "I'm on to you, mister. You're not going to engage in any mischief in my place of business."

There was a *beep* and the silk coffee began to pour down into the cup. With my morning ritual commencing, I could begin my workday. Outside was the worst, and the rain droplets on the dark-tinted windows seemed to be the size of basketballs. I could barely see the line of adjacent monolith office tower buildings because of the growing storm.

When I walked around my desk and moved my chair to the side, I glanced up to the corner of my office where I had my own sitting area, my own arrangement of plush chairs around a glass table, all on another neon dark blue rug. Then my attention returned to all the printed messages in different piles on my desk. It was PJ's system: the "hot" pile; the "hold" pile; the "hell no" pile; and a few other miscellaneous ones, which was always changing. But there was no "hot" pile.

"PJ!"

My son looked up at me holding a toy in each little hand.

"I know! The hot pile is here!" She strolled in with a thick pile.

"What is all that?"

"Money—that's what it is. And your next client will be here soon. They're running late because of the storm."

I took the wad of messages from her. I didn't care for my messages being on the computer or on my phone. I wanted them printed "in the flesh," so I could physically sort them, carry them with me, or PJ could re-sort them. If it's not on the computer, no one can hack it. I scanned through it quickly. "What next client?"

"Last minute booking, but you had a reschedule so it works out."

"And they can pay?"

"They paid their retainer, as standard."

I looked up with a grin. Another of PJ's unilateral systems: charge potential client a fee to simply talk to me. Back in the day, PJ was a soldier in the punk-posh gang, Les Enfantes Terribles, in Neo-Paris, France. Haute-couture designer clothes—the most expensive right off the ranks of Goodwill—with fashion-matched combat boots, knuckle-studded, leather, half-gloves, and Devo-style half-helmets on their rainbow colored, punk hair. They were "royalty." Now my ex-felon employee was a real-life "corporatista" charging people just to talk with me.

I laughed.

"As long as it's no crazy clients."

"You have your super-desk now, so you don't have to worry about that."

My super-desk could withstand any kind of gunfire, laser-fire, even a bazooka attack. All my cases weren't super dangerous or "save the world" ones, but when they were a ton of serious violence came my way. My desk was going to be my impenetrable shield against any human, cyborg, robot, or weapon.

There was a steady beeping from outside at her desk.

"Be right back," she said, and dashed off.

It was the proximity alarm and meant that someone was coming. We had security cameras installed to watch the parking bays, elevator, hallways and main entrances. The front door had a metal detector arch embedded to detect weapons or cyborgs. My office had to have state-of-the-art security. I was "famous," which meant I attracted trouble. But PJ and I could handle it.

As I took my seat behind on my new chair to scan through the hot messages, I heard PJ speaking. There were two other voices, one male, one female. PJ would spend a bit of time with them doing "client care."

I could laugh, but it worked. She weeded out the crazy clients and would physically throw them out of office, if needed. My precious time could be spent with legitimate clients only.

"Now what is that?" I said with displeasure. My super-desk was less than a month old and I noticed a scratch. "Unbelievable." I rested the messages on the desk and opened my desk drawers until I found a cloth. "Junior, you have no idea how good your life is. No bills. No responsibilities. No headaches."

He just grinned at me, having no idea what I was saying. At first, I knelt down on the ground to inspect the damage to the bottom of the desk. I rubbed the scratch at first but then began to buff it, just like my days as a hovercar restorer. I hated scratches as many could attest to, and I had to obliterate them. Nothing else could be done until order was restored to the universe. At this point I was using serious force. Did PJ kick my desk with her combat boots? I was imagining all the ways the damage could have happened.

"Cruz! I'm gonna tell your wife on you! Your son is 'gun-baby' again," PJ yelled.

I looked up from behind my desk and there was a woman and man standing at the door frozen in place with looks of fear frozen on their faces. My eye caught sight of the empty Cruz Jr.-less playpen area on my desk. I jumped to my feet to see the little gremlin standing on the ground—with a gun in his hand—staring at me sheepishly.

"Oh, snaps!" I yelled.

CHAPTER 3

The Cosmos

This was a critical junction. Cruz Jr. was looking for that parental sign from me—even the most minute of facial twitches would speak with the whisper of thunder. For some reason, I was a natural when it came to baby psychology. If my wife, Dot, were here in my place, she'd yell at him, snatch the gun from his hand, and that would lead to a bawling fit—crying, screaming, and spitting that would last for hours. My wife was always focused on punishment; I was focused on not wanting to claw my ears out after thirty minutes of baby bawling. I walked to him and casually took the gun from his hands. I still did not understand how he got down from the desk with ninja-like efficiency and found the (unloaded) gun. PJ and I had so many guns around that it probably was under a table or couch that we couldn't see, but from his vantage point screamed "pick me up and put me in your mouth." Once the gun was in my jacket pocket, I picked him up and placed him back in his play-pen area on my desk.

All this time the husband and wife clients were watching me silently. PJ stood there with her bionic arms suppressing a smile. I walked around to my chair behind my desk, sat down again, and opened the top cabinet. First my hand pulled out the little fedora I recently bought from Harry's Haberdashery. Mine was tan, but I didn't want Cruz Jr.'s to be the same—his was pinstripe black. I removed his skullcap and placed his hat firmly on his head, then I got the other item. His little Sherlock Holmes Jr. plastic magnifying toy. It was the only toy that he didn't put in his mouth. My son was now "in uniform" and he became all serious, he tapped the magnifying glass toy a couple of times against his leg, and then he was done. He looked up at our potential clients. I looked at them too. "You both can have a seat now," I said.

The husband burst out laughing. The wife's eyes narrowed, giving me a disapproving stare. "Thank you, PJ," I said. She grinned, turned, and left my private office, closing the door behind her.

The door opened suddenly. "Oh, this is Mr. and Mrs. Cosmos." She disappeared again.

"Thanks, PJ." I gestured again to them to the chairs, as I sat.

The man was still laughing. The wife punched his arm and he began to quiet down. They slowly sat down in the chairs. Cruz, Jr. was watching them intently. The clients noticed and looked at me.

"How can my business partner and I help you?"

"Business partner?" the wife asked.

"Yes," I said. "This is the Liquid Cool Detective Agency. He's Liquid. I'm Cool." I looked at my son who was looking at me now. "Isn't that right, Liquid? You're the one who excretes massive amounts of liquid—nasty!" Cruz Jr. grinned with his toothless baby mouth.

"Do you always allow babies to carry guns in your office?" she asked.

"My business partner isn't a baby. He's a toddler. How can I help? I don't think you came all this way to talk about youth and guns."

They looked at Cruz Jr. again. "Is he going to sit there watching us?" she asked.

"Are you all going to be saying something inappropriate to me?"

"Well, no—"

"Then let's get on with it. He can't even talk yet."

"Shoot them," Cruz Jr. said.

The wife's eyes narrowed, and the husband laughed.

"Pretend you didn't hear that."

"We were told you were a professional, Mr. Cruz," she said.

"That assessment will be made entirely by you. Usually I'm judged by how I solve my cases, not by the behavior of my toddler son. But it's your choice, of course. Let me call my secretary back in and she can refund you your retainer—"

"Hold on a minute." The man made a "hold" gesture with his left palm. "That's not what my wife meant. We did come a long way, and we're not going to go all the way back in this storm for nothing." He turned to his wife now. "Stop alienating everyone. We need to hire him."

She gave a heavy sigh.

"What's the problem, Mr. Cosmos?" I asked.

"It's her brother, Mr. Cruz. He's missing. We heard you're one of the best when it comes to finding missing persons."

"I've been very successful with previous cases. Where in Metropolis did your brother go missing?"

"He didn't go missing in Metropolis. In fact, it didn't happen here on Earth."

Now, I was suspicious and they noticed my expression change.

"We didn't say it was a simple case, Mr. Cruz," he said.

"Mr. and Mrs. Cosmos, aside from the obvious two questions, how long has he been missing and what authorities are involved?"

"To answer all three of your questions, Mr. Cruz," the wife said with authority, "he disappeared on a space freighter en route to Earth a year ago, and the Martian and Interspace Police are involved. We're Earthers to them, which means they won't even give us the courtesy of a response to any of our inquiries."

I leaned forward in my chair. "Mr. and Mrs. Cosmos, I don't mind a difficult case, or one with some danger." I pointed to Cruz Jr. quickly. "Don't tell your mother." He smiled, as I turned back to the Cosmos. "But the case has to at least be in Metropolis on planet Earth. What is it that you were expecting me to do with a year-old missing persons case that didn't even happen on the planet?"

"The case is coming to you, Mr. Cruz," Mr. Cosmos said.

"Coming to me?"

"The space freighter has been in flight from Mars to Earth for the past year," Mrs. Cosmos said. "It is scheduled to land on Earth, right here in Metropolis, in just over two weeks."

I may have been a private detective without decades of on-the-street experience yet, but I had better-than-average street smarts. This was one of those clients who brought you a case that had the kind of backstory that meant it was either dangerous, unsolvable or both. The wisest course of action was to stay away from it with a ten-foot pole.

"Mr. and Mrs. Cosmos, I may not be the detective for you. My business partner doesn't want me taking cases like this anymore."

"But you don't even know all the particulars yet," Mr. Cosmos said.

I shook my head. "I haven't even told you the instructions I've gotten from the wife. Space freighters, Martians, Interspace Police. What else do I need to know? Something like this even Metro Police wouldn't have jurisdiction, so what exactly would I be doing? When I do missing person cases I am always very upfront with those that hire me. If it's an open case with the police, I have to tread lightly. Only if it's a cold case, can I do whatever we like. A case, any case, that involves Up-Top police authorities is what I call a 'radioactive case,' meaning we have to stay away. You don't want to get entangled with Up-Top police. But you both know all this already."

Mrs. Cosmos was one of those people who made judgments about people very quickly, rightly or wrongly. If she thought you were a bum, then she would keep that impression of you for the duration. I could tell Mrs. Cosmos thought I was a bum. "I bet if we paid more money you'd help."

"In the past, yes, you're right, I would. But now I'm a man with a wife, a kid, a Pony, and a cool hat. I need my life to be as boring as possible for a detective. People want to hire detectives for everything under the sky—legal and illegal. Sometimes, it is simply to use them as a patsy. The detective gets into the trouble that you want to avoid for yourself."

"That's not the situation here," she said. "We need someone to help us. We were told with your connections and reputation that it was you."

"See my secretary on your way out. She'll refund your retainer, and you can find a detective from the Net who's less danger-adverse than me and can solve off-world cases with their feet on planet Earth. Unfortunately, that's not me."

"And doesn't have a wife, kid, car, and hat," the wife interjected.

"A Ford Pony is not a hovercar. It's a high-performance vehicle."

The man burst out with a laugh.

"We're not lying about anything," the wife said.

"I never said you were lying about anything, which now makes me wonder."

"We haven't told you the whole story, but you're kicking us out before we can."

"I'm saving you the trouble."

"Why can't you decide *after* you hear the whole story," she snarled.

"Okay, let's skip ahead." I pulled my desk vid-phone closer. "Give me the name of your son and the name of the space freighter. I have contacts within both Interpol and the Martian police. I can get all the details within two minutes." I looked at them with my finger above the dial button of my desk vid-phone. "Son's name? Freighter's name?"

"You know Up-Top police?" the husband asked.

"Yep, at the very top," I answered.

Both of them sat there with their eyes darting around in their heads, thinking.

"We didn't know that," the wife said, looking down at her hands rather than at me.

I glanced at Cruz, Jr. "See what I have to deal with."

He shook his head, too, as he briefly banged his magnifying toy against his leg.

"It's not what you think, Mr. Cruz," Mrs. Cosmos said. "We're not trying to be deceptive. We're actually trying to shield you from them."

"Them?"

"Yes, them." The man pointed upwards to space; the wife nodded in agreement.

"Another conspiracy case. I'm definitely not doing any more of those."

"We're not trying to be funny," she said. "You make that call, they'll send their agents after you and us."

"Their agents? Them?"

"The men in black," he said.

"Men in black? Is that capital 'M' and capital 'B' or is the 'I' in 'in' capitalized too?"

"He thinks we're crackpots," the man said to his wife.

"Or practical jokers," the wife added. She stood from her chair. "We're neither, Mr. Cruz. My brother's disappearance is every bit as real as your baby is. But at this point, you won't believe us no matter what we say. Investigate us then. You'll see that it's all real. My brother is missing, and his space freighter will arrive for planet touchdown in two weeks."

"What does your brother do?"

"He's a...xenobiologist."

"Why did you hesitate in answering that question?"

"Never mind." She looked at her husband with a frown. "Get up, you. We have to get back. I bet you left all the windows in the apartment open, even though I told you to make sure you closed them."

The husband stood. "I did close the windows."

"Our place is probably already flooded with this storm."

"I closed the windows."

"No, you didn't."

"Well, Mr. and Mrs. Cosmos," I interrupted, "my secretary will refund your retainer and good luck with your case."

"Good luck on 'your' case?" she asked. "'Our' case Mr. Cruz. You're our detective, Mr. Cruz. I have full confidence that you'll find my brother, no matter what happened to him. You'll find him."

I had already pressed my under-desk signal button. PJ opened the door and came in to show the Cosmos out. They didn't say goodbyes or anything else, which was fine with me.

As PJ did her thing, I had to do mine. Bundle up Cruz, Jr. to pass him on to the wife. PJ appeared back in the office.

"Are they gone?" I asked.

"On their way to the elevators."

"Refunded their retainer?"

She gave me a look. "They said they hired you."

I shook my head, as I re-acquired Cruz Jr.'s fedora and magnifying glass toy for the safety of my desk. "I want you to do a media background check on them and full background on any family they have."

"Yes, full checks."

"Is xenobiology a real occupation?" I was walking to my personal office reception chairs for Cruz Jr.'s hoverstroller.

"Study of extraterrestrial life?" PJ began to laugh. "Is that what they said their missing person does? Mon Père used to say from prison that was an occupation for people who didn't want to work. They want to play but sound like they work, but they do nothing."

"Do you know you just mixed French and English again?"

"What? When?"

"You said *mon père* instead of 'my father.' This is not the French territories. English, s'il vous plais!"

She grinned. "Ah, so you can speak some French after all. No, not *Papa*—though he was in prison too—Mon Père. He was a crime boss in Neo-Paris."

"The world of an ex-posh gang member." I was not about to wait around to hear more about her criminal family and associates. "I need to go get Cruz. Jr. to Dot on time."

She held up her bionic arms. "But don't dump them as clients, even if they're mental. These Cosmos have lots of money."

"So, running illegal financial checks on people again, are we?"

CHAPTER 4

The Doorman

Mr. Post was the Concrete Mama's doorman-in-chief. He worked the day shift and personally oversaw the security of the entire building and was a welcome presence in the main ground-floor lobby, especially for the seniors in the building many of who still braved the rain for their daily power-walks outside for exercise. Mr. Post was Puerto Rican like me, but unlike me could speak other languages like Chinese, Japanese and Hebrew. He was also a retired cop which more than made up for the building's previous "bad" hire.

We were both working on a situation that involved the Concrete Mama and all its tenants. I took the elevators to the lobby to see him and he gave me the address of the ring leader of a new Rabbit City gang terrorizing the district.

"Hi little Cruz." He wiggled his fingers at my son. Even he wasn't immune to the spell of newborns.

"This is the leader?" I asked him.

"The head gangster himself, but the police can't touch him. He has these kids do all his crimes for him, and he sits back and collects the profits."

"Rabbit City may not be Silicon Falls or Opus Fields, but decent people live here and should be able to live here without being harassed by street punks."

"They know what they're doing. They never kill anyone, so with everything the police have to deal with—"

"It remains low priority." I wasn't happy, but it was the largest supercity in the world, and the police had to prioritize. "My wife and kid live in this building. My parents visit."

"Your wife's parents."

"They don't count," I said. He chuckled. "I'll see what I can do."

Mr. Post nodded. "I know that you will."

"The leg?"

"Nothing broken."

"Our own doorman can't even get to his hovercar without being mugged. This is not cool. I deal with madness at work; we don't need it following us back here. I'll take care of it."

He nodded again.

The Concrete Mama was a like a chunk of granite set down on Earth from space in the middle of Rabbit City. The district wasn't an upscale neighborhood, but it wasn't the dumps. Working-class and legacy babies all mixed in together, but regardless, it was no reason for the streets not to be safe. Every few years street gangs tried to move in, but there were always parents and residents to lead the charge to get rid of them. Now—it was my turn at neighborhood action. I was a parent, and strangely the people in our tenant building looked to me for leadership. Not too long ago, they were all trying to figure out ways to get me out of the building despite my legacy housing; now I was the "leader." I had to thank Dot more than anyone in changing attitudes, and the doorman. Mr. Post had the respect of everyone, so if he liked me, they would too. (I'll skip the circumstances where I shot dead the previous, and first, doorkeep—who was actually a psycho gang leader who was planning to blow up the entire Concrete Mama to get me.)

CHAPTER 5

China Doll

The Concrete Mama had been home for fifteen years—Dot moved in when we got married. My legacy housing was willed to me from my maternal grandparents. My parents had their own, so it was passed to me. I was on the 100th floor, but we switched with a couple who wanted a smaller and more modest apartment. Now, Dot and I were on the 150th floor.

I'd made good time getting home with Cruz Jr. despite the rain. In such weather, the problem wasn't the rain, but the people in the sky who suddenly didn't know how to drive with more rain. It always rained so whether it was light or heavy shouldn't have made any difference with their hovercar driving.

I was proud of myself. I got back to our place before Dot. She was going to take charge of Cruz Jr. for the rest of the day. Here I was, completely free to do my baby duties, which meant diaper changing. This one task above all others separated the men from the boys. If you were a germophobe, like me, and could accomplish it, then you deserved special recognition from the human race.

There was nothing like a good, clean bio-suit. Babies had their blankets and fluffy robot toys. Adult germophobes had good, clean bio-suits. Nothing like it could give that cosmic confidence to protect you from the invisible world of nasty germs. It didn't take me long to put mine on. Amazing was the word that always came to my mind when I pulled it on. Back in the day, they were bulky and it took like an hour to put on. They were thick, hot (despite inner climate control), suffocating and uncomfortable. These days they were like a second skin that you could put on in less than three minutes. They were so comfortable you could dance in them. The faceplate never fogged up and you always felt comfy—inner climate control systems had come a long way. My bio-suit even had internal lights and enhanced visuals. The gloves were so precise you could pick up a pin. I loved my bio-suit. It was the perfect protection for any kind of biological strike, plague, or contagion, nuclear blast, the zombie apocalypse (okay, that's not real) or changing diapers.

Even better was the inner lining of the modern bio-suit was so supple, I swore they treated it with some kind of cat-nip for human germophobes. You didn't want to take them off. Then, there were the aromatic filters! Stuffy internal climates of previous bio-contamination suits were a thing of the distant past. Your nose was treated to the beautiful delight of lilacs, daisies, "new car" smell—

"Cruz!"

My wife's voice rang in my ears despite my gear. I turned to face her, fully-clad in my bio-suit. She went by China Doll, but women who knew her called her China; men called her Doll. Only her family and me called her by her real name—Dot.

"Cruz, what are you doing?"

She was the consummate fashionista with every piece of clothing, every accessory, and every piece of jewelry being the trendiest and the most stylish. Today, she was adorned in a luminescent halter top under a glossy leather jacket, a sapphire blue pearl belt wrapped around her waist, black skintight pants, and topped off with black heels, adorned with faux-diamond glitter. Her hair was tied back, with the ponytail carefully resting on one shoulder, always a colored neck scarf—today was basic black—and her makeup was always perfect and never overdone. Every finger had a colored ring, and each wrist had multiple bracelets.

She stood with hands on her hips. This was not going to be a friendly conversation.

"Cruz, I know you aren't in a bio-suit to change your son's diapers. A bio-suit that is used for post-nuclear fallout—"

"And diaper-changing."

"Cruz!"

Even the dumbest man would have advised me to keep quiet, but I had to interject. "Dot, I have suppressed most of my germophobia. Can't I have one psychological crutch?"

"No!" I frowned in my bio-suit, but she could see my face clearly. "Considering how your son was brought into being—" I grinned. "Your germophobia seems to be very selective—comes and goes whenever you feel like it."

"That's why it's called a psychosis. It doesn't make sense."

"Whatever. Next time you come by me with fish lips—"

The Hellspawn appeared at the doorway! Dot was actually the spitting image of her father, only female. Mr. Wan was dressed in an almost glowing white shirt, with what looked to be various animals embroidered around the collar and the sleeves. Mrs. Wan was in black pants but wore a beautiful electric blue top. She was shorter than Dot, with shoulder length hair.

"Fish lips?" I protested, not to be distracted by Dot's parents.

"I'm going to put up my hands and tell you I cannot participate in the willful corruption of a germophobe with OCD tendencies."

Mrs. Wan, Dot's mother, was watching me with a sneer. Mr. Wan was laughing as he made fish lip faces at me.

"Dot! Your parents are in the room!"

"Kiss my burrito." He was making the fish-lip faces again.

Good grief! I had no idea what Mr. Wan meant by that, and I didn't want to know. This whole situation was going from bad to worse. Mrs. Wan was yelling something at Dot in Chinese. Cruz Jr. was wiggling around lying on his back on our changing table in the bedroom, sans pants.

"Okay, okay. I'm taking it off. But, not the surgical gloves. Diapers are nasty! Don't they have robots to do this?"

"No!"

"How about the Hellspawn? What if we pay them?"

"My parents are not here to change their grandson's diapers."

"Why are they here?" I said in half-whispered tone.

Mrs. Wan shook her finger at me, yelling something in Chinese at me. I'm so glad I couldn't speak any Mandarin, Cantonese or whatever version they spoke. It spared me from the insults. Mr. Wan was continuing his fish-lip pantomime.

"Cruz!"

I muttered something as I took off the helmet first, then the rest of the bio-suit slowly. How dignified was—the "famous detective"?

"Diaper changing is nasty!"

"Cruz!"

Even Cruz Jr. Was laughing, watching me with big eyes.

"Why are you laughing? You're not laughing at me. I'm the guy about to change your diapers without my bio-suit. I should get hazard pay."

"Cruz!"

"This is the future! In the future robots are supposed to do the things humans won't."

"Cruz, there will be no robots touching my child, let alone anywhere near his private parts."

My face winced. She had a point there. It would be nice to have grandkids in the future. I looked up, and the Hellspawn were pointing and laughing at me. It was time to vacate the premises.

CHAPTER 6

The Cosmos

I drove a bright red, classic Ford Pony—my public statement to separate myself from the masses. A sleek, bright red muscle-vehicle—high-performance, super-charged, advanced nitro-acceleration hydrogen engine.

I had found the shell in a junkyard as kid in middle school, and it took me a few years to build and restore it, spare part by spare part. I had been upgrading it ever since. No one believed that I found and built such an expensive muscle hovervehicle from scratch, but it was true, and I drove it every day. It was considered a true classic and got me solid offers to part with it almost every week, but you don't sell a classic Ford Pony; it's a purchase for life—like legacy housing. My Pony had been featured (without my permission) in so many hovercar magazines that I lost count. My latest modifications to my vehicle was making it baby-friendly. That was the phrase I used with the wife and her colleagues; the real phrase was baby proof. My Pony was a classic in mint condition, but even it couldn't withstand the onslaught of an average baby. I had installed a retractable baby seat in the back that my wife thought was so cool (Yes!) I also installed a hard plastic barrier that covered every inch of the backseat area, and protected any exposed part of the front area that could possibly take incoming spittle-fire from Cruz Jr., all activated with the touch of a button.

Before the modifications, the very thought of a baby—any baby—in my vehicle made me break out in a nervous sweat. Now, it was no big deal at all. I hit the "baby button" and the plastic covering and baby seat disappeared from view. The Pony was now in "Private Eye" mode for me to do some real work.

I noticed that hovercars were avoiding one particular vehicle like the plague, and I was staring at it to figure out why. The storm had tapered down a bit, but visibility was still not the best. Cautiously, I neared the vehicle that was driving in the fast lane, but was definitely not driving fast.

"Oh no!" When I saw the "STUDENT DRIVER" neon sign on the back of the hovercar, I slowed and dove my vehicle into another lane.

The only thing more dangerous than a criminal maniac in a hovercar trying to escape the police was a teenager in a hovercar talking to all their friends on the dashboard vid-phone. Even more dangerous than that was a student driver, usually a 15 or 16 year old, arms gripped on the steering wheel, pale-faced, sweating from fear. Whenever you heard of an accident where one or more hovercars crashed and "returned to the surface," the first question you asked was: high-speed chase or student driver?

As a contrarian, if people went left, I wanted to go right. But in this case, everyone was right. I increased my distance from the student driver who wasn't even flying properly in the sky-lane. No sane person would be a student driving instructor, so that left the insane and criminal to take those jobs. I was about to call 911 on them—I had to be more civic-minded these days with a kid of my own now—but a police cruiser descended from the sky behind them with flashing sirens.

I was on my way to see the Cosmos. The bickering husband and wife team said I was going to be their detective. I wasn't. I had learned my lesson the hard way that when your instincts tell you to avoid a potential client as if they have the Bubonic Plague, then do it. But then something peculiar happened.

The Cosmos lived near the Hinterlands. This was the scene—both beginning and ending—of my last major case, The Electric Sheep Massacre, and where I had the "pleasure" of playing Death Race 3000 with crazy feral hover-roadsters. I had avoided the area for most of my life, and now I was going back to same place again. Again, my instincts were yelling at me to leave this one alone, but I ignored it because of that peculiar thing that happened before.

I didn't even know that farms existed anymore. Well, that wasn't true, I did know. My own Good Kosher market had their own farms that customers like me swore by for natural food produce. It was reasonable to assume that others, unlike the general public who didn't mind assembly-line-created food products, would also want to grow their own food away from the government or megacorporations. The Cosmos were part of their own autonomous, self-sufficient community.

Free Earth. Their own little city was called Free Earth, nearly 30,000 people outside of Metropolis proper on the way to the Hinterlands. The place looked desolate, spotted with dozens of geodesic domes. If I had seen a photo of them, I would have incorrectly thought it was a picture of the early lunar colony settlements. I wondered if that was the intent of their architectural design.

As I landed the Pony, I surveyed the land through the dust cloud created by my vehicle. Just because I didn't see anyone didn't mean there wasn't anyone. Unfortunately, being so far from the supercity meant I couldn't call for any mobile security to watch my vehicle. Wherever I landed, my Pony would be as alone and helpless as I was.

I lifted my driver's door and stepped out into the rain. *Pop!* I heard the sound, but didn't see where it came from. I stood and looked around me. *Pop!* The shot landed six feet away from me, throwing up a geyser of dirt. I drew my omega-gun without a thought as I ducked down.

I saw two, no three figures running to me from the domes. Another shot landed near me. I did not like getting shot, especially when I didn't know who or why. But what was foremost in mind was that these maniacs might hit my vehicle. I ran away from the Pony to keep their shots as far away from it as possible, and showed the maniacs that I could play cops and robbers for real too.

I pulled my new monocle device from my coat—it fitted over my right ear and hung over my right eye—now I could see them plainly. Two men and a humanoid robot were doing the shooting; I aimed and fired. I blew that robot to bits, showering and knocking the two men to the ground.

The rain had started to pour again, but it was not going to deter me. I ran to them, ignoring the falling rain and growing water pooling on the ground. I wanted to be upon the two men before they could do anything else.

"Why are you shooting at me?" I aimed my weapon at the two men, still on their backs, stunned. "Don't make me ask you again! You should know I don't like to get shot or shot at."

"This is private property!"

"We are on public land. Are you telling me the surface of the Earth is your private property? Okay, let me just shoot you and I'll go about my business." I aimed at the man.

"No! We didn't shoot you. The robot did it."

"The robot did it? Is that supposed to be funny? Judge, I didn't shoot that man. My robot did it."

"Okay, we told him to shoot at you," the other man chimed in.

"Is it wise to have lethal robots running around shooting people? Some of those people might shoot back."

"They're not to shoot people. We need them for the super-rodents."

"Super-rodents?"

"Rats."

"I know what a rodent is! You said super?"

"Because they're huge. We need the robots to keep them away from our crops, or they'd eat everything—crops and small animals, babies even, if they could get to them."

I closed my eyes for a second to focus. Rats, rodents, meant nastiness. Before I knew it I would be running to my Pony like a screaming infant.

"I'm not interested in your baby-eating super-rat myths. You had your robot shooting at me, and despite what you may want to think, I'm not a nasty, furry, beady-eyed rodent. Rats don't drive red hover-vehicles, at least not yet."

"We wanted to keep the firefight away from our city."

"Firefight? What firefight? I'm a private detective coming to see some people."

"Private detective?"

"You do know what that is?"

"You're not with the government."

"Are you two high on narcotics? You shoot at people who you think are working for the government. Does that strike you as intelligent behavior?"

"Well, when you put it like that, no, but we didn't know what else to do."

"What people are you hear to see?"

"The Cosmos."

"Oh!" The men said it in unison and their whole demeanor changed. "You're Cruz."

"Yes, I'm Cruz."

One man smiled. "You blew up our robot with one shot." He looked at the other man. "We got him on our side and we'll stop those MIB goons good!"

"MIB? Whatever they are, I'm not stopping them or anyone else until I speak with the Cosmos."

The men began to get to their feet. "We'll tell them you're here."

I reluctantly put my omega-gun away. "What about my vehicle? I'm not leaving it out there unguarded."

"Oh, we have more robots. We'll have them stand guard."

"Yes, program them to shoot anyone that comes near it—but not me!"

The men laughed. "No, we won't have them shooting at you again." I was glad to see that I was their pal now rather than the target of their lame homicidal tendencies.

"Mr. Cruz, I knew we'd be seeing you again."

I turned, and there was Mrs. Cosmos approaching me clad in a gray slicker, holding a large umbrella. Behind her, not too far away, was the husband.

"Mrs. Cosmos, good to see you again. I met your friends and their late robot."

She reached us and looked at the burnt out remains of the robot. She threw the dirtiest look at the two men.

"We thought he was M.I.B." one of them said.

She was about to let loose on them for their unacceptable response when Mr. Cosmos saved the day. "Why are we standing here in the rain? Are we ducks or some other aquatic mammal? Mr. Cruz, follow us inside."

"Howard, ducks are not aquatic animals," Mrs. Cosmos added. "They're birds."

Maybe I should have let the robot shoot me, so I wouldn't have to hear the Cosmos's nonstop bickering with each other.

Outside their geodesic multi-dome community looked decrepit, like they were in need of centuries-old repairs. Inside was a completely different story—it was a ruse. Inside was state-of-the-art tech, clean and, even I had to admit, homey. I was ushered into an elevator. When we stopped, and the rusty door opened, I was in awe. An underground cavern carved out of the rock with the pedestrian street level at the lowest level, and underground towers—the tallest seeming to be about 10 stories—rose to the cavern's ceiling. Was any of this legal? I put the question out of my mind immediately—not my concern. It really was a city with the inhabitants underground—the people looked like residents of any of part of Metropolis—men, women and children. However, there were also plenty of armed male and female guards with big laser rifles.

"Why are you living underground?" I asked. I had never been to the lunar colonies—one of the space stations was the closest I got and I was not eager to ever return to space—but I had seen plenty of photos of them. "And why does your city look like the lunar colonies?"

While the average city street in Metropolis, from a pedestrian standpoint, was filled with an endless display of neon moving pictures of every product under the sky, all their advertisements had to do with space: newsfeeds of space flights, freighter transports, space stations, the lunar colonies, Mars and—

"There are no colonies on Jupiter and Saturn," I said.

Everyone around me started to laugh. I didn't know I had told a joke. The elevator had gone all the way to the bottom level and we exited onto a street with skyscraper towers, as tall as twenty floors. The massive ceiling was covered with holoscreens to project the stars.

"What is all this?" I asked. "You all created your own lunar-like colony underground? Why would you do that? You like the moon so much, move there."

"We're Earthers and like the Earth. Besides, all of Up-Top is controlled by *Them*."

"Here we go again. Them. There is no 'them.'"

The couple stopped. "Why are you here then, Mr. Cruz?"

"I want you to tell me your case, and then I'm leaving."

"Tell you our case and find my brother? You met *them* didn't you?" Mrs. Cosmos was no dummy. She knew something prompted me to semi-change my mind.

"I had a very peculiar situation happen."

"Wait," Mr. Cosmos said. "Let's get inside and tell everyone. They'll want to hear too." Mrs. Cosmos nodded.

I thought I was being led to their apartment; instead, they brought me to room that truly looked like Mission Control at the Metro International and Interspace Airport Transportation Authority. The screen had visuals on all departing and arriving spacecraft to Metropolis. I shook my head as I looked around. I had seen the psychosis before—civilians monitoring authorities. In the police world, we called the civilians who monitored the police bands 24-7 scanner junkies. It followed that other government authorities would have their own versions. Mr. and Mrs. Cosmos were spacecraft watcher junkies, and they even created their own city.

"I have one question for both of you," I said. "How many medications do you take—for real?"

"I'm glad we amuse you, Mr. Cruz," she said.

"Mrs. Cosmos, I have a wife, a kid, a red vehicle and a cool hat. I'm in a profession as dangerous as being a street police officer. I do not need to look for any additional trouble or craziness. Look at all this from my point of view. I come down to an underground city that looks like a lunar colony. You're monitoring space flights. You're watching satellites. You're watching who knows what else. You're civilians! This is not normal behavior for civilians."

"I know you think we're crazy," Mrs. Cosmos said, "but as citizens we have every right to monitor the space activities of the government."

"What about the megacorps?"

"We monitor them too."

"I'm leaving."

"Wait, you said you had something peculiar happen to you. What was it?"

I was going to leave. I was, but the re-asking of that question made me pause. I had an audience now. A room full of people watching me— all ages, ethnicities, nationalities, and walks of life—the entire rainbow of crazy people.

"Well, I was coming out of my office—"

PJ had noticed the man. Right after the Cosmos got out of their hovertaxi and ran out of the storm into the lobby for the elevators, she noticed him get out of a black hovercar that swooped down. He missed them in the lobby, but watched the numbers to see what floor they were getting out on. I always hated those indicators. He then went to the lobby directory display to scroll through all the businesses on the 100th floor.

PJ was onto to him and from her reception desk/command center quickly logged into the building directory database with those bionic fingers and changed the floor of Liquid Cool to read 10th floor instead of 100th, so he couldn't find us. Good plan, but he just decided to come up anyway.

I whirled around and pointed my gun at the man standing in the hallway. He stopped in shock. I was very suspicious about strangers in the hallway, especially after my NeuroDancer case.

"Do you always point guns at strangers, mister?" he said.

"Do you always sneak up on people in dark hallways? Who are you? What do you want?"

"I'm government."

"Show me some ID."

"I don't have to show you any ID."

"Why don't I shoot you, and then I can get your ID off the body?"

"I wouldn't do that, Mister. That's a felony. They lock people up for that here and off-world."

"Are you a spaceman, spaceman?"

"Why do you think that?"

"If you were from Earth, you would have said Up-Top, like everyone else. Only spacemen and Martians—space women too—say off-world."

I could see he was annoyed with himself.

"Why is a spaceman sneaking around, and this ain't space?" I cocked my weapon for show.

"Hold on one minute, mister. Can I make a call?"

"Why should I?"

"One call. Your mobile."

I began to lower my gun a bit. I took out my mobile phone. The man rattled off a number. "Voice." I repeated the number. The man smirked, as we waited—I didn't take my eyes off of him.

"Cruz," Chief Hub's voice answered, annoyed. "How did you get this number?" It was Chief Hub, the Chief of the Metropolis Police Department.

"Chief Hub," the stranger called out. "Can you have your man stand down? Agent Sol on assignment."

"He's not my man," Hub said.

"Do I need to call my director?" Sol asked.

"No, you don't need to call your director." Hub was even more irritable now. "Cruz, what trouble are you causing now?"

"It was Them!" a man yelled.

Conspiracy theorists weren't a new thing to me. When I was in the hovercar racing scene, they too had their conspiracy theories. It was endless: megacorps making hoverengines that exploded after a certain mileage so you would buy a new one to keep up sales, or the government using "secret" rays that added alcohol content to your blood, so when the police pulled you over you could never "beat" their alcohol breath-test. You'd go to DUI jail; they'd get your vehicle. It was the mental rabbit hole that had no bottom. I was talking to such people.

How did an average government agent have Chief Hub's private mobile number? Why were government agents following my not-clients? If it wasn't for that, I would have put the Cosmos out of my mind for good and moved on with life. Up-Top government agents sneaking around...*now* I was interested, even if it was out of pure curiosity. I was the boss, so I could take a case out of simple noisiness, if I wanted to. Besides, and more importantly, they were already paying me.

"Mr. and Mrs. Cosmos," I said in a soft tone. "Why don't the three of us—only the three of us, sit down. I'm a silk coffee man myself."

"We don't have anything so fancy. Coffee black and we're in business."

"Then coffee black it is. I want to sit down and have you tell me all about your brother. I don't want to hear about 'them' or anything like that. Tell me about your brother."

As a subterranean city, the apartments went down into the ground not up in the sky. Their housing complexes were much smaller, and when they led me down a few hallway turns I noticed that all the apartment doors had Roman numerals. Didn't think they were in use anymore. In we went into their place—much smaller than a standard apartment I was used to, even compared to Free City, but home was home. This was theirs, and they didn't need to please or impress anyone but themselves. We sat in the living room after we got my coffee from their auto-beverage dispenser.

It was the first time I had seen Mrs. Cosmos act like a human with feelings rather than someone always trying to prove how smart she was. Even Mr. Cosmos seemed different. They gave me my cup of coffee—they didn't take anything—and sat across from me. Mrs. Cosmos fidgeted with her hands and Mr. Cosmos had his in a death grip, visibly nervous. It was as if no one had ever asked them the simple question before.

"Now, tell me about him. What's his name?" I asked.

The wife glanced her husband for a moment, then turned back to me.

"Neil. Parents named him after the first man on the moon. I used to call him Neily as a child—when we were both children."

"What did he want to be when he was a kid?"

Mrs. Cosmos smiled, looking down at her hands, as a fond memory came to mind. "He always wanted to do something that had to do with the stars. He always was looking up at the stars, even when most of the time he couldn't see them through the rain clouds.

"Neily always said there was life in the universe, and he wanted to be one of the ones to find it. He was so smart. Read through books that most of the population could never understand themselves, but it was basic to him. He finished top of his class and in half the time. I always knew we'd be losing him to the stars."

Mrs. Cosmos's eyes were tearing up. She looked at her husband. "All three of us grew up together. Actually, most of us here at Free Earth, we all grew up together, almost as one huge family.

"Neil rose very quickly in the scientific ranks on Mars, despite being an Earther. But he got very disillusioned with the bureaucracy. He wanted to do more, go everywhere, but the bureaucracy was holding him back. He transferred to the Jupiter Outpost. Yes, Mr. Cruz, there is one. It's a mining colony, mostly robots mining the asteroids. That's where he ended up. He said that Mars was too much under the thumb of the authorities. He said he had to go further and went to Saturn.

"We didn't hear from him as often as before. He was busy. He was their chief exploration scientist, the head scientist, in fact. Then his messages stopped completely. We tried not to worry. Then about 18 months ago, we received a message from him."

"More than one," her husband added.

"Yes, more than one. He said he was coming back to Earth and told us that when he got back—everything was going to change."

"Meaning?" I asked.

"He found proof—incontrovertible proof."

"You know I don't believe in that."

"Why, Mr. Cruz? Why don't you believe there can be life from other worlds out there? My brother said he found proof of extraterrestrial life."

"That's not the question, Mrs. Cosmos. The question is why we believe said aliens are any more capable of interstellar travel than we are. Why is that? Why do we always assume they—whoever they are—

are more advanced than us? Why can't we be the most advanced ones in the story?

"Let's skip that part. You believe and so does he. What I believe is not relevant. What is relevant is why you believe he's missing?"

"Because he is, Mr. Cruz, and we don't know the details."

"As soon as we received those messages, Mr. Cruz, that's when the government increased their activity on us," Mr. Cosmos said. "They've always watched us."

"Maybe because you're monitoring government space flights."

Mrs. Cosmos snickered. "Yes, Mr. Cruz. You're a cheerleader for all things government."

I laughed. "Cheerleader? They think I'm a jerk. They tolerate me because I've solved some big cases and embarrassed them. Honestly, I simply don't like people—government, corporate, the public. Family, excluding parents-in-law, and friends are the only exception."

Mr. Cosmos laughed. "No one likes parents-in-law."

"Howard, enough of that from you. Your parents are no exemplars of humankind either."

"Tell me more about the messages," I said. "What did they say?"

"Exactly what we said. They found the proof, but—the messages seemed—off."

"Off how?" I asked.

"Very—stiff, unemotional. Like they were censored or it wasn't him sending them, but it was his private account. Then the messages became cryptic. He was referring to things and we had no idea what he was talking about. Not scientific language but cryptic. We were worried. He also said he had to get the proof he found back to Earth. He said when he arrived it would change everything. After that message, they all stopped, or—we felt the messages were being blocked."

"Like I said, Mr. Cruz, that's when things started happening."

"What things?"

"Increased surveillance, tapping our communication, strange people watching our city—who came and went, showing up at our places of work, strange hovercar flybys of the city. Our city's power inexplicably going out, our city's satellite monitoring systems being jammed, a sudden increase to the local rat and bug population."

"What?"

"Out here there have always been rats. But we went from seeing a couple a day to seeing hundreds a day. And we're not talking normal ones—"

My body tensed. "Super-rodents, your men at the perimeter said. I thought they were exaggerating." Please can we change the subject, I thought.

"No, it's true," Mr. Cosmos said, "and we never saw isopods before, but we got them too."

Isopods! I had to fight my growing flight instinct.

"We found out from contacts there on Mars that he booked a passage on the *Nostradamus*—a commercial Martian freighter bound for Earth," Mrs. Cosmos said. "That's all of it, all that we know. That's why we need a detective."

"What do you want me to do? This isn't a missing persons case. You're alleging some kind of government conspiracy."

"It is a missing persons case, Mr. Cruz. My brother went on that space freighter and disappeared. We can't reach him and no one else can. The freighter has been out of contact for its entire 13-month journey. All you have to do to solve this case is get a communication channel open to that freighter. Regardless, we plan to personally be there when it lands at the spaceport in two weeks."

"This seems like a stretch. I'm a detective, not a communications tech or spaceship greeter."

"You solve missing persons cases, and that's what this is. It's just a bit different." Mrs. Cosmos stood from her chair and walked to the common desk in the room. She walked back to me and handed me a disk. "We already downloaded all the files. All my brother's vid-messages for you."

"We even were able to record some of the government messages," Mr. Cosmos added.

"Government messages?"

"Mr. Cruz, whatever happened to my brother is their doing. Neil suspected this was going to happen."

"Why would the government care if your brother found or didn't find extraterrestrials?"

"Mr. Cruz, extraterrestrials have been coming and going to Earth for centuries," Mrs. Cosmos said. "They work in the government and all the top megacorps."

I had been thrown down the rabbit hole. "Them?"

"Yes, Them," Mrs. Cosmos said, nodding. "Them is not the government. Them is the extraterrestrials working in the government."

"They don't want the public to know they're here," Mr. Cosmos said. "They'll do anything to prevent that."

I put a hand on my forehead. I hadn't been thrown into the rabbit hole. I had always been there. "Are you telling me your brother was made to disappear by extraterrestrials working in the government?"

"Yes!"

"Mr. and Mrs. Cosmos, what exactly do you expect me to do then? I'm a private street detective. I'm not a galactic James Bond with my own personal spaceship."

"You're resourceful. You can use your contacts to find out what happened to him. We know he is on that space freighter bound for Earth. We've been tracking it. But we need you. No one will tell us anything. We've even tried normal channels and illegal methods to contact the freighter. Nothing! It like it's a—dead freighter."

Mr. Cosmos huffed, "Mr. Cruz, the freighter has been incommunicado for 13 months. If they know we've hired you, the government will cooperate to make you go away."

"Or," I added, "they'll stonewall even more. So the government or Them did what? A freighter has a full crew. What are you alleging is the conspiracy? What happened to the crew? I'll play."

Alarms screeched and I jumped so high in my chair I thought my head would have knocked the ceiling. The alarms were that loud. "What is that?" I yelled.

"It's the warning alarms," Mrs. Cosmos answered.

"For what? What are those sirens for?" I could barely hear myself yell.

"Something's falling to us from above," Mr. Cosmos answered.

"What?"

People burst into the room, and the Cosmos ignored me as they all ran. I followed them into the express elevator back up to the surface, then outside. I saw a name on the side of one of their hovertruck plow-pickers, but the words completely emptied from my mind when I looked up to the sky.

I stopped in my tracks looking up like everyone else. I must have still had rats on the brain because as I stared up at the massive object falling from the sky, all I thought was that it looked like a giant turd. However, there was nothing funny about the situation. I realized that this was a real rock, a real meteor, and it was much larger than I originally judged. It was heading straight for us!

"What are you standing here for? Run!" I yelled to everyone.

Suddenly, the panic was unleashed and everyone ran, most screaming. I had always been told that meteors burnt up in the Earth's atmosphere. Then why was this humongous rock almost on top of us?

I greatly misjudged—we all did. All I remembered was running, but the ground collapsing beneath me, followed almost immediately by being blown up into the air. The sound was deafening, and a wave of heat and dirt covered me.

I was a simply private street detective. Was I about to be killed by some random meteor from space? The wife was not going to be pleased. Didn't this space rock know I was "famous"?

PART TWO

In Space No One Can Hear You Scream
Like A Girl

CHAPTER 7

Space Cowboys

Thirteen Months Earlier

The *Nostradamus* was a multi-use commercial space freighter built for comfort and safety rather than speed. Civilians called it a "space frog"—one command sphere with two corridors sprouting forward northeast and northwest ending in triple pronged struts that did look like forelegs in a way; separate corridors extended southeast and southwest to the rear of the craft with the same design. The entire craft was covered in indicator lights, satellite-dishes, and antennas. Along the side of the command sphere read: NOSTRADAMUS.

"*Nostradamus*, this is the *Bradbury*. Please respond. *Nostradamus*, are you receiving?"

The first officer kept repeating, but no one responded. The *Bradbury* was a Martian quasi-military recon and retrieval craft. Out here, both Jupiter and Saturn were under the authority of Mars. The only action that the *Bradbury* ever saw was the occasional robot craft that went on the fritz, operating erratically or losing power altogether.

They were a team of both scientists and military, but out here they were simply glorified, overpaid mechanics. This was different.

On the bridge the captain sat at his center station, the navigator and first officer sat at the front crew seats directly in front of the main bay windows, but the sunshields were engaged. There was no atmosphere out here to block the fury of the sunlight.

The first officer glanced back at the captain. "Are we sure they're receiving?" he asked.

"The channel is open."

"We're still unable to patch into their internal surveillance."

"I can't believe it's a system malfunction—all systems, the vids down too? What about their autonomous cambots?"

"None seem to be online."

"Let's look at their registry again. Crew of twenty-nine—15 crew, six heavy robots, 12 bots, two passengers. Cargo of ore and supplies."

"Maybe the robots revolted and killed the crew," the navigator joked.

"Maybe someone went Pandorum and spaced the crew," the first officer chimed in.

"I really wish I had a first officer and navigator without such vivid imaginations. Maybe their comms are not working. Send the recon team in."

"Yes, Cap." The navigator looked back at him. "Maybe it's aliens. We heard that they've been on Pluto, hiding all these centuries. We're close. Jupiter, Saturn, just a hop, skip away."

"Maybe they're on Ur-anus instead," the captain said and his crew laughed. "Stop with the chatter and get the recon team over there. I don't want to be out here all day and night."

"Aye, aye, Captain," they said, still chuckling.

The six-person recon team slowly floated to the *Nostradamus* in formation. The freighter was still on a flight trajectory to Earth and with the engines engaged the *Bradbury* captain did not want to dock the freighter. It meant a naked space hop to the ship. A person in their spacesuit, out the air lock of one ship, flying in the void of space to the airlock of the next ship. Such maneuvers were not ordinary, but they weren't rare either.

The recon team entered the *Nostradamus's* airlock without a hitch. The dome of the freighter was merely an outer protective shell; the real spacecraft was nestled inside. The team made their way from the airlock at the outer space corridor to the inner airlocks. One by one they floated through and the last team member closed the hatch behind them. One of them tapped on the wall displays and then gave the thumbs up; she began to lift the tinted protection of her visor.

"All internal artificial atmosphere is normal—oxygen all within normal levels. We can take off our helmets if we want," she said.

"No, let's keep them on and breathe our own air until we know what's going on here," their team lead said.

"How much you want to bet they are all sleeping in their bunks after days and nights days of a drunken orgy?"

"Enough at that."

"I'll take that bet."

"I bet a crewmember went Pandorum and spaced the whole lot."

"Stop it, all of you." The team leader floated to the front to enter through the inner air-lock.

"That's right, boss. You take that lead position. Crazy crewmember or space alien, you'll be the first to get it."

They all started to laugh.

"We love you, boss, but if it's an E.T., we're leaving your ass behind."

"My team, my lovely team." The leader floated into the low light inner chamber. He didn't float far until all the lights powered up as normal. "Let's check out their bridge and find out what's happening. Juliet, what's on the scanners?"

Juliet was the third person through and banged her right arm against the back of the team member in front of her. "Stop hitting me," he said.

"Boss, I'm not getting any readings."

"Why?"

"I don't know. I don't want to get paranoid or anything, but I looks like my scanner is being jammed."

"Okay, let's keep the paranoia to a minimum."

"Boss, do we need to be armed?"

The boss continued his floating forward but flipped around to face the team member. "Armed? Why would we need to be armed?"

"Precaution, boss."

"No, we do not need to be armed, nor will we be. Let's keep our cool, people, find the crew and be off on our way."

"Boss, I would really be more comfortable if at least one of us was armed, just as a precaution. I'm not talking about ET. I'm talking about criminal activity. Crime bosses have tried to hijack freighters in the past; maybe they succeeded this time."

"Okay, at last someone is speaking logically. Kilo, draw your weapon."

"Thanks, boss. Feeling better already."

"Let's get this over with—before I start to get paranoid too."

The captain stood at his console, impatiently. "Can we open the sunshields?"

The navigator reached down and the steel doors began to lower to the floor, slowly revealing the bay windows. They could see the *Nostradamus* freighter clearly.

"That's better." The captain walked to the bay windows. "Any progress on patching in?" he asked the men.

The first officer shook his head. "We're being blocked, Cap. I'm 99% positive. Diagnostics are all negative."

"Why would they be blocking us?" the navigator asked. "It's a Martian freighter. They're not answering, and we're Martian."

"Call the recon team. I want to know what's going on."

The first officer pushed a button on the comm. "Recon Team, status report, over." Seconds turned to a minute. The first officer stared at the speaker. "Recon Team, status report, respond, over." The navigator glanced at the captain.

"What the hell is going on over there?"

"Cap, do we need to call Martian Control?" The Captain thought for a moment. "Please, something is not right."

"Send a message."

"Yes, sir!"

"Keep trying them."

The Navigator reached over to push the comm. "Recon Team, respond, over. Rob! What's happening over there?"

"Nav! No names. What's wrong with you?"

"Sorry sir."

A noise flashed over the speaker. All three men stared at the comm speaker; the captain moved closer.

"Recon Team, were you transmitting, over?" Nav asked.

There was a scream. Nav stood from his chair, the First Officer stopped his text message, and the Captain had a nervous look of fear on his face.

"Get that damn message sent!" the captain yelled, and the first officer sat back down and typed as fast as he could. "Anything on sensors?" he asked the Navigator.

"We're the only two ships out here."

"This us Recon Team! Get us out of here! We're coming! Get ready to rocket out of here!"

The three crew officers looked at each other in panic.

"Oh my God!" The first officer pointed. The captain and navigator turned around.

The recon team were jetting out of the airlock of the *Nostradamus*, flying at them so fast that if they missed the *Bradbury's* airlock grapple holds, they'd drift into the void of space, possibly to their deaths.

PART THREE

Lost Up In Space

CHAPTER 8

M.I.B.

I landed on my back with a hard *thud* and a shower of dirt, but I was alive. Suddenly, images of soil infested with rodents and isopods popped in my mind. I jumped up like a jack-in-the-box, spitting dirt and frantically dusting myself off with my hands.

I looked around; people were lying everywhere. I ran from person to person; each as stunned as I were, but no more. I didn't have to find the Cosmos. All I had to do was listen. They were yelling at each other—again.

"I told you that we needed a missile defense system!" she yelled.

"Who's going to pay for it? You? Your parents?"

"You're useless! The aliens tried to whack us right here on our own planet!"

I couldn't believe what I was hearing, but continued surveying the area. We had lucked out big time! No one was killed or injured, but there was the ginormous crater in the ground. It was surreal. We all stood at its edge in stupefied shock.

"What used to be there?" I asked.

"It was the town hall auditorium," the man standing next to me said.

"Are you telling me that the very place you all were going to meet with me is the place that just got obliterated by a rogue meteor from space?"

"Yep. Lucky for us."

"Lucky for you. What about me? I could have been killed. How would that have looked in my obituary? Famous detective killed not in a violent laser gun-battle with gangsters but a rogue meteor from outer space. That's just plain wrong. That's like an Olympic swimmer drowning in a freak accident in his own bathtub."

"Yep. Lucky for us."

I looked around and saw the name on of their hovertruck plower-pickers.

"Crop Circles?"

"Yep."

"What does that mean?"

"Means it's the name of our farming company."

"That phrase has other meanings."

"That's why we picked it."

There was a scream and we both turned. I instinctively ran to Mrs. Cosmos; she was the one who had screamed. Mr. Cosmos was clutching his chest, his face wet and pale. Underneath his shirt it was glowing white in the heart area.

"What's wrong with you?" I asked.

His face winced and he dropped to the ground on his knees.

It was as if God—or for this bunch, a UFO—switched on a light and caught him in the brightest spotlight there was. I looked up, and the hover-EMT dropped from the sky like a rock. It stopped literally a few inches from the ground, landed and out popped two med-bots. The robots ran to Mr. Cosmos.

"Sir, you are having a heart attack. Please be calm. We are here to assist."

"I can't breathe." Mr. Cosmos was now so many shades whiter that he looked dead.

"Hon!" She tried to pull him back to his feet.

"Ma'am, we are here to assist."

A third arm popped out of the chest plate of one robot to hold her away and its other two arms steadied Mr. Cosmos. The second robot set him on the ground, then placed its palms on his chest. "Hold on, sir!"

"Don't you need to put something in his mouth to keep him from biting his tongue?" someone in the crowd forming around them said.

Zap! I almost fell down laughing as Mr. Cosmos froze with his teeth clenched.

"All clear, sir. Your medical incident has been resolved." The robots looked at their forearm displays. "Sir, you are overdue for your annual check-up, which includes a full cardio exam."

"A giant meteor fell from the sky and almost killed us!" Mr. Cosmos was back to normal, natural skin tone and all.

"Why don't you give him a bionic heart, robot?" Mrs. Cosmos yelled. "If his heart is bad, then give him a new one. A natural heart at his age, with his family history, it's unnatural!"

"It's not my heart! Nothing is wrong with my heart! A giant meteor fell from the sky to kill us!"

The thing about yelling at robots was that they truly couldn't care less. The two med-bots stood there nodding at preprogrammed intervals to feign real concern. "Sir, can we schedule your annual checkup at this time?"

"No!"

"His heart monitor implant did its job," Mrs. Cosmos yelled. "You two are here."

"A cardio-monitoring implant will not resolve the underlying problem of heart disease, ma'am."

"Then give him a new heart!"

"Ma'am, we're robots, not physicians. However, at your husband's annual checkup he can discuss heart replacement and all other options available."

"No! I'm not getting a new heart!" he yelled at his wife. "All we need is for giant meteors not to fall from the sky to kill us."

"This is your fault!"

I had been ignoring them, but realized that Mrs. Cosmos was pointing her finger at me. "My fault?" I said. "What is my fault? You all said that the aliens were trying to kill you. How is that my fault?"

"Kill us?" she sneered. "Not us, Mr. Cruz. Kill you!"

"Why would the little aliens want to kill me?"

"Why don't you ask them?"

I realized that the Cosmos, their friends, and even the two med-bots were looking at something past me. I didn't want anything behind me. I slowly turned. There were several black hovercars descending from the sky.

The med-bots in their little white and red hovercar ascended and flew away into the storm clouds. However, no one was watching the med-robots depart; they had their eyes focused on the black hovercars. Then I realized that they were landing not too far from my Pony, which was what I wasn't pleased with.

The men who exited did look like stereotypical government agents to me. I couldn't tell you what a government agent looked like, but they had that "look".

"It's Them," said the man, who was still standing next to me.

"Them? Them who? Government?"

"Yep, and more."

"Government and more? More meaning what?"

"It's Them. Be careful around them."

"What does Them do?"

"Don't let them know where you live."

"The government knows where I live. I'm in Legacy housing like most of Metropolis."

The man shook his head. "Not good."

"Not good. Why not good?"

"Not good." The man stepped away from me, as if I had a sudden attack of bad body odor.

I turned my attention back to the black hovercars and the approaching "agents." There was a man in a black-slicker suit, and blade shades (which seemed odd). "Mr. Cruz," he said as he approached. He looked like the head guy.

I never liked it when some stranger knew my name and I didn't know theirs. I had the frequent misfortune of criminals using that tactic to verify my identity before trying to shoot me.

"I'm with Metro Police."

"Are you now? I know every cop in Metro, and I've never seen you. What's your beat?"

His eyes may have been blocked by his shades, but I could see him changing his mind. "Actually, I'm with Federal Police."

"Really? Are you lying again because you know I don't know every Fed by sight?"

"I know you don't know every Metro police office by sight either. But you can feel free to call Chief of Police Hub or anyone else at Metro PD you like."

"You know the name of the Chief. I'm still not impressed. Where's your badge and ID if you're a Fed?"

He flipped it open in front of my face: "Agent Weborg, Mr. Cruz." He flipped it closed.

"What are you doing on our land?" I turned to see my friend Mr. "Yep," but he wasn't alone. There were a dozen people with him, and more were coming. No one was smiling, and some of them were carrying metal bats. At least, they had learned the lesson of not shooting at strangers first.

"This is public land and—"

"This is not public land," someone in the crowd shouted. "It's private land, and it's Earth land. Why don't you go back to your own planet?"

"He's a Martian?" I asked.

"He's from a planet a lot further than that." Weborg was smirking.

"That's right alien! Get out of here!" someone else yelled.

"You missed!" Mrs. Cosmos startled me; she was standing right next to me. "You thought you could launch your meteor from your secret government Cydonian base on the moon to kill us. You missed! Nothing will stop us from exposing your plot to take over Earth! We know you run Up-Top! But never Earth!"

What the hell had I gotten myself into, I thought. Free Earth was a city of Alienists, which meant their brother was one, too, and probably as nutty as a fruitcake. I had a very low tolerance for craziness. But I looked at that crater—it, and what had caused it, were not figments of the imagination, nothing funny about that either, or the fact I could have been killed.

City Hall in all its faux-splendor may have stood taller than any other monolith tower in Downtown Metro's business district, but no one cared. It was Metropolis Police Central, a foreboding cubical fortress at the other end of the street, that the people both respected and feared—just like the criminals. Rumor was that it was the deepest building in the world with endless levels underground—a holdover of a past era when nuclear annihilation and civil unrest of a biblical proportion were the daily fear of the government. It was headquarters to 500,000-plus police force, the largest in the nation.

I wasn't going to get dragged down the mental rabbit hole where the Alienists lived with their "Them" conspiracies, but I did want to check out Weborg. I didn't believe he was a Fed, but he did have a real badge, as far as I could tell. I sat inside the station in the general waiting room, which was like a massive zoo, but of people. The bright, bold, and cheery colors did nothing to offset the station's grimy exterior. There was a constant march of police with their combat boots and the steady stream of captured criminals in and out. Here was where I waited to be served DMV-style by the police at the counter. None of my police "contacts" were available, so I had to wait my turn like the dozens and dozens of other citizens seated in row-after-row of large chairs.

"Mr. Cruz." I looked at the two officers that strolled by. "Why you waiting out here? Come on down." I smiled and stood from my seat.

"Wait a minute," an elderly woman stood from her chair. "You better not have him cutting in front of all of us."

"Oh no, ma'am. This is my CI. He may have pertinent info to a crime that could save a life or solve a crime. You want him to stay here, or tell me his story?"

"This better be on the level." The woman was actually scolding me, not the officers. "You don't look like a CI."

"He's a CI, ma'am. Come on back, Cruz, my confidential informer." They both were trying to hold back laughs.

They brought me back behind the counter area and barrier wall, through the door to the inner waiting room. It was the difference between night and day—outside was the noisy zoo and here was the quiet bull pen of dual cubicles where the street police worked when not on the beat, elevated single cubicles where the detectives sat, and the offices for the higher-ups.

"So who are you here to see, Cruz?"

Security at Central, even here, was no joke, despite the relaxed atmosphere of the officers—armed police guards, security cameras, armed sentries at the end of the hallways near the elevators, and scanning archways.

"Officers Break and Caps are not here."

"Cruz, cops like you, but we're not your personal police force."

"No, it's not for me. I want you to look up a name for me. Claims to be law enforcement. I want to know if he's legitimate."

"Okay, we can do that. Have a seat."

I gave them the full name of Agent Weborg and waited in a tiny waiting area in the mega-hallway. I was a police intern back in high school. I knew how long it took to type one name into the system and get a response. It didn't take thirty minutes. I looked around impatiently. Now I was starting to get paranoid, then Weborg waltzed up to me from the direction of the police brass offices.

"Mr. Cruz," he greeted as I frowned. "Maybe we can have a chat."

Another man appeared. It was the lurker from the hallway outside my office. "You again," I said.

Weborg looked at him. "Oh, you met one of my field agents, Mr. Cruz."

"What's going on here? I'm not the kind of guy to play games with."

"Yes, Mr. Cruz, we know it. Not too many Earthers get a reputation in law enforcement both on Earth *and* off-world without being a major crime lord. Let's talk in one of the empty rooms."

"Interrogation rooms you mean."

"One of the rooms."

"Am I being interrogated?"

"We're just talking, Mr. Cruz."

Metro PD had a million of them—small, damp, dimly lit interrogation rooms; and they had the higher-end, all white ones too. We were not in the latter.

"Mr. Cruz, I'm going to level with you," Weborg said, which meant he was about to lie to me. "This case you got—"

"To level with you, Agent, I'm not continuing with this case. The Cosmos are a bit too 'eccentric' for me." Both agents smiled. "But...did a meteor from outer space almost kill me today?"

Their smiles disappeared. "Mr. Cruz, that was not a meteor from outer space."

"I cannot claim to be an expert on such things, but that sure felt like a meteor from outer space."

"Meteors break up and disintegrate to dust in their planet-fall."

"Do the dinosaurs know this Mr. Weborg? Oh, they don't know anything because they were wiped off the Earth because of a ginormous meteor from outer space."

"Mr. Cruz, I can see you're traumatized right now."

"Where did the meteor come from then?"

"That's classified."

"Is this how you want to play this?"

"Yes."

"I was about to drop this case, but now I'll have to continue just for spite."

"Go ahead. There's nothing to investigate. The family is 'eccentric' to use your words, the brother was a suicidal—"

"Suicide?"

"Yes, he committed suicide—on Jupiter colony."

"If that's true, then why don't you tell them that? You can't be that heartless."

"Why should we say anything? Earth civilian authorities will inform them in due course. They won't believe anything we say. They'll say we killed him, killed him in our alien plot to take over the planet Earth. You saw her. This is one of those situations where saying nothing is far better—and more compassionate—than saying anything."

"Suicide how?"

"Spacing."

"He spaced himself?"

"Mr. Cruz, suicide by spacing is not a completely unheard off-world. He was depressed, broke up with an ex-girlfriend again, lost his job—"

"He was fired from his new post?"

"So they told you. Yes, that part of their story is true. He was the new Chief Scientist of Jupiter colony, but he was let go for mental issues."

"What mental issues?"

"What do you think, Mr. Cruz? He was looking for extraterrestrials on company time and was fired."

"That's it?"

"That's it, Mr. Cruz."

"What about the killer meteor?"

He smiled and stood from the table. "I'm sure you can find your way out back to your hovercar."

"Agent, a Ford Pony is not a hovercar. It is a classic hovervehicle. But forget that. Why would you leave it this way? The meteor is the only anomaly in my non-case here. I don't like anomalies. You explain it away, then I'm gone. Unexplained and I'm not going anywhere."

"A killer meteor launched from a secret government base on the Cydonian region of the moon. Good luck with that investigation, Mr. Cruz, from the streets of Metropolis. Some friendly advice, they're your friends now, but when you don't give them the answers they like, then suddenly they'll start saying you were abducted by the aliens and replaced with another alien. You'll be Them. They'll camp out at your apartment, camp out at your Liquid Cool offices, even your wife's fancy salon. Think about that."

"I'm thinking."

"We'll leave you to it then. Have a good night."

"You too, Agent. I can never say I never met a Man In Black anymore." Weborg didn't acknowledge me at all as he walked out of the interrogation room. "And you, don't lurk around my office again." The field agent ignored me, as he followed.

CHAPTER 9

Punch Judy

I returned to my office in the Pony. PJ was on the vid-phone at her desk when I walked in. She hung up just as I walked into my private office to see what messages were on the desk.

"What happened?" PJ was at the doorway, eager to know.

"This case is weird," I said.

"That never stopped you before."

"Oh, I'm sorry. I didn't say it the right way. It's a weird case that will pay no money."

Her whole demeanor changed. "Then you have dumped the client. We are a pay-to-play detective agency only."

I smiled. PJ was consistent.

"Well even if it did pay, I couldn't take it. The case involves Lunar Colony, Mars, Jupiter, and who knows where else up there."

"Jupiter? We got people on Jupiter?"

"Mining. On the asteroids."

"Why do they need to mine rocks way out there? What's wrong with Earth rocks or moon rocks or Martian rocks? Sounds like a scam to me."

"I can't disagree with you there. Refund the Cosmos's retainer for real this time."

"Okay."

"Seriously. There is no case. No case that I'll ever be able to solve from here on Earth. They got detectives Up-Top. They'll can hire one of them."

"You need to avoid all these clients that waste your time. While you were flying out to their place for a case that's not a case, you could have been meeting with real clients with real cases."

"Don't I know it, and not having giant rocks trying to kill me."

"What does that mean?"

"Never mind. I'll be making client calls, so I don't want to be disturbed."

"Oh, you're going to get it! Your wife left a message."

"What are you talking about?"

"What two words don't go with diapers?"

"What?"

"Two words for you: bio-suit!"

"What? What did my wife do to my bio-suit?"

I was pretending. I knew Dot was going to dispose of my bio-suit, which is why I switched it for my old one. She could throw that one away. My new one, straight from London Prime, was safely tucked away in one of my bank safety security boxes in Metropolis. I may not have been able to wear it, but knowing it was safe gave me peace of mind—which was almost like wearing it all the time.

That was all behind me now.

Distractions were normal in the private detective business, but one had to push through it and get back to the solid work. Thanks to the PJ system of organizing my client messages, all I had to do was walk into the main office, into my private office, and grab the hot pile from the desk—all potential cases that were likely to be solved quick and pay fast. That's what I needed. I could deal with the sleazy and unethical clients, but I couldn't waste my limited time with crazy.

I was off for a real case fit for a proper private detective like me—surveillance. That's what I called them, but what that really meant was another cheating spouse case. Five out of six times that what it was. Quick, often unremarkable, but the clients paid right away.

These cases took me all over the supercity—low-end or high-end, it didn't matter to me. The process was always the same. Sit in the Pony and watch. Take up a post inside or outside and watch. Snap the pictures or record audio, done. Next day, collect my money.

I had hated these cases at first but realized that they were more real than any other case. This business was not glamorous no matter how much people wanted to say it was, or detectives wanting to pretend it was. My priority was to avoid another key ingredient of the business—the danger. I never got shot on one of these cases yet. The rain was pouring hard, but I sat warm and snug in my Pony parked on the ground. In this rain the pedestrian traffic was light, but this was a booshy part of town, so pedestrian traffic would have been light anyway. Rich people here didn't walk anywhere. Lucky for me my mark was not one of them. He came out of the ground-level entrance of the bar, arm-in-arm with his female "friend." They were laughing it up, as I began my video-recording—a nice device with shades attachment so you recorded what you saw. It didn't take long until I got the images I needed. With that, I was gone. The last of four "surveillance" cases wrapped up all in one day.

That meant I could swing by and see what Dot and Cruz, Jr. were up to. I could also pretend to be devastated in front of the wife about my "only" bio-suit being "retired." I realized that I had to return to the office first. The sky-traffic on Circuit Circle was extremely heavy and soon I saw the reason: an army of media hovervans around my Liquid Cool office tower. I drove by but then realized that not just one but all the media hovervans were taking chase—after me!

They had their stupid hovervans. I was in a souped-up muscle vehicle. My foot touched the pedal and left them behind in the last time continuum. Actually, I raced until out of view and dove into one of the largest parking structures. It was particularly fiendish—spiraling either up or down. I went up and whipped to the top 250th floor, parked, hopped out, and covered it with my inside car cover. I had no idea what was going on, but I was not going to be ambushed by the media. I promised Dot to stay out of the press for a while; media was good for business at the beginning, but now it was causing more problems that it was worth. It attracted clients, including the insane, but also attracted more than a few criminals who wanted to stuff me in the glove compartment box of my own vehicle.

"What is going on there?" I asked PJ on the vid-phone. I sat in the backseat of the hovertaxi I called.

"You didn't tell me you were almost killed by a killer meteor!"

"How do you know that? Is that what the media is saying?"

"Saying, Cruz? The pictures are on the newsfeed everywhere. That crater is huge! You almost got smushed like the dinosaurs."

"PJ, that's not how that super meteor killed the dinosaurs."

"Cruz, that was a super meteor that almost killed you and those people. When the media found out you were there, they were here like an army. You're famous again."

"I don't want to be famous at all. Now Dot's going to be worried."

"She's not worried. She's mad—and looking for you."

"Since I'm already in trouble and the media is after me, find out where this meteor came from."

"Came from? From space?"

"PJ, you said yourself that the meteor was huge. How could a meteor of that size get through all our anti-asteroid laser satellites?"

I could see PJ's face change. "You're right! What does it mean? Are you still working their case?"

"No, I'm not."

"If you are, they need to pay. Pay-to-play!"

"I am not working their crazy case. Just find out where that meteor came from. In fact, ask the reporters. Trick them into thinking I'm investigating that."

"Yes! Get them to do the work. Smart! At least I don't work for no dummy."

"Yes, good to know that you approve. Go trick those reporters and let's find out where that meteor came from."

As I was talking to PJ, a call came into the hovertaxi driver. I saw his eyes look back at me in the rearview mirror. Were he and his caller talking about me? I ended my call with PJ.

"Mr. Cruz," the driver said, "your main man Flash called. He wants to meet us and have you switch to his taxi."

"Is that okay? Drivers don't usually steal each other's passengers.

He laughed. "Not stealing, Mr. Cruz. Half the fare will go to me. You know how it is at Run-Time's. We're all one big, happy family."

"Yes, I do. Sure, let's meet up with him, and I'll pay you extra to send some mobile security to watch my vehicle."

"Consider it done, Mr. Cruz."

CHAPTER 10

Flash

We waited until a Run-Time mobile security guard arrived via jetpack at the parking bay. His name was Ray, a young kid from Woodstock Falls who was a part-time student getting advanced degrees in fission and hydroelectric sciences. He was super smart and big—very big. He actually looked funny flying around with a tiny jetpack on his broad frame. He wasn't my normal guy for vehicle security, but he was a perfect substitute.

My main vehicle security guy—meaning I used him more times over the years than anyone else—was Flash. He was Black, with a ponytail and a small goatee. Flash was friendly, reliable, and he took his job seriously, whether driving a hovertaxi or car-sitting security. After all this time, we were good friends. If Run-Time hadn't been the Godfather to my son, it would have been Flash. My driver, Mario, zipped through sky-traffic as I watched out the windows.

The thing about Metropolis was that everyone had a favorite hangout—police, firefighters, different unions, cyberpunks, druggies, dope daddies, VLers, gangsters, you name it, there was a bar, restaurant, or club that they hung out in. Of course, there had to be a place for hovertaxi drivers too, but I had never been to it in all those years.

The diner was called The Acid Rain, which made me smile. My driver set his hovercab at the end of the huge parking lot that was packed with hovertaxis of every color under the sky and not just one company, but all the major taxi transportation companies in the supercity. Across the freeway was the higher-end diner that all the hoverlimo drivers hung out in.

I bobbed my head around from my seat to get a better look inside The Acid Rain. "I don't see him."

"Flash is inside," Mario said, looking at me in the rearview mirror.

"Oh, there he is."

Flash stood at the main entrance waving with a smile. He was in his brown overalls, but he had a nice suit underneath.

"See you next time, Cruz." I shook Mario's hand from over the seat and opened the door.

I stepped out into the rain, closed the door, and gave a quick thumbs-up. Mario rose ten feet, then zipped into the sky-traffic like a rocket. All seasoned hovertaxi drivers were like that—better drivers than any.

Boom! The thunder almost startled me; thunder was rare for the supercity. I ran into the diner to Flash, who held the door open for me.

"Cruz." He greeted me with a handshake, then a pat on the shoulder.

"I've never been here."

Flash led me in. "Oh, the food is really good." The diner was a beehive of activity. The far end in the back was the smoking section, closest to the door was non-smoking. Inside was as diverse as any in Metropolis—not ethnicities, nationalities, or languages. Here in this diner were all the representatives of the ruthlessly competitive hovertaxi industry, all under one roof, hanging out like a happy family. "I have a booth for us over here."

"Don't tell me you have another case for me."

"Kinda."

We had barely sat down when a short-haired waitress on hoverskates popped up and place a menu right in front of me on the table. "I'll give you a few minutes." Then she zipped away.

"Service here is great too," Flash said.

I glanced at the menu. "I think I already know what I want." Flash raised his hand. It wasn't even a minute when the same waitress popped back. She took my order and was gone. Flash already had his order so he resumed eating.

"How's work?" I asked.

"Never any complaints."

"Family and life?"

"Same there. How's little Cruz Jr.?"

"A giggling ball of energy."

Flash smiled. "Wait until they start walking."

"He's already doing it, in spurts. He pretends he can't when you're watching him, but the second you turn your head, he's halfway across the room."

"I remember when the kids were like that. Seems like yesterday. My oldest has already told me he wants to be a driver too. I take him up in the hovertaxi with me a couple of times a week."

"At least you don't have to deal with diapers."

Flash laughed. "How exactly does that work for a recovering germophobe?"

"Not well, but I'll survive. It's like it never ends. Food goes in and it like multiplies ten-fold on the way out. I don't get it. It doesn't seem human."

"It is human, Cruz."

I shook my head. "Crazy cyborg in a dark alley or change diapers for the day. I choose the cyborg every time. So what's the secret, Flash? You snatched me away from a colleague. That can't be normal."

"In the fraternity of hovertaxi drivers, we do favors for each other all the time." I saw in his face that he remembered something. "How is it that you can get in the news so easily? Megacorps pay millions to get good press and it's not guaranteed. You get in the news all the time for free."

"It's not all the time, only a few times."

"More than a few times. And it's always big news."

"It's not my fault. I'm trying to keep a lower profile these days with Cruz Jr. in the world. How on Earth did I know I was going to almost get hit by a meteor from outer space? How does one plan for something like that? When was the last time a meteor like that crashed on Earth? It's like you can't even leave your apartment."

The waitress returned with my order. She placed my cup of silk coffee and breakfast-for-brunch plate in front of me with a fork and knife bundle, smiled and was gone. I placed the utensil bundle to the side and took out my own from my jacket—my own utensils nicely sealed in a hermetically sealed pouch. Flash had seen this before, so he wasn't surprised by a detective—me—who carried his own germ-free utensils on his person.

"Are you going to take that case from the Cosmos?"

I sat back in the booth before taking my first bite. "You know Mr. and Mrs. Cosmos?"

"I do actually."

"I know you have a tendency to sometimes intervene on the behalf of a customer, but it sounds like it's more than that this time."

"That's how I met them originally. I was interested in what they were saying. They gave me some literature, and I got to know them from there."

"You took literature from them? Flash, tell me it ain't so."

"I'm not sure what you're thinking, but taking literature from a person is not a bad thing."

"How do you know about their case?"

"I talked with them yesterday."

"Just in general."

"I was the one who recommended you to them."

"Oh." I said it in a somewhat off-handed way, which I shouldn't have.

"Yes, 'oh'."

Flash was a long-time friend and he had sent me tons of good clients. I definitely did not want to offend him. "Here's the thing. I'm a local private detective. They need someone Up-Top to take this on."

"Cruz, I know you think they may be living in 'crazy town' with their 'theories,' but that's exactly why I recommended them to you. You can keep them on the straight path. The true fact is the brother is missing, and everything associated with it is not right."

I started to nibble at my food. "Okay, convince me. Why should I take their case?"

"Well, there is the Godzilla in the room. The meteor—start there."

"No, don't start there. The meteor isn't the case. The missing brother is the case. Convince me about that. If I do any investigating, it will be about him, not a big rock from space."

"The rock doesn't interest you."

"No, I'm not a media reporter. I'm a street detective on the mean streets of Metropolis. People may think I need to tie up every loose end, but I follow the tenets of my posthumous mentor, Wilford G.: "Focus on the facts and principals of the case like a pit bull with a big, fat juicy steak in your mouth. That's how you solve it."

Mr. Wilford G., Metropolis P.I., died at 92. I never got to meet him but I memorized his 60-page book titled, *How to be a Great Detective with 100 Rules* cover to cover.

"Following the rock takes me away from any case. Following the brother, takes me to the case, if there really is one," I continued.

Flash nodded. "You're right."

"Why should I take this missing persons case for the Cosmos then?"

"He's her only sibling. She practically raised him from a child. We're both fathers. We know what that's like."

"There's lots of missing people in this supercity. Why go after one who's not even on the planet?"

"But he's coming here—to Metro Space International."

"A freighter is, yes. Whether he is or was ever was on it is nothing I'd be able to verify even if I was on the case. You know those spacemen barely cooperate with the real police."

"But you could find out."

"I could make calls, but that's just calls—relying on others rather than seeing for myself. There's nothing for me to do with this. It's all Up-Top bureaucracy. We're at their mercy."

"I'm going to tell you something that I shouldn't, but I'm going to anyway. I know you think the Cosmos are not playing with a full deck, but it's all harmless. Like lots of people here on Earth and Up-Top, they believe there is life in the universe besides us."

"Nothing wrong with that."

"Exactly, especially now with us on the moon and Mars, other colonies being planned. It would be strange if people didn't think there was other life in the universe doing the exact same thing we are doing—exploring space to find other life different than themselves.

"I don't disagree with anything you've said. How does this relate to the missing brother?"

"Cruz, I've seen it with my own eyes. I've been to Free Earth—their city. The government persecution is real—harassment, surveillance, just strange things. I agree with you that Mr. and Mrs. Cosmos are a bit out there, but I think people are purposely trying to make them seem crazy."

"Why?"

"To discredit Neil. I've met him a few times. The first time when he was a teenager. He was a genius even back then."

"A xenobiologist."

"Cruz, it's a real occupation. They're actually a lot like you. They investigate and look for clues."

"The government is messing with Free Earth to make its inhabitants seem crazy to discredit their real scientist brother who lives on Jupiter Outpost?"

"He found something. That's when this all really started. The Cosmos didn't tell you that."

"Found what?"

"They probably told you that he started sending messages about 18 months ago. It was more like over two years ago. He wasn't just coming home. He was bringing the proof of his findings."

"To who—Free Earth?"

"No, NASA—all their lead scientists. They have xenobiologists too."

"Flash, what did he find?"

"Proof of extraterrestrial life."

"This is exactly what I'm talking about. I do surveillance, cheating spouses, corporate espionage, fraud cases, an occasional counterfeit case, missing persons, civil investigations. What am I supposed to do with this?"

"You've solved a government conspiracy case before."

"Not with extraterrestrials. There is nothing for me to do. The freighter is Martian, so neither me nor anyone on Earth is going to contact it without their permission. There is no case."

"The Cosmos think that the government is going to try to harm Neil to keep him from revealing his findings."

I was so tempted to tell Flash what the government agent told me at Metro PD—that the boy was dead, suicide by spacing, but that would have been cruel, and possibly false. For a detective, nothing was true unless you could verify it. People lied all the time. I knew because I did.

"I have one favor to ask."

"Flash, don't burn up any favors on this. I get that they feel helpless, but that's life sometimes. They have to work the bureaucracy to get answers."

"Come with me to Metro Space International when the freighter arrives."

"That may be on Earth, but it will still be a Martian freighter, and they're not going to allow any Earthers anywhere near it."

"We'll be able to get onboard."

I stopped eating completely. "What does that mean?"

"I'm asking for this one favor, Cruz."

"This is not some kid's prank you all are plotting. This is felonies in four jurisdictions—Metropolis, Earth, Up-Top, and Mars—serious jail time, and not on Earth. This is not fun and games, Flash. Does your wife know you're contemplating something so reckless, since we're both married men now?

"She knows. She's going to be there too."

"What? You're lying. There's no way your wife would let you do this."

"You can call her and ask her for yourself."

"You're not helping the Cosmos. You're part of their group. That's what this is about."

"He found the proof. That's what it's about."

"So the government naturally wants to kill him to keep him from talking."

"Yes, and they tried to kill all of them—and you!"

"We're back to the rock again."

"It's all connected, Cruz. That meteor didn't just wander into Earth space. I know you know that without me having to tell you. Meteors are supposed to come from space, not be launched from secret bases on the moon."

I let go of my fork and touched my temples with hands. I thought I had escaped from the rabbit hole but realized that I had been pushed further down into it. It was worse than a bad dream or lousy virtual reality sim. This case was like a demonic, fat, juicy isopod that had latched onto my leg with its nasty sucker. I suddenly had an uncontrollable urge to run away, even if it meant changing diapers without a bio-suit.

CHAPTER 11

Chief Hub

I rarely watched the live newsfeed; I preferred to read the news text—less sensationalistic, more factual, and less annoying. There was audio-only, too, and I sat in the Pony listening. I had no idea how huge the meteor story was—it was on every channel, and it was the only thing people were talking about. Media frenzies were not new to me—we had a bad one in my last Electric Sheep Massacre case—but this was worse. I was in the center of it. Because I was at the scene and almost killed, every conceivable theory and conspiracy theory was being tossed around by news anchors, commentators, experts and crackpots.

I dialed the wife from my vehicle vid-phone.

"There you are, Meteor Man." Dot was staring at me. She reached out of frame and there was Cruz Jr. with some kind of fabric on his head. Dot cradled him so he could see me.

"What's that on his head?" I asked.

"It's called a hat, Cruz."

"That is not a hat. That's a sock. Don't put a sock on our son's head; I already have a cool hat for him."

"Where is it then?"

"Hey Meteor Man!" All of Dot's Eye Candy colleagues appeared behind Dot and Cruz, Jr.

Now I was Meteor Man. This was why things like this in the media could be so devastating. An entire life's reputation could be ruined, though in my case I was only a private detective for a couple of years. However, it was the principal of the thing.

"Where did this Meteor Man label come from?"

"The media, of course."

"I told you I wanted to drop this case like a hot meteor rock—"

"That's a good one, Cruz," Dot interrupted. "Isn't that right, CJ?"

"C.J.?"

"Yes, Cruz. You do know what the initials stand for."

"CJ is a girl's name. Don't mess with the boy's head. Call him Junior then."

"Hey CJ," it was one of Dot's work colleagues.

"Hi CJ," another one said. "CJ, Meteor Man wants me to shower you with the glitter after we do your nails, eyebrows and lashes."

They started to laugh and even I couldn't help but to chuckle. "Okay, have your fun. I was just checking in, Dot. I have to go to work, because this Meteor Man nonsense will not stand."

"As long as you keep your feet on planet Earth."

"After what we've gone through in space, I'm never leaving Earth again."

"What happened when the two of you were up in space?" a colleague asked.

"Bye Cruzie—"

"Cruzie?" Dot asked. "What happened to Junior?"

"Love Dot." I disconnected before I was drawn into more silliness.

I sat there for a moment. I did not want to do what I was going to do. I said the meteor was an accident, but I knew all along that it wasn't. I didn't believe in a government conspiracy or aliens, but whatever the true explanation was, it was attempted homicide—multiple homicide.

I dialed my dashboard vid-phone again. This time PJ picked up.

"There he is!"

"PJ, call the Cosmos. I'm taking the case."

"Yes! I knew it! The second the media started calling you Meteor Man, I knew you wouldn't stand for that. It's Liquid Cool to you, I told them! And the Cosmos, nothing to worry about. I saved their paycard details!"

"Illegally retaining people's credit card information again, are we?"

I hated it. As soon as I landed the Pony and exited, the media were on me like a pack of jackals on a fluffy bunny rabbit. Reporters with microphone wands and hoverlights pushed in my face, hovercameras buzzing around. But I kept my cool. I wasn't going to regain my rep by hiding.

"What falsehoods have you been spreading about me in the media?"

The reporters got a kick out of that. "Mr. Cruz, is it true that you were almost killed by the falling meteor?"

"You know that's true, so why are you asking?"

"Mr. Cruz, why were you visiting the secret compound of an anti-government cult that claims that extraterrestrials have infiltrators at all levels of government and the business sector?"

I started to laugh. "You can't be serious. They're joking with you! You can't tell when people are joking with you."

"They are true believers, Mr. Cruz."

"I am working a case on their behalf and it has nothing to do with ETs; ironically it has to do with the kind of cases that started my career and first brought me to your attention."

"Kidnapping, Mr. Cruz?"

They fell for it. "Let me talk to the police and call my client afterward. If they give me permission, then I'll happily tell you what we know."

"What about the meteor, Mr. Cruz?"

"Are you the one who called me 'Meteor Man?'" The reporter gave me a nervous smile. "That wasn't funny, Jay. We're professionals. Honestly, I don't know anything. It's one of those surreal things that occur to you that you'd swear wasn't true, except for the fact that you were there. Imagine walking outside turning, and a humongous rock was falling from the sky at you. The only thing on your mind is how fast you can run at that very moment."

I continued, "You all probably know more about it than me. Didn't one of you report that you're investigating some secret government Cydonian base on the Lunar colonies? Some media person said that no one can say where the meteor came from because it wasn't picked up on any tracking. Someone mentioned this secret government base."

They were all screaming at me the same question. "Mr. Cruz, are you alleging that the meteor was some kind of strike from the Moon by Up-Top against Earth?"

"I didn't say that. I'm not the reporter. I'm just repeating what I heard." I should have stopped talking at that instant, but I wanted to end with something so inflammatory that I'd get everything I wanted from them. "Maybe Up-Top was testing some kind of meteor-launching weapon or something."

That sent the reporters into a frenzy. They ran in a million different directions, as if bombs were about to drop—they were off to their respective media hovervehicles to get on the air. With the snap of a finger, I had done what I set out to do. I had replaced the "Meteor Man" story with the "The Spacemen are testing new meteor death weapons against Earth."

I smiled and proceeded to the main entrance of Metro PD.

For the average beat cop, I was in their "good book"; the police brass, though, loathed me. I helped them solve a few high-profile cases, but the fact that a civilian helped them was why they hated me. Police on the street couldn't care less, as long as the bad guys were off the streets; they had no time for politics.

I came into Metro PD, and there stood a reception committee in blue—blue suits, not blue uniforms, which meant they were police brass.

"Mr. Cruz, are you happy with your performance?" one asked me.

"I am actually. I want to set up an appointment to see the Chief."

"Appointment," another sneered. "He's waiting for you this minute."

"We should drag you there by your toenails," another said.

I pointed at the large man. "Keep your nasty hands off my toenails."

"You're not funny. You just caused a world incident."

"Are you telling me the Up-Toppers really did send that meteor?" I sincerely asked. "I was making that up."

"Come on with us!"

We were in Police Chief Hub's office. It had been a while, but he was unhappy to see me just the same. My five police brass goons sat me down on a chair in front of the Chief's desk and stood behind me. I didn't like people standing behind me, which is exactly why they were doing it.

"Before you start," I began to the Chief, "strangely, I really don't care about this meteor. Everyone thinks I do, even though it almost killed me, I don't care. I have two clients with a missing sibling. I think I already know what happened to him, but they wouldn't believe me if I told them. There's a Martian freighter arriving in two weeks, less than that now. All I'm going to do is be there when it arrives with them, and the Martians will either let us inspect it or not. After that, my case is done. I'll go back to my normal cases."

"Normal case?" the Chief asked. "There're thousands of private detectives in this city, and not one of them has been in my personal office once, let alone all the times you have been; not one of them I've been to their personal residence after a homicide—"

"Not one of them saved your life and seven sons from being ripped apart piece-by-piece by half a million street police."

He smirked. "Yes. So I tolerate you, Mr. Cruz. But I don't like it."

"I was a police intern in high school. Notice I didn't become a policeman."

"Yet you can't seem to stay away from Metro PD."

"Never been arrested."

"Not yet. You're still hanging around Compstat Connie? I thought you were married."

"Funny, Chief. Compstat Connie won't live forever. Since Police One isn't doing anything to learn all that she knows, I will. Solve more cases and get more money. I got a new mouth to feed."

"Yes, Cruz Jr. I heard."

"As long as he doesn't become a cop," one of the men behind me said.

I ignored him. "Who is Agent Weborg? Your officers blindsided me with him, which is not like them."

"Police Intelligence. I know he's going to want to talk to you again—bad."

"Intelligence from where? Here or Up-Top?"

"Ask him when you see him."

"I don't want to see him ever. Tell me what you want to tell me. I know your buddies didn't bring me to your office to talk about life."

"You don't want to know about the meteor?"

"Why won't anyone believe me? I don't care or want to care about a rock from space. After the arrival of that freighter with my clients' sibling, I'm done."

"Your clients." Hub huffed. "Those Alienists are dangerous. You should stay far, far away from them."

"In a galaxy far, far away?"

"You think it's funny, but it's not."

"If people want to believe in ETs, it's a free country."

"It's a lot more than beliefs. Beliefs are not a crime. Actions are what get people arrested or dead."

"Are we talking about Free Earth? I was there. They're harmless."

Hub shook his head slowly. "You won't listen, but you should stay away from them."

"Just because you believe in ETs doesn't mean you don't love your family member and that something didn't happen to him."

"You know what happened to him."

"I don't know anything. I don't know anything about this Agent Weborg, so I'm not going to take his words as gospel. I don't trust him. He looks like an ET himself."

"And you don't want to know about the meteor?"

I shook my head. "No! I don't want to know. This case is a rabbit hole, all kinds of weirdness. I already had one of your officers behind me saying out loud he wanted to play with my toes."

"Why don't you just shut up!" the large officer muttered behind my head.

"My goal is to get out of the rabbit hole, not get in deeper. Whatever the meteor is or isn't, wherever it came from, you'll handle it. I'm a civilian so it doesn't involve me.

"Don't care that it almost killed you?"

"I have full confidence in the Metropolis Police to investigate this incident. It's beyond my pay grade and I have no desire to interfere with the fine men and women in silver and black on the job."

"Okay then. I've leave you to your Alienist clients. But you can never say I didn't warn you."

"You don't have to warn me. I'm only on this case because a friend asked me to help them as a personal favor and I will. But all that involves is meeting a space freighter. That's it."

"Then I misjudged the situation and there's nothing more to say. My men will show you out."

They did, without saying a word—out the back entrance so I wouldn't run into any more reporters.

Some called it street smarts, gut instinct, your sixth sense, being in tune with the Force. Whatever one called it, you had to be able to read people and read situations correctly. For a street cop, or a street detective, to not do so could mean your life.

I would never say I knew Chief Hub well, but I did know him well enough. The meeting we had in his office was deadly serious. I had stepped into something serious. He knew what it was, but wasn't going to tell me. This case had nothing to do with eccentric people believing in ETs or extraterrestrials taking over Earth. Hub might have slipped when he mentioned that it was actions, not beliefs, that got people arrested or dead.

If this was a terrorist thing, promises or not, I'd turn the Cosmos and their entire enclave over to Metro PD myself. I was not liking where this was all going. I needed to bring in an expert who knew everything there was to know on the streets.

CHAPTER 12

Phishy

PJ appeared at the open doorway of my Liquid Cool private office with a gruff look and her hands on her hips. "It's stupid man," she announced and left.

Phishy was basically a street hustler—a little "legal" (his term, not mine) contraband running here, a bit of courier work there, whatever scam he could get into to bring in some cash. Nothing illegal enough that if he were caught, he'd get no more than a mere misdemeanor situation—pay the fine and be off on his way, not even a blot on the record. Cops and courts couldn't be bothered with street hustlers working non-violent, low money scams. In a vile world, you had to set your priorities properly.

Phishy leapt into view with the biggest smile. He always wore a dark-colored vest and pants, but underneath was always some off-white, long-sleeve shirt extravaganza with colored fish all over it. When he appeared at my door, I knew just to remain seated, my hands clasped together on top of the desk, and waited. He jumped in and then it began—Phishy's chicken dance. This was how he greeted me. I waited until he had sufficiently amused and tired himself out. When he was done then he leapt over to my desk.

"Cruz! Did you see that jump? I could be in the Olympics."

"If you say so, Phishy." I leaned back in my chair as he took a seat in one of the two chairs in front of my desk. "Phishy, I need information."

"Oh!" He jumped up from the chair. I was about to ask, but he closed the door and returned. He leaned forward. "Confidential, huh? That meteor thing, huh?"

I threw up my hands. "Why does everyone want me to investigate a meteor? The meteor is not a case; it's a rock. It can't pay my bill."

"But Cruz, you almost got killed. The rock was sent by someone. You said it yourself on the news, it was an Up-Top death weapon."

I could feel myself wanting to laugh. "Phishy, don't believe everything you see on the news."

"But it was you saying it!"

"Phishy, don't believe everything you see on the news. That's not why I called you here."

"Those Up-Toppers shooting lasers at us, sending flying saucers over our cities, now death meteors."

"Phishy! Focus. I need information. Tell me about the town Free Earth."

"Free Earth was almost flattened by that meteor. Cruz, what did it—"

"Phishy, focus. Tell me about Free Earth. What do I need to know, because the people who live there aren't going to tell me."

Phishy began to laugh.

"What's so funny? The police call them Alienists."

"Alienists? That's a dumb name. They're called, wait for it—Free Earthers." He started to laugh.

"What's so funny about Free Earthers?" Phishy now broke out laughing so hard that he fell out of his chair and on the ground. "What is wrong with you?"

"They believe space aliens abduct people and—probe them." He starting making gestures with his hands to various body parts.

"Hey, stop that! This is a family-friendly establishment. Alien abductions is as old as the Abominable Snowman and the Loch Ness monster."

"Cruz, don't use those examples!" Phishy started another round of laughter. "They believe the Abominable Snowmen are a lost space alien tribe hiding out on Earth and the Loch Ness was one of their pets that's escaped from their starships."

"It seems that I picked the right man for intel on the Free Earthers. Get up from the floor and back in the chair. Your mother didn't raise you in a barn."

He got back in his seat. "But Cruz, the case is the meteor."

"I'm not investigating the rock. Leave me alone with the rock. Back to the Free Earthers—are they dangerous?"

His eyes looked up, thinking.

"Phishy, why do you have to think so long? Are they dangerous? If I go there again, do I need my weapons?"

"You're a detective, you need your weapons at all times."

"What is it that you have to think about for so long?"

"Most of them are nice people."

"And the others? The not-nice ones."

"If one thought that the Earth was run by space invaders and they had an elite group of humans as their task masters, one might be a little dangerous."

"Phishy, it's not like you to be vague. I got Dot and Cruz Jr. to think about. Are they dangerous?"

"Okay. Yes."

"How? Believing in space aliens and alien conspiracies isn't dangerous. What have they done? Are these people terrorists, Phishy?

"Oh no. Don't use the T word."

"Then what word should I use?"

"There are different groups. There's the Roswellians."

"Yeah, I know the Roswell Area 51 myth."

"They're the original Free Earthers, chapter's been around for centuries. There are the Blues and the Grays."

"Phishy, what kind of craziness is this?"

"That's the names of their groups. I didn't name them. Bet you can't guess that the difference between the Blues and the Grays? The Blues are from the North. The Grays are from the South." He started to laugh.

"Phishy!"

"I'm serious. I'm not making this up. I promise."

"You can go then. You're not going to be serious so I can't confide in you."

"Oh no, Cruz, give me one minute. Phishy leapt from his chair and was out the closed door so fast it was a blur.

I leaned back in my chair. My friends. Only I could have friends like these. There was a knock and the door opened. In walked "serious" Phishy, but he got halfway to his chair and burst out laughing again.

"That didn't last long."

"I'm okay, Cruz. Promise. I just can't stop thinking about the alien probing."

"You can do that kind of thinking on your own time."

"I asked you if these people are dangerous in any way. I think they're crazy, but harmless. The police think they're dangerous, but won't tell me anything. If the police think you're dangerous, they did something, are doing something, or about to do something."

"Most of them are simple space UFO watchers. They look for space aliens, talk about them, go to space alien conventions, but when you have a community like that—sub-groups form and it's not always fun and games."

"Are the ET watchers terrorists? What are you not telling me?"

"You know I'm a licensed gun dealer."

"Phishy! Are they stockpiling weapons?"

"Yes, but not to use."

"Phishy! ET watchers who stockpile weapons are no longer ET watchers. That's dangerous."

"I don't believe they would ever use them."

"Why do you say that?"

"They're scared of space invaders not humans. Not even the humans they think are working for the space aliens. It's all for defense. No real space aliens ever show up and they'll never use them."

"Stockpiling ET-watchers. And Phishy is their weapons dealer."

"Only a very small part of their stash."

"Small. Says you."

"Cruz, they aren't the only citizens in Metropolis and around the world stockpiling weapons."

"Well, that's definitely true."

"People have all kinds of reasons for 'saving for a rainy day.' Their reason just happens to be fear of a space alien takeover. There's people who are actually stockpiling weapons waiting for the zombie apocalypse, you know."

"Okay, you made your point, and I agree with you, Mr. Defense Attorney." Phishy smiled. "Let me ask you this then—"

"Is it about the meteor? Cruz, I'm telling you, that's the key to your whole case."

"Whether it is or isn't is irrelevant. How am I supposed to investigate a meteor from the moon?"

"You're the famous detective. You'll think of a way. How many people do you know who can build a hovercar as a teenager?"

"The Pony is a hovervehicle, not a hovercar, but your flattery is also irrelevant. The full weight of the planet Earth is going up against the full weight of Up-Top. I am not getting in between those two. It's all interplanetary politics. Now that's dangerous. You see Phishy, you made me forget what I was going to ask you!"

He laughed again. I lowered my head to remember what I was going to ask him. That was the contagious effect of Phishy. He could make those around him lose focus too. "Oh, I remember now. Since you're an expert on stockpiling citizens—"

"Thanks, Cruz."

"Is there anything else I need to know about them? I'm not so much concerned about the weapons stockpiling anymore, since I don't expect the arrival of real ETs anytime ever. Is there anything else?"

"Yeah, there are no real space aliens, except for Spacemen and Martians, but they don't count. They're human. I mean real space aliens."

"I'm on my way back to Free Earth, so as long as they don't think there are real ETs on the way to Earth, I'm safe. And the police won't have to raid them. But is there anything else? I'm going to visit Free Earth again."

"Umm."

"Phishy, what is it? What else did you not tell me?"

"Nothing. Only there's someone else who knows about Free Earth much better than me."

"And I know them? Who?"

"But it's not what you think."

"Who?"

"Don't tell him I told you."

"Who?"

"Flash."

"Flash? Flash is an ET watcher? I thought he was just a friend. Read their literature once."

"He's a Roswellian."

"What!"

"But it's not what you think."

"What is it then?"

"I said too much already. Ask him. He'll tell you."

"Flash believes in ETs?"

"Cruz, 50% of the planet believes in space aliens."

"And 50% don't care. Flash is one of the most level-headed people we know."

"It's not what you think. Ask him."

"Why can't you tell me?"

"Ask him. It's business corporate stuff."

I practically put it together right there. "Okay, Phishy you're off the hook. You gave me the information I needed."

He stood up from his chair, smiling. "See, I always come through for you, Cruz."

CHAPTER 13

Flash

Dot told me, no matter how tempting, not to listen to the news. That meant it was bad. Metro PD heavy police hovercruisers were in the skies blanketing the supercity in force. I tried to avert my eyes as I flew by in the fast lane of sky-traffic, but the news was even on the neon digital billboards streaming by. More than a few were not only quoting me, but some featured my picture: "Up-Top testing meteor-launching weapon against Earth!" That's not what I said, but no one cared. Earth versus Up-Top sentiment had existed before I was born and would be here long after I was gone from this plane of existence.

The police brass that loathed my media performance probably were mild in comparison to those of City Hall. The Mayor and the City Council were probably in their offices yelling every curse word they could think of at me in every language possible, including binary. It was a calculation I had to take. I knew what I was doing. At least, I killed the "Meteor Man" story.

I arrived to pick Flash up from his apartment tower. At first, I didn't see him, but he came running out of the main entrance in the heavy rain, jumped down the steps, and into the passenger seat after I lifted the door.

I had called him from my office right after Phishy left. Besides getting to talk more, Flash was going to be my chaperon for my return to Free Earth. I had also talked to his wife. She did know that her husband and the Free Earthers had a plot to get past Spaceport security to "inspect" the Martian freighter when it landed.

"There's no keeping secrets when it comes to Phishy," Flash said, after he greeted me.

"There's always a chance."

"What did he tell you, and I tell what he should have told you?"

"Roswellian. This just keeps getting better and better each time."

"It is not what you think."

"That's what Phishy said."

"It's funny."

"What is?"

"Your first case—the kidnapped girl. That's what started it. She was kidnapped in Alien Alley."

I nodded, remembering. "Alien Alley. So naturally you had to join the space aliens."

"You're telling me you don't believe in extraterrestrial life."

"I'm telling you I don't care."

"Well a lot of us do."

"And the relevance to life is what?"

"Not everything has to be relevant to this life."

"Yes, it does, because in my business I deal with the real life here in front of me. Whether ETs exist or not doesn't pay my bills, help me keep my vehicle clean, or buy the million and one diapers Cruz Jr. is going to fill to the brim in the years to come."

Flash laughed. "That is one way of looking at it. But seriously, it's not what you think. The Cosmos are a lot more than you think. They also are part owners of a community corporation called Crop Circles."

"Community corporation? What exactly is a community corporation? Isn't that the same as a regular corporation?"

"It's the term for do-gooders who hate corporations, but have to start their own, but don't want to feel like they sold out to capitalism."

"The word you're looking for is hypocrite."

"Cruz, you get more cynical every time I see you."

"I saw one of their hovertruck plow-pickers."

"Crop Circles is a multi-billion dollar operation."

I always kept my eyes on the lane when I was driving, but I shot Flash a look of surprise. "Flash, that's not a corporation, that's a megacorp. The Free Earthers are rich."

"Filthy. The reason none of it is tied to their names is because all profits go into a communal bank account."

"What are you saying? You became a Roswellian to get on the board of their communal bank account?"

Flash laughed again. "I wish. No, my wife and I were sincerely interested in the Extraterrestrial Life Movement, but not for us, for the kids. They really do run the best space museums and space amusement parks. My wife and I are amateur astronomers. All the best amateurs are part of the movement.

"It's like when you were part of the hoverracing scene. You were a part of the scene but not part of all the clichés, because they were the best of the racing scene. I like astronomy for the science."

"You're part of the club but not the cult of it all."

"That's it."

"But Flash, that doesn't explain why you know about their communal bank accounts. That's not science. Sounds like business economics or maybe a little—espionage."

"It's not that either. Run-Time has me exploring a possible joint-venture."

I smiled. "Run-Time still wants to get into space."

"Always."

Run-Time was my long-time best friend, the best man at my wedding, and the godfather of Cruz Jr. He was also the founder, President, CEO and COO of Let It Ride Enterprises, the top hovertaxicab and hoverlimousine service in Metropolis, and Flash's boss.

As with any good business, he always had an eye to expansion. He had been trying to get his services into the highly competitive (and dangerous) commercial world of the off-world colonies for years. What was stopping him was the existing Up-Top megacorps.

"Crop Circles has turned astronomy into a major business," Flash added.

The Free-Earthers had taken science fans and sci-fi fans alike throughout space to view the moon, the planets, the stars, other galaxies, and more through the magnifying view bays of their shuttles. Crop Circles had the tour guides; Run-Time wanted to take their business to the next level by providing the transportation they didn't have. Crop Circles would dramatically expand their clientele, Run-Time would be in space to bring Let It Ride to all the off-world colonies.

"He's thinking partnering with the ET watchers will allow him to bypass all the Up-Top megacorp gangsters."

"Exactly. They are very bare essentials operations. Simple shuttles. Run-Time wants to upgrade the accommodations dramatically with premium Let It Ride space shuttles."

I nodded approvingly. "You do know a lot about them."

"I do. Regardless of what you think of their beliefs and motives, the situation with the brother is real. And I know you don't want to hear about it—"

"Flash, don't say it—"

"It's about that meteor."

"What is with this meteor? Phishy was about the meteor. You. My wife calling me Meteor Man. The Chief wanted me to ask about it. A space rock is not a case. Why won't people see that?"

"Cruz, the meteor isn't the case. It is *the* case. Someone tried to kill you."

I took my eyes off the lane a second time to look at him. I quickly returned my gaze to the front. "That's ridiculous. Someone wanted to kill Free Earth, but to what end?"

"That's what you have to find out. That's why it's the case. Cruz, maybe the reason everyone is saying the meteor is the case is because it actually is the case?"

"Flash, let's put the meteor to the side for a moment. What if Neil Cosmos found proof of ETs out there—so what? What's the big deal? What's the motive to make him disappear, and to try to kill us using a previously never-before-used weapon to destroy a 'Space Aliens Rule the World' community from space? I don't see the reason. I'm very good at reasons—money, sex, revenge, power, insanity. What's the motive? Just give me a theory—any theory."

How to be a Great Detective with 100 Rules. The book by my posthumous mentor, Wilford G, who was a private eye in Metropolis for 70 plus years.

"What makes a great detective is having a theory to the crime," I said. "How else can you solve it? How else do you know which way to go, who to talk to, what clues to look for, and follow? Otherwise, you're just a blind, one-winged pigeon flopping around on the asphalt doing nothing but flopping around."

Flash grinned. "You really have memorized that book."

"Every page. Well? Do you have a theory for me?

"I do, but I'm not going to say it out loud. Next week at the Spaceport."

"I don't know what you and your new friends have planned, but there is no way in Hades that the Up-Toppers will let any of us anywhere near their Martian Freighter. Then what?"

"Then that's it—the end of the case."

"Flash, you get too caught up in people's problems too easily."

"If I didn't there would be one lonely woman in Metropolis without her little daughter. I brought that woman to my boss to help and he brought her to you. You helped her. You saved her daughter from a vicious animal gangster, and your new detective career was launched. All I'm asking is for you to help them—the Cosmos—find Neil. That's all."

I sighed. Flash caught me off guard with the emotional plea. Neither of us talked again in the Pony, as I drove to Free Earth.

CHAPTER 14

Sid and The Detective

I could see that Flash realized that instead of driving to the outskirts of Metropolis that I had taken an off-lane to fly to another part of town. However, he said nothing. He continued to quietly stare out the passenger window.

For anyone in the hovercar racing or restoring business, the place I was going was sacrilegious—the automatic hovercarwash. Any real classic hovercar owner would rather have their flesh peeled from their body than to subject their vehicles to the robotic brushes of an automated hovercarwash. You wanted to wash your vehicle? You did it by hand!

When Flash saw that we were headed into one, he immediately straightened up in the seat and looked at me. The structure looked like short tunnels stacked on top of each other from the tenth story to the one hundredth. Such a place made me and every other real hovervehicle owner sick, but to the average Metro supercity dweller they were cheap and convenient. I flew right into one of the washing tubes and down. I didn't stop; I kept driving past the robot brush arms around a corner, stopped, and then ascended fast.

Flash looked at me again as we rose straight to the 100th level in minutes. I drove forward a bit and landed my vehicle. Flash followed me as I left the vehicle and knocked on what looked like the wall, but it was a door. It opened.

"Cruz, my man." Inside the hidden room was a rotund man, gold bracelets and necklaces galore, with one hand opening the door for us and the other holding a box of Chinese food with the chopsticks inside. "What brings you to my domain?"

The room was not very big at all but the wall were covered with vid-monitors of every tube and the surrounding area. Even automated businesses needed full-time human surveillance.

"Hey Sid, I wanted to see if I was being followed."

"Looks like you were," he said, pointing at a monitor with his chopsticks.

We all watched the monitors and there were black hovercars everywhere illegally hovering in the sky-traffic. They all looked like Feds, but Feds didn't wear stupid, black cheapie shades.

"What agency do they look like to you?" I asked Sid.

"Not Feds."

"Up-Top police?"

"I would say so, but look how many. Metro wouldn't allow it, but—"

"I know him!" I pointed to one display screen. It was Agent Weborg.

"I know who they are," Flash said.

"Sid, can I borrow a vid-phone? Looks like I'll be hiding out here for a bit."

"Sure, you know where it is."

I left Flash and Sid there to watch the agents swarming in front of the tubes looking for my red Ford Pony to pop back out. I made my call.

Sid was an OG, "original gangster," in the classic hovercar racing scene. He had retired and used his winnings over a lifetime to open up a string of auto-hovercar washing facilities all over Metropolis. He also owned some of the most beautiful and highly prized hovervehicles around, which is how we came into contact—he hired me as his restorer. I restored three of his thirty vehicle fleet. The last job, I purposely drew out my job so I could stay in his garage vault as long as possible to be with the vehicles.

He personally would never have his pride and joys near an auto-hovercarwash, which he viewed as taking sandpaper to a vehicle's high-gloss, high-grade paint, but he had no problem pocketing the money from the masses. He made a lot of money racing hovercars; he was making a king's fortune with this business.

Sid was nice enough to order more Chinese, and we all sat at the table, eating as we watched the agents on the screens. They were angry knowing I had ditched them.

"What did you do to these guys?" Sid asked me.

"Other than be born, I don't know."

One of the cameras was in one of the elevator capsules. I wiped my mouth with a napkin and got up from my chair. "I'll be back."

The elevator opened. A semi-well dressed man stood there, leaning against the back wall.

"Detective Cruz."

"Detective Crux."

"Never thought I'd hear from the famous detective again."

"Yes, it's your lucky day."

"Are you serious about this? Is this a gag?"

"No, it's not a gag. Do you want the job or not?"

"Oh, I'll do it all right."

We quickly did our transaction. I gave him my credit card; he swiped it with his wallet scanner.

"You're on the case."

"A detective hiring a detective."

"Can't do much detecting myself when I have a lot of unfriendly people looking for me."

"Yeah I saw all those Feds out there. But they're not Feds are they?"

"Who cares? Get back to me when you got something."

"Maybe this can be a regular thing."

"If you get what I need, maybe it can be."

I saluted him and left; he grinned and tapped the elevator call button.

CHAPTER 15

The Cosmos

I'm glad we had the Chinese food before we set out again. I flew the Pony down a secret underground tunnel that only Sid, me, and a handful of former hovercar racers and aficionados knew about. It took us fifteen miles away from Sid's auto-hovercarwash tower. At least, I wasn't going back to Free Earth on an empty stomach.

Flash said the movement came out of the ancient UFO community before we had hovercars, our first off-world colonies, and real spaceships. That's why it all seemed like a group psychosis to me. "The ETs are hiding on the far side of the moon. Well, we put our lunar colonies there, then, no, they're hiding on Mars. We put a colony on Mars. No they're on Jupiter's moons—no Saturn's moon Titan—no on Pluto—no, they're hiding in the center of the sun itself in their secret base in a force globe with cloaking technology." It never ends—a rabbit hole. A rabbit hole with no bottom in sight.

As I neared the location in the Pony, at first I thought there was a fire because it looked like a black cloud in the distance wavering up from the ground. Then we realized that it was thousands upon thousands of hovercars in the sky.

"Oh my goodness." I was looking to see if I could do a U-turn.

"Don't turn around," Flash told me. "It'll be fine."

"It's a circus, Flash. The proverbial mother-lode of circuses from crazy town."

No," he laughed, but then two hovercars whipped past us designed to look like flying saucers—made out of tinfoil.

"Flash! We got to get out of here. I don't want any of these crazy people near my vehicle."

"Okay, you're right. It's not safe."

I U-turned out of there as fast I could fly.

The driver of the hovertaxi we took back there spent more time peeking out of his open driver side window than watching the sky. It was even worse than we first thought. The entire area around Free Earth near the meteor crater had become an ET watchers Holy Land. The hovertaxi landed and the driver was already out of his seat, leaving Flash and me in our seats.

"Where are you going?" I yelled.

The driver threw up his hands and spun back around, grinning.

"Yes, you left two passengers in your cab and didn't even collect your fare." He said nothing but pointed to the side of his head. "Yes, you are mental. No, the big crater isn't going anywhere."

We paid him and grudgingly gave him a tip—at least I did. Then the man was gone—into the crowds he went. Flash and I looked at each other. We had no idea what was in store for us.

People in silver gowns, big alien-head masks, clip-on antennas (not the Martian play ones), silver visors. Tons of signs: TAKE ME, I'M YOURS; BEAM ME UP, NOT THE OTHER GUY; EARTHERS FOR ALIENS.

It was a dizzying display of madness. I attempted to turn back twice, but Flash grabbed and kept me going forward. Who knew how many undercover reporters there were? Who knows how many undercover police there were in this bunch?

"We're almost there," Flash said.

We bypassed the crowd to walk to the main entrance domes of Free Earth. They had an army of robots at the front to block people. Several feet back, their citizens watched through binoculars. Flash waved and one of them waved us in, two eight-foot humanoid robots stepped aside to let us pass.

"Why do they get to go through?" a woman, with some guy behind us yelled. The silver-skinned couple rushed the robot to get around us, but another robot stunned them.

"Why did you stun me?" the guy said on his back.

I looked up and noticed that the rain had stopped. Great! That meant more ET watchers would be on their way.

"Let me do all the talking until we get to the Cosmos." Flash smiled, realizing what it sounded like he said.

"I know what you meant and that would be best."

I had told Flash what Mr. Weborg told me about Neil Cosmos. Flash shook his head, not believing a word of it. "Neil would never commit suicide," he said emphatically, without a hint of doubt.

Flash insisted I tell Mr. and Mrs. Cosmos immediately. Hence, we were here in the middle of the madness. That Martian space freighter couldn't arrive fast enough, but I had a sneaking feeling that when that day did arrive the whole thing was also going to be a fiasco, but I put that out of my mind.

We had been ushered into an elevator to their subterranean streets of the real Free Earth; a crowd was waiting for us, but unlike my first visit, the crowd wasn't dressed like normal Metropolis residents. Flash saw that I was already having trouble keeping my composure. One side of the crowd was dressed in silver gray; the opposite site was in neon blue. Mr. and Mrs. Cosmos were near the middle with the "normal" members of the crowd.

At first, I couldn't make out the object coming through the crowd, then I did. A man with a large conehead on his head came through the front. I had had enough.

I walked up to them, turned around, bent down and looked up from between my legs. "Take me to your leader!"

Mr. Cosmos burst out laughing. His wife smacked him in the arm. "Mr. Cruz, that is not funny."

I stood up and spun around to face them.

"Do you think you're the first person to think of that? You aren't funny, you know."

"Your husband thinks so."

"He doesn't count."

Conehead glared at me, as if he wanted to punch me. "For your information, the conehead is a portable missile defense system that I invented. If the government tries to attack us again, we'll be able to defend ourselves this time."

"You're joking, right?"

"I am not. I am a real defense systems engineer, and I am not doing this for your personal amusement."

"You look like an idiot."

"Says the man in the hat."

"Says the man in the hat? You have a conehead on your head. Missile defense? I don't believe you."

He held up his palm. "Venus!"

The underground streets of Free Earth were not congested like Metropolis. There were a few hundred people, all clustered around us at the elevator, so the main street was practically empty. A woman in the front raised her hand to her mouth and began talking into a wrist comm. I could see something rising in the air from the corner of my eye. I turned. A hoverlimo was arcing up in the air to us—must have been some kind of catapult machine. There was a loud metallic sound. I whipped my head around to see that Conehead's conehead open, and a mini-missile launched. My eyes followed it to its target. The hoverlimo blew up into a million pieces. I looked at him with my mouth hanging open. "It's real!"

"Yes, it's real, Detective Cruz."

I wasn't shocked. I was impressed, and I wasn't a man easily impressed. Conehead had impressed me. "How many missiles does it hold?" I asked like a little kid standing at the feet of Santa Claus.

Conehead's top lip started twitching; then he ran.

I was mad. My original assessment had been right; Conehead was an idiot. He was running with a couple of Free Earthers right behind him. They disappeared into one of the buildings down the street. "How can you only have one missile in your head? And you waste it showing off! Now we're defenseless again! What's wrong with you? Missile defense with only one missile." I looked at the Cosmos. Mr. Cosmos was literally trying to choke himself to keep from laughing again. His wife glared at me.

"Should we wait for him to load another missile in his conehead?"

Mr. Cosmos dropped to the ground laughing.

"Yes, have another heart attack you!" his wife yelled at him, then kicked him.

At this point, half the crowd was laughing; half the crowd was glaring at me. I smiled. Half of them hated me and they had just met me. I was proud.

There was a man in the group, whose face was very familiar. I knew him, but couldn't remember from where. He wasn't a major criminal; I had committed the faces of most of Metropolis's crime boss population to memory. I knew him and he tried to move back into the crowd so I couldn't see him directly. He knew I recognized him. He was probably an undercover police officer.

They didn't lead me to a huge auditorium or common meeting room. It looked like one of those Old European-style sitting rooms with the expensive plush leather chairs. It actually looked like the executive smoking rooms at Fat Nat's Joe Blows in Old Harlem. It was the place where real business took place among the elite.

"Have a seat, Mr. Cruz," Mrs. Cosmos said to me. "Wherever you want."

I sat down in a chair and got comfortable. Flash was very talkative before when we arrived to them, but hadn't spoken since we entered the room, and sat closest to the door. When Mr. and Mrs. Cosmos also sat, several new people began to enter, as if on cue.

"Is this the Crop Circles Community Corporate Board of Directors?"

"Right you are, Mr. Cruz." A bald man with a pure white goatee answered and sat. He leaned back in his chair with a smirk. At least it was close to a smile; the others had blank expressions or, like Mrs. Cosmos, were outwardly contemptuous of me.

The man's name was Geo. He had piercing albino eyes—more likely than not contacts, since he didn't outwardly look like a real albino. He began the smalltalk as people got settled in their seats, and something to drink for everyone was brought in. We were in Free Earth so what would a discussion be about—ETs.

"But your colleagues believe the ETs will enslave humankind," I said.

"ETs, Mr. Cruz?" It was a larger woman named Terra in a one-piece florescent outfit that was constantly changing colors. It was annoying, frankly. "That's a small-minded, human-centric word."

I laughed. "Human-centric? When we meet real ETs, I'll stop using the word."

"Mr. Cruz, do you think we're unbalanced people because we are certain that there is other life besides ourselves in the universe?"

"No. I'm agnostic myself. I couldn't care less either way. But when you start talking about abductions, probing, and the takeover of humankind, and start running around with fake antennas and coneheads, what should outsiders think?"

"Fair point. You've been a private detective long enough. Would you say you're an average representative of your profession?"

"Absolutely not."

"You could no more regulate who can call themselves 'detective' than we could regulate who is part of the Alien Life community. To use your phrase, 'we could care less.' Sadly, most in the movement can barely comprehend the enormity of our beliefs. If humankind ever did encounter true extraterrestrial life, the result would be profound. Humankind would never be the same. Unlike most of our colleagues you met outside, we are real space scientists."

"Yes, I met Mr. Conehead."

"You always have a dismissive comeback, or is it just for us?" Mrs. Cosmos asked.

"Okay, I'll compromise then. I'll say space aliens, but I really mean ET, just so you know."

"Some do believe space alien life will try to conquer and control humankind," Geo said. "Their views are every bit as valid as ours. That is why we both live in Free Earth, both sides must be represented. We prepare for either possibility, because that's what responsible adults do. Everyone is represented here, and we don't mind those who wish to make fun of all of us, because of a few. When we do meet outer-life, when everyone else is panicking, we'll be the only ones ready and prepared to seize the opportunity for mankind."

"And if they turn out to be hostile or evil?"

"That answer is simple. Kill every last one so that the message is clear—humankind is not to be trifled with."

It wasn't Mr. Conehead that was the most dangerous Free Earther with his cranial cone-hat missile launcher. It was the ones sitting in front of me now. If ET was friendly, they would be dancing and spooning each other all day long. If ET was hostile, then ET would get a double-tap to the back of his space alien skull by concealed laser gun. As long as humankind was the priority. That's what I really wanted to hear.

"Well, Mr. Cruz, what have you found?" Mrs. Cosmos asked. "Flash said you had news. Honestly, I haven't been much impressed with you at all. You're openly dismissive of our beliefs, openly hostile—"

"Mrs. Cosmos, you and your husband came to me."

"Why did you take the case then?"

"Firstly, I didn't. If you recall, I refunded your retainer. You were the ones who insisted I was your detective."

"Because of Flash's assurances."

"That's why I reconsidered and am taking it, though in a very limited way. Mrs. Cosmos, clients don't have to like their detective or vice versa. Flash already told you what I found out."

"Suicide?" Mrs. Cosmos huffed. "Are you so easily thrown off track?"

"Whether I believe what this agent said or not doesn't change the fact that we're here on Earth. There's no way for me to find out either way."

"You could if you wanted to."

"No, I couldn't. They have all the power here. Not only is it Up-Top, it's Up-Top law enforcement. They say your brother committed suicide on Jupiter Outpost."

"Our contacts confirmed he's on the freighter," another board member snapped at me.

"How do you suppose I would prove or disapprove any of it from here on Earth? I'm good, but I'm not a magical super hero. We have to go through channels, that's all we can do. But you know that, Crop Circles Board Member.

"You still haven't told me why you're so certain your brother didn't commit suicide like that government agent said. However untrustworthy, he's in a better position to know than any of us. I have to ask, because I've been led astray by clients before: is this about Neil Cosmos, or this space freighter? Are you all also illegal contraband smugglers? The last husband-and-wife clients I had were also child prostitution pips on the side. Are you all smuggling drugs or something on that freighter?"

"That is completely outrageous and very much uncalled for," the woman Dawn said.

"There it is. You're comparing us to other people without giving us a chance. We're not criminals, Mr. Cruz. Do my husband and I look like we could be criminals?"

The husband squinted, thinking. "Why couldn't we be criminals? We could be criminals."

"Shut up, you!" Mrs. Cosmos snapped. She turned back to me. "Mr. Cruz, we're not criminals. People with our beliefs can't afford to be anything other than upstanding citizens or outside forces will use it to taint all of us."

"Yes, but Mr. Cruz did ask some fair questions," Geo interjected. "We'll answer them simply. The reason we know Neil Cosmos didn't commit suicide before he boarded that space freighter is because he sent us a transmission *after* he boarded. So the agent lied to you. We lost contact with him when his freighter entered Martian space. That's all we know because everything has been jammed since."

"Jammed by who?"

"We don't know."

"The freighter is the only thing we care about because Neil is on it," Mrs. Cosmos added. "There is something else on it, which is why we believe Space or Martian authorities are involved. Proof of extraterrestrial life that Neil found on an asteroid between Mars and Jupiter. Proof, not fantasy or myth."

"That's why we need you, Cruz," Flash spoke up. "We need you there when we get onto the freighter."

"Hold on a minute! You all are smugglers and criminals, maybe even much worse. That freighter can't come to Earth with a potential—" I had jumped up from my chair. "That freighter has to be put into possible xenomorph-level quarantine. Earth must be informed now, and any space station or lunar colony that may come into contact with that freighter before it gets here."

They were all uniformly smiling. I stood there looking back at them. "What?"

"Mr. Cruz, you've made all the right assumptions," Geo said. "A space freighter carrying a possible extraterrestrial in whatever form would be put under the most draconian of quarantines. Any involved in such a plot would be subject to the most severe off-world felonies. However, for one thing."

"Which is?"

"He disclosed everything on the manifest."

"My brother is a scientist. He's not a criminal," Mrs. Cosmos snapped. "He put all of it, in detail, on the manifest and they approved it."

I sat back down in my chair to think. I suddenly felt very, very vulnerable. "Where's Mr. Conehead?"

"He's on guard above-ground," one of them answered.

"No need to be nervous, Mr. Cruz," Geo said. "They wouldn't send another meteor after us—too much publicity, no chance of deniability if they were to do it twice."

"Why can't I get scummy little cases like every other detective in Metropolis?" I asked myself. "The Up-Toppers are sending a quarantined spaceship to Earth without telling Earth authorities."

"Yes, Mr. Cruz. It's the only thing that makes sense."

I shook my head. "No."

"What do you mean 'no'?" Mrs. Cosmos asked.

"I will not buy into your mob paranoia and government conspiracies. The Space Colonies and Mars would never do this—never. They'd blow it out of space, not let it land on an unwitting Earth. I don't like Up-Top like every other good Earther, but I don't hate them. I reject your conspiracy theory."

"It's not conspiracy theory, Mr. Cruz. It's what they're doing."

"Yet, you plan to meet it at the Spaceport."

"Neil is on that freighter. We confirmed it," Mrs. Cosmos said. "And he's alive—we believe in suspended animation."

I was suspicious again. "How would you know that?" I asked.

"We have ways," she said.

"How many other passengers are on this freighter?"

"We don't have the exact number, but it's a standard crew with a couple of civilians."

"How did you find that out?"

"We know."

"What do you think will happen when the proof of this extraterrestrial life is exposed to the world? You said it will change everything. How will things change? How will my life, my family's life, all Earther's lives change?"

Geo was happy to answer me. "Mr. Cruz, we will not only know that we are not alone in the universe. It will be revealed that they have always been here among us. Unlike what others in the movement have feared, we believe a group of them have likely been benevolently steering human evolution from the beginning. Once the world knows what we have found and accept the proof of their existence, we can join the intergalactic community, side by side."

A whole community of people with their minds lost in space.

"Alrighty-then," I said.

When I exited their ground floor elevators and had just started walking, I heard the yell. "You're Cruz, aren't you?"

The tone of voice let me know whoever it was, wasn't interested in a friendly conversation. I turned to see two men in dark slickers, one with blue-tinted shades, walking to me, and I had my arm under my jacket with weapon in hand. The two could see I was packing and stopped.

"Are you going to shoot us in the open, P.I, with cameras everywhere?"

I stood there and they could see in my face that I was not playing around.

"You better not talk to the media again!" he yelled. "Keep your mouth shut with your lies."

I said nothing. I just stood, stared and was ready to draw. They were both nervous and slowly walked away, back into the crowd—a crowd totally oblivious to what was happening around them.

When they were out of sight I double-timed out of there.

CHAPTER 16

The Detective's Wife

When I took off running it was to where Flash had been waiting in the crowd. The hovertaxi he called arrived quickly. How the driver was able to spot us in all the pandemonium of people and vehicles on the ground and in the sky was nothing short of magic. Neither one of us could pick up our vehicles, so it was back to the Acid Rain.

Somehow the same booth was free when we showed up, so we slid into our seats for a waiter to serve us.

"A colleague of the guy I hired is coming here. PJ said it was urgent, so we'll meet here."

Flash was still focused on my Free Earth visit. "I don't know why you left it there. I'm not a detective, but I could see you had many more questions to ask."

"Yes, and I'd still be there. I got what I needed. They're scientists. Scientists, like all academicians, tend to talk forever, and often you have no idea what they're talking about. After I talk to this guy's colleague, I'll head over to see what Cruz Jr. and the wife are up to."

"Oh, no." The look of fear that came over Flash's face made me drop my cup of silk coffee to the table. I stood but it was already too late, my hand couldn't reach my weapon fast enough for whoever was approaching me, from behind. I turned to see a woman menacingly reaching into her coat. She pulled out her mobile phone and put it right up to my face. I cocked my head back to see the picture of Detective Crux on the display screen.

"Where's my husband?" she said.

I looked at her, then I noticed them. There was one kid standing behind her—no, there were like nine!

"Where's my children's husband?"

"I'm sorry, ma'am, but I don't—"

"I know you hired my husband for something shady. Now he's gone. What are you going to do about it? What am I supposed to do? Me and my kids!" I felt something and I looked down at her other hand—a laser pistol aimed at my belly. "I want answers now, mister famous detective." She and her snarling child-brood had me trapped in the booth.

"Why would you have nine kids?" I asked.

"Stop trying to change the subject, or I'll shoot you."

"I can barely deal with the diaper changing of one kid—but nine! I'd kill myself."

"Yeah, you new fathers are never the paragons of bravery. What did you get my husband into?"

"If you let me sit down, so we can talk, and send your demon brood to go play out in traffic, we can find out what's what."

"Mommy, what is a brood?" one of her kids asked.

"Never mind what he's saying. Ignore him. Mr. Cruz, my kids are staying right here. They'll help me keep an eye on you."

Flash had been silent all that time. "Well, Cruz, I'll catch you later." He slid out of the booth and was gone for the back exit. *What the heck?* There were some people in the diner watching what was going on, but for the most part, no one cared. They were on the same page as Flash, letting me fend for myself.

Mrs. Crux let all of the brood in first, before she slid into the booth in his place. Nine kids, one adult, all staring at me.

"I cannot conduct business under such conditions. I have one word for the ten of you—Tarima!"

Arcades were every bit as ubiquitous as virtual life parlors. The latter crowd wanted to disappear into their virtual worlds through time and space. But for the arcade-goer it was the group experience that was the fun—one or two players with a group gathered around to watch.

It wasn't that I minded the kids hearing our conversation or anyone in the Acid Rain diner. Maybe all of the patrons were hovertaxi drivers, but I didn't believe it. Flash and I were followed to the auto-hovercarwash, why not the diner?

I had taken Mrs. Crux and her brood to the arcade that was right down the street. I started them off on Ultimate Tarima dancing on a hover floor with multi-colored flashing squares and copying the dance moves of the holo-man in the floating screen in front of us—in my case it was a holo-man who looked a lot like me. I sure hope it wasn't supposed to be me—I still was annoyed at seeing Liquid Cool T-shirts everywhere courtesy of PJ and Phishy franchising me.

What made it such a great game was that not only did the holo-man's dance moves become more elaborate as the game went on, but included moves that took full advantage of the entire dance floor—jumping, sliding, and spinning. I went for a good five rounds and then turned to the kids.

"No, I can't do any of that," the youngest girl said.

"Then two of you come up," I said. "Two of you at a time against the holo-man."

With the kids completely immersed in the dance game, and a laughing, cheering crowd, I was free to speak with Mrs. Crux.

"What happened?" I asked.

"My husband was picked up."

"By who?"

"The Feds."

"Why would Feds pick him up?"

"What did you have him doing?"

"He was investigating the meteor for me. That's all. Why would the Feds pick him up for that?"

"It was government agents. I'm sure of it, but no one will tell me anything. I went to Metro PD, the Feds—" We both had the same thought at the same time. "What happens if someone is picked up by Up-Top Police?"

"They get transferred to holding on the Praetoria Space Station."

"Oh my God! What am I supposed to do?"

"Nothing. I'll handle it."

"Will you? Will you really handle it? As you can see with nine kids, I'm the one who stays home. I don't work."

"Raising nine kids is more than work."

"You said it! You need to promise me that you'll get my husband."

"If they got him, I'll get him out. "

"You better. I need my husband back. The kids need their father!"

"I'll get him out."

Mrs. Crux's eyes were tearing up, but she believed me. She composed herself and returned to the side of her laughing children with the crowd on the Tarima game. The kids were also glancing back at me and I smiled, but inside I was far from happy. I had hired another detective to take work off my plate. Now I had another missing person's case with me as a joint-client. Two clients for a case and neither of one of us would be paying a retainer. I'd have to investigate the killer meteor from space after all.

PART FOUR

Arrival (of Some Very, Very Crazy People)

CHAPTER 17

P.J.

"Why did you hire another detective to do your investigating?" PJ asked me from her desk. I had returned to my office to be interrogated by my own employee.

"Because I didn't want to investigate the meteor."

"Why are you avoiding a key part of the case? Now you have to."

"Now, I have two things to investigate: the meteor and what unknown persons snatched up my detective who was investigating it."

"That's what you get for not doing your own work."

"Well, that means I have a job for you because I can't be everywhere and I'm not hiring more staff."

"We need more staff."

"No. But—I will have you hire temp employees, to report to you until this project is done."

PJ was now interested and grabbed her electric steno pad. "Now we're talking. I can be a boss too."

"I want you and your team to pull the pictures of every bystander at the crater and around Free Earth. Everyone. Then run those faces through the facial recog databases."

She smiled again. "I know what you're doing."

"What am I doing?"

"Whenever a bad thing happens the bad guy comes back to the scene and mingles in with the crowd to watch for himself. Very smart. You're being very smart right now."

"Glad you approve. It's going to be a huge project because there were a lot of people there, so a lot of people talking pics and vids."

"But all on the Net. Got it. Identify all the people, so we can find the bad guy."

"Or bad guys."

"Got it."

"But—be careful. Remember my detective guy was snatched up."

"Because he wasn't working here. Liquid Cool can be a fortress when we need it to be. Besides, I got my laser rifle under the desk handy and more weapons too in the drawers. Can I arm the temps?"

"No, you cannot arm the temps! You, yes. You're an ex-felon so you know how to handle weapons. There's no reason for any temps we hire to become felons too. Just you."

"Anyone comes snooping around, I'll punch them through the building to splat on the ground." PJ flexed her bionic arms.

"Punching is okay, but let's avoid sending bodies to the ground 100 floors below. Hire your team."

"Yes, boss, so I can be a boss too."

CHAPTER 18

Up-Top E.T. Watchers

I had tried to avoid any and all news. Honestly, I was scared what I might hear since I probably had a lot to do with it. I didn't know how the media could let me use them so often, but to them, I was good person of interest that gave them big headlines and contributed to their bottom line. My first case put me on their radar and they'd never let me go, so I had a right to use them for my purposes when it suited me.

However, I couldn't avoid hearing people talk about it, wherever I went: Earth and Up-Top were not on speaking terms. But it meant that something was not right because the Up-Top authorities wouldn't just come out and deny the "meteor death weapon" allegation. Why? More importantly, why did they snatch up my detective, if that's what happened? I had a case that I didn't want that had turned into three cases I didn't want.

It had never occurred to me that the Space Station, Lunar and Martian colonies would have their own Alienist societies. They did.

Flash was the one who called me at the office and, despite my better judgment, I decided to see for myself. Curiosity was one reason—I wanted to see what ET watchers from off-world looked like—but more importantly, I needed intel. They would be the best source outside of the Up-Top police, who would never talk to me, of getting some possible answers.

Geo sat at the farthest table in the back of the restaurant. His tea was probably cold by now, but he kept stirring it. He smiled noticing his guest enter. The man who approached was dressed all in black with a gray skullcap covering his ears too. He took off his white shades with his gloved hands as he sat across from him. For a spaceman, he looked like any other person on the street.

"Who's your friend?" he asked.

"My name's Cruz," I answered, sitting in the chair adjacent to both.

"Geo, I thought we were meeting alone."

"Ares, we are."

"What do you want Mr. Cruz? Tell me so you can leave and I can conduct my private business with my Terran colleague."

"Yes, I'm sure there're lots of ET things you need to discuss."

He smirked. "What can I do for you?"

"Did you spacemen purposely try to wipe out Free Earth?" I asked, point-blank.

Mr. Ares laughed. "We Martians may not think the highest of our Lunar and space station brethren, but they wouldn't be that stupid. Also, they have much more sophisticated weaponry than shooting rocks at Earth."

"Maybe that was the point. Make it look like a natural event."

"Does anyone on Earth believe it was natural? No. You were there. The meteor knew where it was going."

"Exactly," I said.

"Yet here you are alive and well. Were you all caught unaware?"

"No—"

"No, because Free Earth's early warning defense systems did what they were supposed to—they warned you and you all ran away in plenty of time. He looked at Geo. "Surely, you don't believe this too."

"I didn't have to dodge it like Mr. Cruz, but many of us did. It was a miracle no one was killed."

"Then you do believe it."

"The secret Cydonian base," Geo said to him.

"Their Cydonian base has no meteor weapons. Listen to us talk—meteor weapons. There is no such thing. Why would someone have a meteor weapon when everyone has laser weapons. Seems too retro-useless to me. You're all being played."

"By whom?" I asked.

"The M.I.B.s of course. This is exactly the kind of thing they do to stoke the paranoia."

"We were almost killed."

"*Almost*, Mr. Cruz. I don't believe you were ever in any real danger."

"Then what is this situation between Earth and off-world?"

"That is real, which is why I'm to talk to my colleague, after you, Mr. Cruz, excuses himself."

"How did you get to Earth?" Geo asked.

"You don't honestly think we'd take a commercial spacecraft and land at one of your airports. We have our transportation."

"Flying saucers?" I asked.

"With cloaking technology," Ares said with a grin. "Are you still here, Mr. Cruz?"

"If the meteor wasn't launched from the moon, then why doesn't Up-Top provide the proof. There have satellites everywhere—taking pictures, recording images."

"Why does Up-Top, as you call it, have to do that? It's the moon, Mr. Cruz, not the far side of the Andromeda Galaxy. Earth authorities have satellites, too. They know exactly what happened and where the meteor came from."

"I don't get it then."

Geo took his hand off the spoon in his cup. "I don't know what to make of it, Mr. Cruz. Mr. Ares is an off-worlder, so maybe he's protecting his government."

"That's a dirty lie, Geo. We mistrust off-world government every bit as much as Earth's, but that said, we're not going to buy into Earth's anti-off-world prejudices. Off-world is playing games, but so is Earth. Or are the two of you trying to protect your planet?"

I shook my head. "I'm simply asking questions about this meteor because everyone wants me to, including Mr. Geo and his Free Earth friends. I didn't want to investigate it. Can I ask a question?"

"Please do, Mr. Cruz," Geo asked.

"What are you two going to talk about when I leave?" Ares smirked. Geo starting stirring his cold tea again. "Then I'll be going."

The men watched me leave the restaurant. Even when I was out of the building and walking to the parking bay, I felt I was being watched. The Up-Top ET watchers were on Earth. Why?

"Oh, Mr. Cruz." I turned and there was Mr. Ares standing with something in an outstretched hand. "You accidentally left your secret little listening device behind."

I took it from him. "Thank you. I was wondering where I had left it."

He grinned and walked back into the restaurant.

Oh, well. I had tried.

CHAPTER 19

Run-Time

It was only a matter of time before my best friend—the best man at my wedding and Cruz. Jr.'s godfather—appeared in the flesh in relation to this case. Already one of his employees, Flash, was in the center of it. Run-Time was a middle-school drop-out at eleven years old, body shop go-fer at twelve, hovercar mechanic at thirteen, valet attendant at fourteen, hovertaxi driver at seventeen. By nineteen, hovertaxicab owner, bought three more at twenty-one, millionaire at twenty-two, started *Let It Ride Enterprises* at twenty-five, mega-multi-millionaire by thirty.

His megacorp was headquartered in the trendy business district of Peacock Hills. This particular day he wasn't at his business tower, but another larger one. His office had called me and I had arrived, landing the Pony in the valet. There were an army of hoverlimos in the parking bay, so it was some kind of major megacorp meeting.

Run-Time had three main VPs and Mrs. Role, the West Indian, was waiting for me. "Mr. Cruz, good morning."

"Hello."

"Follow me. The meeting has already started."

"What's the meeting about?"

"It looks like Earth is threatening to boycott all Up-Top commercial traffic."

I almost stopped walking. "The meteor?"

"The meteor."

"How likely is it that Earth would ever do something like that?"

"Not likely at all, but even idle threats are dangerous. Up-Top is threatening to boycott all Earth transports of any kind to any space, lunar, or Martian destination."

"Why am I always involved in these kinds of things?"

She smiled. "You're not. How many cases have you solved without any fanfare at all?"

"A lot."

"When you're that active, you're bound to have a few high-profile ones mixed in there. This is simply one of them. It'll be alright. The level-headed adults will prevail over all the political children on all sides."

"Maybe I need to hire me a VP like you. I can be a glass-is-half-empty kind of guy sometimes."

"What about that secretary of yours?"

"If I want someone punched through a wall, that's her."

She laughed. "That can be a valuable skill too."

The mega-tower had its own auditorium-sized meeting hall filled with business types, standing and seated. Mrs. Role said it was only threats, but from the yelling and chatter in the room it felt that everyone felt that boycotts were imminent.

I spotted Run-Time in the crowd right away. He was standing at the back wearing one of his slim fit business suits and slim ties. The only casual thing he wore was his trademark flat cap. You'd never see his head without it. He saw me too and waved; I gave him a temple salute.

Run-Time ducked out to meet with me in the hallway. Ms. Role stood a few steps away to give us privacy and at the other end was a male aide who stood quietly at his post.

Phishy greeted me with his silly chicken-dance; Run-Time greeted me with a handshake and a hug like normal people.

"My man, Cruz. How's Dot and Cruz Jr.?"

"Family is good. Yours?"

"Wife and the kids are wonderful."

"I've been dying to ask—when it came to diaper changing, did you ever consider getting a robot?"

Run-Time began to laugh so hard. "Cruz. Well, of course."

"Don't tell Dot I asked that. She already took away my bio-suit."

"Bio-suit? I won't even ask."

"When we have a casual lunch."

"Well, let's not talk about it. What are you and Dot doing this weekend?"

"Yeah, we can do Saturday."

"Come over Saturday then. The women can do their thing. We can hang out in our place."

"Good. Deal. Your VP, Mrs. Role, put a very positive spin on this meeting here, but that crowd didn't seem very positive."

"Negative talk from politicians and law enforcement can move markets overnight, turn a rising stock into a nose-diving one in seconds. A business can lose market share, a senior exec can lose their 'permanent' job. None of us like this climate, which is why we're meeting."

"Is your business being affected?"

"The businesses of Metropolis have already been affected. And, confidentially, Flash told me you talked. That 'venture' is already on permanent hold. I was about to sign contracts this week."

"I'm so sorry. I know how long you've been fighting to expand there."

"Not your fault."

"No, but I'm in the middle of things again."

"Also, not your fault."

"What can I do to help then?"

"The meteor—"

"Not again. Everybody's asking me about that space rock."

"I don't know about other people, but since you were physically there—"

"What do you want to know?"

"A very important question, especially since I know you dabbled in amateur astronomy when we were kids."

"In other words, was it a real meteor from space or made to look like that?"

"Yes."

"It's been a while, so I'm not a 100% sure. Is what I think a meteor falling through the atmosphere to the Earth, what it really looks like, or based on some movie I watched on my mobile? I'm not sure, but I know I don't believe it was from space. And I'm suspicious."

"About?"

"Everything. Up-Top's denial that the meteor came from the moon was weak. Earth's insistence that it came from the moon was weak."

"We all thought the same thing."

"They both know if it did or didn't come from the moon. No investigation needed, just pull the satellite image files."

"What do you think is going on?"

"I don't know, but it isn't some grand conspiracy like the ET watchers would have people believe, but it sure plays into their hands."

"ET watchers." Run-Time laughed again.

"Also, where is the meteor? Government agents were in there and scooped up all the fragments like they were radioactive, but they weren't radioactive within an hour. When they behave like that, it feeds the paranoia and conspiracies."

"You do know if it didn't come from space—"

"Means it came from Earth. I'd say some kind of giant catapult machine."

"You've already been figuring out the means?"

"I've been playing out the scene in my mind over and over. To achieve that kind of trajectory to make it seem like it came from space—the machine would have to be huge, and it would have had to come from a long way so no one on the ground could see where it came from. I suspect some kind of heavy hovertruck, so it could fly away afterwards.

"I don't know why I'm even involved in this. I was hired to find a missing person. That's the job of a private detective. I'm not a secret agent, and this feels like a job for a secret agent."

"Never bothered you before."

"With Cruz Jr. around, I need to lessen these crazy cases I'm involved in."

"I hear you."

"That's why I want nothing to do with the meteor. I know what the meteor means, and I want nothing to do with it. Missing person, yes. Fake meteors, no."

"You've already concluded it was fake?"

"Yes, staged. Free Earth has radars, sensors and defensive systems. They have the ability to see anything coming at them, and the ability to shoot it out of the sky."

"Lasers?"

"The Feds could arrest them up for that, but they have their own mobile missile defense system. I would give you the details, but you'd fall on the floor laughing, it sounds so ridiculous, but I saw it, and it does the job.

"I don't believe the meteor was sent to kill anyone. It was sent to mess with the Free Earthers, and to cause the aftermath, which I elevated to the nth degree with my media performance.

"Or, just as likely, the meteor scam was perpetrated by the Free Earthers themselves. Not Flash, of course, but one or more of the others. Create a big news story to get attention in the media. The space alien controlled government tried to kill them with a meteor, just when they were going to hire a 'famous' detective. Scams like that have been done throughout history and will be done in the future. Either way, I didn't want to be a part of it. I had hired someone to dig around anyway, but that has run into complications. Why did you need me to come down here?"

"We need to calm the situation down. Would you be willing to talk to some of the megacorps leaders about the meteor attack—tell them your theories like you told me? It would mean far more coming from you—physically being there and a licensed detective that everyone has heard of—than me reciting it."

"Of course. However I can help."

"Good. Let's walk back in and I'll introduce you to some people."

CHAPTER 20

The E.T. Watchers

Run-Time was the ultimate business insider. He knew all the corporate and government players in Metropolis. I remember once when I asked him if he enjoyed the politics, he gave me a funny look and said, "I'm a CEO. It's my job." I liked that about Run-Time—all about business, no games. That's the standard I wanted to keep with my Liquid Cool business—whether I was successful was another matter. However, one employee of mine had come through in a big way.

I was flying back to Free Earth in the Pony. It was getting annoying, but there was no other way. I didn't want to speak to them on the vid-phone, for what I had.

When I neared their "city," I could see that the madness had increased, not decreased. I realized that now their crazy-town didn't just have the Earth ET watching groups, but now had all the Up-Top ones too. I had set down half a mile away; two big burly guys were waiting—my mobile car security guys.

"Hi guys. I don't know how long I'll be," I said as soon as I exited the Pony.

"No problem, Mr. Cruz," one answered.

"Keep those ET watchers away from my vehicle."

The duo laughed.

Just my luck that the rain had started again. I didn't care, because, unlike a lot of people, I did not mind walking in the rain. It was the life a true hovervehicle owner who actually drove their vehicle in this supercity—you would do a lot of walking because you would park your vehicle as far away from others as possible.

Nothing could prepare you for it. It wasn't just the Earth ET watchers, and their Up-Top counterparts, it was the media, and all the regular citizens who were drawn to the spectacle like moths to a zap-light. There were far more hovercars and jetpackers in the air. Normally, this whole area was virtually empty; we were on the outskirts of Metropolis, which is why the Free Earthers had picked it. Today, it looked like a scene out of a bad sci-fi movie, ravaged by overpopulation. I hated crowds. Lots of people meant concentrated germs. I walked through them with my head down and a handkerchief cupped over my mouth. My skin had begun to crawl, which was just my psychosomatic reaction to feeling like I was immersed in a sewer.

Once again the Free Earth robots let me pass. People again tried to rush their robot line of defense and were meant with stun blasts. It was funny to watch but nothing was going to get me to remove that handkerchief from my mouth until I was inside.

My reception committee included Mr. and Mrs. Cosmos, Mr. Geo, the she-hulk Terra, Dawn, who always looked like she was about to cry, and the Up-Top ET watcher leader, Mr. Ares. There were others, but I didn't care who they were.

I reached into my jacket and held up a photo gallery. It was all the people that PJ and her temp team identified as suspicious—one in particular, but I wanted to show all the pictures. "Tell me who these men are in the photos."

"Oh no!" Dawn gasped, pointing.

They were all gathered around the photos. Mrs. Cosmos grabbed it from my hand so they could all stare at it. All of them were pointing at the same man.

"How did you get these photos?" Ares asked. "Are you working with government?" He glared at me and I didn't like it.

"No, I'm not working with the government. I'm a detective, remember?"

"All the other men in the photo are known to us," Geo said. "But I suspect that you only wanted to see if we knew the man that you really wanted us to identify."

"First, who are the others? ET-watcher groupies?"

They all looked at each, shaking their heads with looks of disgust.

"Didn't we tell you not to call us that?" Mrs. Cosmos said. "Yes, they are groupies."

"They're harmless," Geo added. "They show up at all the Alien Life conventions and have, on more than one occasion, tried to break into Free Earth. But they're harmless, simply over-eager."

"The man in the center is another matter. Do you know who he is?"

"My team—" I liked being able to say that I had a team—"identified him as a Mr. Merlin, but as soon as they found that out, all hell broke loose as far as the file on the Net being flagged. Fortunately, they'd piggybacked through all kinds of other systems. Who is he? I know I've seen him before."

"Of course you know who he is, you probably watched his TV show as a kid," Mrs. Cosmos said.

I snapped my fingers. "Merlin! The guy on TV who exposed all those alien life hoaxes." I smiled.

"You probably didn't miss one episode," Mrs. Cosmos added.

"That guy was good. Can you tell me why you're scared of a former TV celebrity?"

"Because he's not a TV celebrity anymore," Geo answered. "He no longer disbelieves in alien life anymore either."

My memories were vague, but I stood quiet for a moment. "There was an incident."

"Yeah, he tried to kill someone who he was convinced was an extraterrestrial," Mrs. Cosmos snapped.

"What's the problem then? He's one of your people now."

"*Our* people, Mr. Cruz?" Terra looked like she wanted to slap me.

"Certainly not, Mr. Cruz," Geo said. "He's a delusional psychopath. Oh, Mr. Ares told me that you attempted to leave a little toy behind to illegally listen in on our conversation. Mr. Ares, tell Mr. Cruz what we talked about."

"Merlin is planning on meeting the freighter too."

"Meet the freighter. Our freighter? To do what?"

"Ask him when you see him," Mrs. Cosmos said to me.

"Why don't you call the police on him then?"

"We have!" Dawn yelled.

"Mr. Cruz, Merlin is wanted by both Earth and off-world authorities, and more than a few megacorps," Geo said.

Mr. Cosmos looked at Geo, and for a moment I thought they were speaking telepathically.

"That could be an idea," Geo said. "You have a chance to make some more money, Mr. Cruz."

I was grinning. "Can you teach me how to talk telepathically too?"

Mr. Cosmos laughed, but no one else found me amusing.

"We are a never-ending source of amusement for you, aren't we, Mr. Cruz?" Geo managed a smile.

"Where's Mr. Conehead?" I asked.

"He's hiding from you. So are you interested?" Geo asked.

"I'm not capturing Merlin the Maniac. I'm a private detective, not the police. They arrest people. I tell them where to arrest people."

"It would be a citizen's arrest," Dawn said.

"If a police officer mis-arrests someone, they have the entire Metro PD legal defense behind them. If a citizen does it, and you get sued, say goodbye to everything you own. I like my stuff and so does my wife and son. We want to keep it."

"But there are civilians that do that kind of work all the time—" Dawn began.

"Those are bounty hunters—special licenses, authority, and legal protection. I'm not a bounty hunter. I must say this is the longest week I have ever lived through. I can't wait until that freighter arrives."

"Don't worry, Mr. Cruz, it will be here soon enough," Geo said.

"I am worrying. Did you see outside? Mr. Ares is here, Up-Top ET watchers are here, Merlin the Maniac is here. The longer this goes on, who else will show up? I still don't know how you believe we'll be able to sneak into the Metropolis International Spaceport to meet your freighter. Are you watching it?"

"Our telescopes are training on it every second of everyday, Mr. Cruz," Geo answered.

I was not happy with that fact. A freighter that should be quarantined was on its happy way to Earth without a care in universe. I realized that Ares was standing near me.

"I know you think this is all a joke."

"Actually, I don't think any of it is a joke, including getting blown up by a meteor, which is why I want to drop this case like a meteor."

He pulled up the sleeve of his left arm to show me his cybernetic forearm. "I had the 'pleasure' of meeting Merlin some years back after his nervous breakdown—"

I remembered now. Merlin disappeared when his TV show was canceled for undisclosed reasons because the show was extremely popular. People felt that Up-Top had it canceled from behind the scenes because they didn't like how it portrayed Up-Toppers. "Yes, his nervous breakdown. The rumor was that it was a lie to taint him so he could never get another show."

"It was no lie. I was there, Mr. Cruz. Merlin thought that extraterrestrials had implanted a mind-control device in my arm, so he proceeding to remove it by biting it out of my arm.

"I tell you this, Mr. Cruz, not to get sympathy but for you to understand that this man is extremely dangerous. Lots of people are looking for him. Government agents are looking for him to arrest him. Megacorporations are looking for him to kill him. Neither have found him in ten years. You see him, kill him. That's how dangerous he is."

"The real reason Mr. Conehead, as you call him, isn't here is because he's leading the effort to find him. Merlin has moved to the top of the list of threats for us. He's killed members of the movement before and we have every reason to believe he will continue to do so until he's stopped. In his delusional mind, all humans controlled by the space aliens must be killed. And it would seem those humans would be everyone here on Earth and off-world, including us." Geo moved next to Ares. "If you were to see and—shoot him in self-defense—we might be persuaded to add a bonus to your fees."

I smiled. "If ETs exist and ever do arrive on Earth, they better be good, or they'll have to deal with the ruthless, homicidal likes of all of you. Shoot him in *self defense*."

CHAPTER 21

The Martian Cow People

I had killed someone in quote, unquote self defense before and was so close to being hauled off to prison that I literally saw my life pass before my eyes. The only thing that saved me was the guy I shot dead happened to be in the middle of blowing me and everyone else to bits in the Concrete Mama. I took that as my first and last time I would ever do that again.

However, the meeting with the ET watchers was productive overall. The key to getting as much information from people was to pretend you didn't know anything. They would confirm what you knew, but often would add the little nuggets you needed. When PJ showed me Merlin's picture when I got to the office, I remembered him right away. PJ knew him too. Before she became the great posh-gang member in Neo-France, she watched the show too. We remembered the "nervous breakdown" story, but no one in the public believed it. The ET watchers said it was true. I believed them and Ares didn't have to show me the aftermath of Merlin practicing to be a cannibal to believe him.

I was back with the handkerchief cupped over my mouth, making a beeline through the crowds; I now noticed the multi-colored skin and hair. A pencil-neck kid underneath his umbrella approached me.

"Mr. Cruz?"

"Go away."

I brushed past him, quickening my pace.

"I'll follow, Mr. Cruz, until you get to your hovervehicle."

At last, a civilian referring to the Pony by its proper designation. That meant I'd give him at least five minutes to talk, except if he was trying to shoot me. "Where do you want me to go?" I stood with my back to the Pony, a mobile hovercar security guard on either side, their arms folded but ready to pounce.

"The Euphoria Hotel in Paisley Parish, Mr. Cruz. My employers need to speak with you urgently. They'll pay you for your time whether or not you take their case."

"I have a case now."

"You'll be able to take theirs, too."

I glanced at the card. "When?"

"They're waiting for you now, sir."

I put the card in my coat pocket. "Okay, I'll be there. But go away. You're making me nervous."

He smiled. "Yes, sir. I'll meet you there."

He disappeared into the crowd of crazies. I released my vehicle security and the duo jetpacked away into the sky—a sky as crowded with hovercars and other jetpackers, as when I arrived. I drove six feet from the ground to skim out of there to avoid any possible person that could even remotely scratch my vehicle.

I had been to the Euphoria Hotel before during my Blade Gunner case and like a lot of the high-end luxury hotels in Metropolis the price of a room for a night was more than I made in ten months, and I needed all the diaper money I could get. This particular hotel loved the color purple and it wasn't too far away from where my wife worked.

I hadn't even made it through the main entrance when I was greeted by that same kid. "Right this way, Mr. Cruz." I was certain I had left the scene ahead of him, but here he was leading me through the hotel's palatial main lobby to the meeting rooms. He led me in and there they were.

It was a motley crew of what looked to be cowboys, business suits, and a few who looked like mad scientists. The largest man in a Stetson walked to me and greeted me with a handshake to break an average man's hand. "Mr. Cruz, I've heard of you. You wear a hat like me. I like a man who wears a hat and stays away from those sissy umbrellas. I won't introduce everyone because we are here as a unit. Have a seat."

They had set a chair in front of them as if I was about to be subjected to one of those panel interviews. I sat and he returned to his seat.

"What is this unit of yours?" I looked up and that kid set a cup of silk coffee in the chair's cup holder. I smiled. So they even knew what I drank.

"We represent the off-world cattle, beef, and dairy interests for the entire off-world colonies," said the man sitting closest to the cowboy.

I sipped from my cup. "Okay. What can I do for you?"

"We understand that you became aware of a man named Merlin," the Cowboy said.

I looked at him. "How would you know that? I only became aware of within the hour."

"The Metro Police are aware of your progress," the other man said, "and they are keeping us informed."

"Are they now. Why is this man an interest to you?"

"He's a murderer," a man sitting in the second row of chairs yelled out. "A mass-murderer."

"Mass murderer?" The ET watchers didn't tell me that. "How many people has he killed?"

"People?" the man asked with a perplexed expression. "We're not here about people. We're here about cows."

"Cows? He killed cows? You kill cows."

The men smiled. "Slaughtering cattle for human food consumption is not the same as a deranged man breaking into our facilities and disemboweling thousands of helpless animals," the man said.

"Leaving them to suffer in agony." The look on the cowboy's face was genuine hate.

"Let me guess. He believes your space aliens and the cows are part of your plot to take over humankind."

"You're not guessing, Mr. Cruz," another man said. "You've deduced it correctly. He spent his life debunking alien life hoaxes and conspiracies. Now, due to his psychotic break with reality, he's creating them. Cow mutilations was the extraterrestrial myth from the past."

"What is it that you want me to do?"

"Apprehend him, dead or alive, Mr. Cruz."

Was I caught in a repeating time loop? "I am not a bounty hunter. I'm a detective. I can't do that. I might take such a case to locate him and then call the police, but I was told that both our governments and other corporate entities are after him, and have been for a decade. I'm not sure what I would be able to do when all of them have come up with nothing."

"You, Mr. Cruz, are the only one who has come up with direct proof that he is on Earth. None of them have done that."

"Luck," I answered.

The Cowboy stood from his chair as he scribbled something on a card. He handed it to me.

"Mr. Cruz, I like to speak plainly and am not one for bells, whistles, and the frills of life. We want this man bad, but none of the other bounty hunters have done jack-spit for us, and we have most of them on our retainer. Luck you say? I don't care what you call it. From my vantage point, you've been getting a whole lot of luck here on Earth and off-world ever since you became a detective. Maybe some of it can sprinkle into this situation. If you find him and cause him to be arrested—or killed—call that number and that sum of money will be deposited into your business bank account. We want him bad, Mr. Cruz. He's a vicious, cruel cow-killer, and we want him. I don't care how, or who makes it happen."

He walked past me and all the other men stood, too, and left their seats to follow him out of the room.

"Thanks Mr. Cruz," the kid popped into view to tell me, and then he ran after them.

I sat there staring at the number the Cowboy wrote on his business card. My mouth wasn't hanging open as wide as when Mr. Conehead fired that missile from his conehead. But I would never need to buy another diaper every again in my life, even if Dot and I decided to have nine kids too.

CHAPTER 22

Chief Hub

The Cow People said they were being kept abreast of my activities. So I was under the surveillance of Metro PD and others. I didn't get paranoid about such things. My attitude was that I had a higher than likely chance than the average citizen of being under some kind of surveillance because of my profession and being "famous." Also how could I be bothered by it; most of my cases involved me spying on people.

However, I had to admit that in this case I was annoyed. Watching me was one thing, but running to the Cow People to tell them my business was another matter. I didn't mind police knowing but not Up-Toppers. Earthers should not be informing on other Earthers to Up-Toppers.

That meant I had to return to Metro PD but a strange thing happened when I walked back to my Pony in the hotel's parking bay. There was a standard five-seater police cruiser hovering near my vehicle, waiting.

"Get in," one of the two police officers said.

When a Metro police officer said to do something, you did it. They may have had the words PEACE in big bold white letters on their chests, but the people of Metropolis expected them to be ready to go to war with the supercity's criminal world. In their silver-and-black body-armor, high-powered binocular attachments over their visored half-helmet, and state-of-the-art weapons, they were not to be fooled with.

"Who am I going to see? Is it Chief Hub? Am I going to need my union rep?"

They liked my sense of humor. "You're not a cop, Cruz. Just because cops like you and you're buddies with Wilfred G. Jr., you're not one."

"But I was a police intern back in high school."

They remained focused on watching the sky-lane traffic. Police cruisers usually flew above all other traffic, and that's what they were doing—driving faster than the fast lane. It didn't take long for us to arrive at Police One and land in their police parking bay near the express elevator capsules.

I wasn't taken to a grungy interrogation room or Hub's office. Then set me down in the higher-class, white interrogation rooms, but of course, no silk coffee service like the Cow People.

Chief Hub entered, and the man behind I recognized from my NeuroDancer case, the Chief of the Metropolis Marshal Service.

"The Marshal. I didn't think I'd see you again," I said smiling.

"Somehow I knew I'd be seeing you again." He stepped forward and placed a badge and holder on the table in front of me.

"What's this?" I picked it up, the badge I didn't recognize, so I read the card in the holder. "Bounty hunter! What's this?"

"You're being authorized for a temporary period of time to also act as a licensed bounty hunter, in addition to your lawful licensed private investigator activities."

I looked at Hub, then back at the Marshal. "Are you going to say anything?"

"No," Hub answered dryly.

"That's it, no explanation?"

"No," Hub answered.

"While I'm here, I need to find out about someone who was picked up by police, possibly Up-Top police—another detective I was working with. His name is Crux. Can someone help me find out where he is in the system?"

"No."

I read it clearly in their faces they had no interest in anything I had to say at this point and it was pointless to ask further.

"The officers will take you back to your red speedster," Hub added.

"Mr. Merlin," I said. "Is this for him?"

"Mr. Merlin gunned down one of my officers twenty minutes ago," Hub answered, making me immediately switch off my jovial tone. "There is a citywide manhunt for him. We want all hands on deck and since you stumbled onto him, you might as well be on that deck too."

"This Merlin is also an illegal criminal alien. When he did live on Earth, he was using a false national ID, but was actually born off-world. He has no authority to be on the planet Earth at all. You are now authorized to apprehend, subdue, or shoot to kill to defend your life should you come across this Up-Top cop-shooter," the Marshal said.

"Chief, I am not expecting to run into this person, and I definitely will not be looking for him with a police manhunt after him."

"It's just a precaution for the 'what if' scenario. We don't expect you to see him either, but if you do, you are to take that attempted cop-killer down first, call us second. I want him brought down by Metropolis law enforcement, not Up-Top law enforcement. I'll even settle for a Metropolis civilian taking him down. Do you understand me, Mr. Cruz?"

"Loud and clear, Chief."

CHAPTER 23

The Friend For Hire

The Chief of the Metropolis Police had given me the full legal authority to quote unquote "defend" myself, no questions to be asked. If you shot a street cop in Metropolis, 500,000 police officers were going to scour the streets until they found and shot you dead. That's how it was, which is why even the biggest and sickest criminals didn't do it. It was bad for business and living, because before they did find you to shoot you, they would get into, mess up, damage, destroy everything you owned. They'd arrest your goldfish just to ruin your life.

That was all fine with me. It meant I would go back to my office, which was my fortress away from home and I'd stay there until this was all over and make client calls. I gave Merlin the Maniac a few days tops before Metro Police caught up with him. It was not like before; he had shot a cop.

I came through my Liquid Cool office door, and there was PJ giving some kind of presentation to a group of college-age kids congregating around her receptionist work area.

"Ah, there he is," she said.

"Is this your team?"

"It is." She smiled and the six temps smiled back.

"Good work everyone. We found our man, and now the police can get him."

That made their day. They were all smiles. "PJ, a quick word in my office. What do you have planned for the team?"

"I was about to send them all off to their next assignments with glowing references and a free Liquid Cool T-shirt."

I marched into my private office not wanting to hear any more. I sat at my desk and scanned the messages of the hot pile. PJ entered and closed the door, "What's up, boss?"

"I want you to be especially focused on office security for the next few days. Until the police capture the guy who shot that police officer."

"Oh yes, we heard. It happened near Shangri-La. That's supposed to be a safe neighborhood. Why would we need to increase security?"

"The perp was our guy."

"Merlin? It was the Merlin TV guy?"

"The one and only."

"Is he after you?"

"No, he's not after me. But people want me to go find him, and you know I'm not doing that. Just keep an eye on the security to give me peace of mind, until they find him."

"Okay. I'll keep my rifle on the desk."

"Well, you don't need to do that. We have cameras in the hallway and everywhere else."

"Yes, but remember that Ichi man from your last big case got into the office."

I looked around. "Why did you have to say that? Now, I'm paranoid."

"Good thing we fried him."

"Just keep an eye out."

"Okay. You make your client calls." PJ opened the door and walked back to her desk.

"Do I have any clients scheduled?" I yelled.

"Two cancellations! But, I booked a new client to fill the slot!"

"It better not be Merlin!"

"No, it's a woman."

I realized that I was still vulnerable with having to see clients. I didn't know why I felt Merlin would come after me, but I did. I was given the legal cover to go after him, but again, there was no way I was going anywhere near him—eating peoples' arms, cow mutilations, attempted cop-killer. This was a situation where fear was a good thing. I was staying put in my office until he was found.

My 3 o'clock client arrived on time. I never had to do anything, because PJ always did her thing when they arrived—offering them refreshments, showing them the wall of Liquid Cool news stories; she also verified they were who they said they were. That's all cared about in my vulnerable state.

"Ms. Green is ready for you." PJ's face popped into my office.

"Send her in."

The woman looked young, though nowadays, she could have been 60 with plastic surgery. I looked at her file that PJ had on my desk display—24 years old. I gestured for her to take a seat. She did and smiled.

"I've never been to a detective before."

"It's painless."

"How can I help?"

"I have a confession to make. I'm kinda on the job."

"On the job?"

"I work for a service."

"Service? Escort service?"

She was almost offended. "Nothing like that. I work as a friend-for-rent."

"Someone hired you to be their friend."

"Yes, this is our second day. He wanted me to come down here and talk with you—"

I stood from my desk with my omega-gun in hand, showing. "Who is this friend who hired you to be his friend?"

"Why do you have a gun in your hand?"

"PJ!"

When I yelled out she was startled. She turned to see PJ standing at the doorway with a laser-sighted shotgun pointed at her. She stood from her chair.

"What kind of detective agency is this place? You always point weapons at potential clients?"

"Who's your friend?"

She raised a hand slowly. "Calm down. Both of you, calm down. I'm going to say a number. Dial it and you can ask him yourself."

"I'm feeling very vulnerable at the moment and you come into my place of business under false pretenses."

"Both of you calm down. I'm not here under any false pretenses. I was hired. Just dial the number into your vid-phone."

"PJ, stand a bit to the side so if you blast her, I won't get showered by blood and guts."

The woman watched PJ step in and move to the left side of her, aiming the shotgun. "You two are crazy. I should call the cops on you. Do the cops know you behave this way?"

"What's the number?" I asked.

She had to compose herself and slowly recited the number. I watched her with a frown.

"Are you going to dial it?"

"I'm thinking."

"Please dial it so I can leave."

I dialed the number. It rang, then again, then I heard something. There was something over the vid-phone screen on the other side. A hand pulled back a black cover. There was Merlin.

CHAPTER 24

The Hunted

Ms. Green wasn't joking. She couldn't run out of the office fast enough. PJ returned to her desk to watch her run to the elevators on her monitor.

"I'll keep an eye on her and make sure she leaves," PJ yelled back to me.

I stood there staring at Merlin on my vid-phone screen. "Why do you need to hire strangers to be your friends? Don't you have friends, Merlin?"

"I don't have a lot of time—"

"Why is that Merlin?"

"I know you already heard, but I didn't shoot that cop."

"You didn't?"

"It wasn't me. I'm being framed."

"Why would someone do that?"

"We can't talk on an open line."

I laughed. "Do you really believe that I'm going to leave my safe office to go out on the streets to meet you? With half a million police gunning for you? With who else is looking for you? After I know you like to bite people's forearms and slice up cow's bellies? Are you under the influence of narcotics, Merlin?—because that's not happening."

"Mr. Cruz, those are all lies. I never did any of that. I need to hire you to help me."

"Why would you want to hire me? There are hundreds of thousands of detectives out there you can hire."

"It has to be you. I can explain, but not on an open line. Find me."

"What?"

"Find me. None of this is what you think. Find me. I need you to clear my name, so we can stop the real danger coming. That freighter—it's on that freighter."

"What's on that freighter?"

"Mr. Cruz, that freighter cannot be allowed to land on Earth. Earth has no idea what's on it. Find me."

The vid-phone disconnected.

I stared at the blank screen for awhile. What was I going to do? I was not leaving my office. But—I believed him—at least most of it. Next week, I was going to accompany the Free Earthers to get onto that freighter. If there was any possibility that something dangerous was on it, I better find out.

Merlin was known as the myth-buster, a hoax exposer. But, it wasn't only hoaxes related to space aliens—he exposed far more about tech-related scams by criminals, megacorps, and even a few government agencies—but he was best known for his space alien life exposes.

But then he disappeared, and life on Earth went on. We all found others to entertain us. I was told he went insane, but the man who was talking on my vid-phone didn't seem insane to me, though I admit I had been fooled before. However, my gut said otherwise.

"What are you going to do?" PJ asked. She stood at my doorway with a worried look. "Don't do it. Don't do what you're thinking. You have to stay indoors is what you should do."

"My gut says that he may be on the level."

"Stay here, Cruz. Don't go after him. It could be a trap."

"He said find him. What does that mean? He expects me to track him down when all of Metro PD are after him."

"He's bad news. Stay away from him. Let the police kill him and go about your cases."

"Why would he think I could find him before the police?"

"Who cares? He's psycho. Let the police deal with him. The police are probably listening in to all our phones too. You go out there, and they could snatch you up too for being an accessory!"

PJ was absolutely right. You didn't want to get involved with anyone who the police designated a cop-killer or who attempted to be one. If you got on the wrong side of the police on this single issue, they'd hate you for all your life. PJ was right. I had to stay away.

"PJ, when you're right, you're right."

I sat back behind my desk to start my client calls again. PJ had already returned to her desk.

"PJ!" She popped back in front of the doorway. "Show me those pictures you and your team found of Merlin."

"Cruz, you have to leave it alone. It's dangerous."

I showed her the card that I fished out of my pocket.

"What's that?"

"The amount of money the Up-Top cow and dairy megacorps will put into the business account if we find him first."

PJ only had bionic arms, not legs, but she moved like she did. "I got them right here."

I was at her desk and she had the file opened on her mobile computer screen. She slowly tapped the keyboard to make the photos scroll one after the other, across the screen. There was Merlin in a black trench coat, just standing there with people around him, watching. He didn't seem particularly bothered by the fact that his likeness was being captured on film or video. There were enough pictures to show him from many different angles. There was plenty of media footage to also get a full view of him.

"For a man on the run supposedly for ten years he doesn't act very stealthy." We looked at all of them again. "If you were hiding from dangerous people, would you allow anyone to take pictures or videos of you?"

"No, I wouldn't, and I wouldn't be anywhere near any crowds either."

"He wanted to be found," I said.

"By who? He couldn't have known you were going to think of the idea."

I was not pleased at all. "Get Phishy. We're going to find Merlin."

"You know where he is?"

"Yes, 525 Junction in Plat-Ville, but we need to get there as fast as we can. Bring your shotgun."

CHAPTER 25

Metro PD

We sat in the Pony just outside of the police tape. The police had shut down every street and sky-lane in a ten-block radius around Plat-Ville—the full name for the district was Platinum Village. What the police didn't know was that I knew my office was bugged and that I'd sent them to the address of a Mr. R.C., the gang leader who had been sending his hooligans into Rabbit City, a gang who'd even reached the steps of the Concrete Mama, assaulting tenants and our doorman. This was what I called "multi-tasking."

We were too far away to see for ourselves, but we watched the "businessman" dragged out of his house in handcuffs and shackles, as the police continued their search for cop-shooter Merlin. The police would rip Mr. RC's apartment to shreds looking for him.

The only people who could have planted a listening device in the Liquid Cool office was one of PJ's temps. She was in the passenger seat stewing in her own anger. "The police planted a rat in my team," she said. "*Incroyable!*"

"We now know how they found out so fast about our discovery. Get on the phone and get Bugs in there to do a full sweep. Besides, that's the boss of those damn punks terrorizing our building."

"Him. That's the gang leader? He doesn't look a gang boss."

"What does a gang boss look like these days? An eighty-year-old great-grandmother could be a gang leader here in Metropolis if they're ruthless enough."

"That's true."

"We're in the detective biz so this will not be the last time people will try to leave their listening devices behind. It's part of the business. It isn't the first time Bugs has swept the office and it won't be the last."

"I guess so."

"Now, I need muscle, but not the Sidewalk Johnny Brigade. I don't want to take any chances."

"I know people," PJ answered.

"Felons?"

"Of course."

"Good. Make sure they're armed. Merlin said go find him. That's what I'm going to do."

"You know where he is?"

"Yes, and so do you."

CHAPTER 26

The Real Merlin

What I was doing was incredibly foolish. I was wearing my bulletproof/laser-resistant vest underneath. I had my omega-gun and pop-gun as normal. I was packing a few other "surprises" on my person—meaning weapons of the extremely illegal kind, but none of it mattered. I was walking into danger, which I had said I was never going to purposely do again as a detective.

We were back to Free Earth, back to the circus. The crowds on the ground were larger, the hovercraft and jet-packers were spread out over a larger area—all with the meteor crater in the center of it all.

I walked through the crowds slowly, by myself, as if I didn't have a care in the world. It was now the third time I had walked in a counter-clockwise spiral around the crater through the crowds and back the other way.

"Follow me." The voice was almost a whisper, but the man in a hoodie brushed past me. The rest of his clothes were black too. I had seen the face for a nano-second—it was some kind of silver space alien mask. Cute!

He was walking fast, but I kept up. The ET watchers had created their own parking lot which was filled with hovercraft that looked like different flying saucers. I was amused by one sign display: PLEASE TAKE ME TO YOUR PLANET! I WANT TO BE ABDUCTED. But a sharp resolve came over me again when I saw he disappeared through the open door of one of the flying saucer hovercraft; I stopped in my tracks. I approached slowly and kept to the side of the open door.

"Mr. Cruz, if you've come this far, you might as well finish it."

I peeked in and there was Merlin sitting inside on a chair holding his alien mask in his hands. It wasn't a real flying saucer-craft but a hovervan made to look like one on the outside. I showed him I was armed and stepped in. "My people know where I am."

"I'm sure they do. Do you know, Mr. Cruz, that before I went into journalism, I was an amateur magician."

"Why are you telling me this?"

"We can't stay here. You were likely followed. The police are not the only ones after me. Underneath us is a series of tunnels."

"Yes, I know. I've been down there before, and almost died in one."

"Then it shouldn't be a problem, except for the almost dying part." He got up from the chair and lifted a trapdoor in the floor. He climbed down and when I peeked in, he was going down a rope ladder down a low-lit tube. "Make sure to close the trapdoor," he called out to me.

I stood there thinking. Merlin the Maniac, who was also a magician, had me following him down the path he wanted me to go. How did I know he wasn't going to kill me, or make me disappear? I swallowed hard and down I went. As soon as I closed the trapdoor, I heard a lock click. There was no turning back now. I peered down and the tube was empty.

"Waiting on you, Mr. Cruz."

As I descended down the rope-ladder, I kept thinking how stupid I was. PJ and company wouldn't be able to find me. I was totally alone with this guy that the police said had tried to kill two of their own. I dropped to the ground and slowly peered around the corner.

I couldn't believe what I was seeing. It was a hollowed-out cavern and some kind of real spaceship. Sitting in one of two folding chairs was Merlin sipping something from a teacup.

"What's this?"

"It's my spaceship, Mr. Cruz. What else does it look like to you?"

I neared him cautiously. The hand holding my omega-gun was sweating, but at least it wasn't shaking.

"Mr. Cruz, I can see you're very nervous. Let me tell you my story and then you can return to the surface. In fact, I insist. I can't be the only one who knows the true story. It's too dangerous. I can't run forever. Eventually, they'll catch me."

"The police are a determined bunch."

"Yes, they are, and there are others. I'll begin."

I slowly sat in the chair adjacent to him, but I was far from being comfortable.

I saw him watching something on a little mobile device on the ground with its own kickstand to stand upright. "Mr. Cruz, what's the largest craft you've ever flown."

"Why?"

"Indulge me."

"A hovertruck, but I didn't like it. When you fly a precision vehicle like my Pony, it's hard to drive anything else."

"Fair enough, but at least you've flown something larger. May we please move to my spaceship."

"Why? What are you up to?" I stood from my chair.

"I am not up to anything, but I have to tell you my story. This may be my last chance to bring someone else into the knowledge. I am going to show you my mobile monitor, but you have to promise not to run away. We'll move to my spaceship and I'll give you the command codes to fly it out of here if needed."

"Fly your flying saucer? No way!"

"Mr. Cruz, please."

"I will not be tricked by you!" I pointed my gun at him as he picked up the device from the ground and showed me the mobile monitor. It showed the interior of his hovervan where we had just been on the surface, or what was left of it. It was crawling with police troopers, and they were ripping up the floor. They couldn't get through the trapdoor, so they were going to destroy the entire floor around it to get through.

"Oh no."

"Mr. Cruz, follow me!" He ran to the spaceship and up the gangplank, inside. I had no choice but to follow. I couldn't be caught with him. If I was, it was over. I would go from being friendly with every police officer in Metropolis to being hated by all.

"I'm not flying a flying saucer!" I protested.

We were in the cockpit. Merlin was flipping buttons all over the place. "Mr. Cruz, you don't have a choice."

"Why can't you fly it? It's your spaceship."

"Because I have to tell you my story, and you're going to be my means of escape."

"Escape?"

"Mr. Cruz, you're going to fly the craft while I jam their tracking means. You can do the former, but don't have the technical expertise specific to this craft for the latter."

I was looking back at the exit, but the doors had already closed. The main monitors had turned on, and the police were flying down into the cavern, and all I heard was the barrage of gun-fire against the hull. The police had far more powerful weapons, and they'd be opening up with those any second. I felt like a trapped rat on the Titanic.

"Mr. Cruz, sit here!" I did what he said. "I'll start us off, but pay close attention to all that I'm doing." He hit the ignition button and the entire craft shook, and I immediately felt it jump up. We were hovering. He pushed the throttle forward and, if I hadn't been accustomed to rocket-like launches before, I would have thrown up, passed out, or passed out while throwing up—that's how fast we flew forward. All I saw was blackness, then we punched through. It was a fake wall and we rocketed upward into the sky.

"Mr. Cruz, take the throttle. You have to get used to the controls."

"I can't fly a spaceship!"

"I'm letting go in 3-2-"

I grabbed the throttle. "I bet you staged all of this. You knew the police were tailing me."

"I don't have time to allay your paranoia. I'm paranoid enough all by myself. I'm going to begin my story. When I'm done, there will at least be two people in the universe who will know."

"Know what?" I couldn't believe it. We were heading out to space. "Where am I going?" I can't fly into space."

"When you pass the stratosphere you'll level off." A warning siren was going off.

"What's that?"

"Slow down just a tad."

A massive space jet ripped past us, and I almost let go of the throttle. "You're going to get us killed!"

"Relax, Mr. Cruz. I've done this many time before. I'm engaging the cloak."

"The cloak?"

"It will make us invisible to radar sensors. Not invisible to line of sight but we'll be sure to stay far away from everyone so they can't see us."

"Merlin, you are a maniac! Why am I flying in space in your flying saucer! We were supposed to be sitting in a hovervan talking! How am I in this situation?"

"That is the beauty of life, Mr. Cruz. It has all kind of surprises for us."

"I hate surprises!"

"Level off now...," he was gesturing with his hand, "...and you can slow down a tad. We'll coast at this altitude for a while. We simply need to also keep an eye out for any satellites. If we play our cards right, they'll never find us.

Now, my story. Once upon time, I believe is how it starts."

"Madness!" I yelled, staring out the main viewport of the saucer.

"I first became aware of this stranger when I was debunking another Cydonia myth, very popular with the Alien Life community. Secret Cydonia bases on the moon and Mars. The variations were always the same: either the bases were controlled by space aliens; humans were holding space aliens there, alive or their corpses; or it was some joint human-space alien consortium using the bases for no good.

"In all my myth-busting, I did come across people, scientists, professional and amateur, who were by no means crazy. There were doing real science, using real scientific methods to search for extraterrestrial life, and were frankly far more skeptical of any potential discoveries than the average off-worlder or Earther would be. Even though they believed in alien life, they wanted to get it right, never give in to false hopes.

"I had worked with a group of scientists on Mars several times in debunking various myths. Their chief scientist was a man by the name of Neil Cosmos. We became friends." My attention perked up. "And he became my favorite go-to person for any Mars focused exposé.

"I had known he was becoming frustrated with the extraterrestrial life exploration bureaucracy and the politics. He wasn't the only scientist out there who had felt the same way. He learned of a new chief scientist role with the new Jupiter Outpost colony. It was a very small operation, but as chief scientist he could do whatever he wanted out there at the farthest reaches. He was his own boss.

"I got a cryptic message from him about two years ago. He said he had found 'it.' Of course, I knew what 'it' meant but simply felt that finally he had crossed over to the nutty side. I received a file three months later. It was from him. He never told me he had sent it. I viewed it and it was the video files of the heavy mining craft used for the asteroids. According to the record, they found an unknown craft crashed on one of the asteroids. They salvaged the craft and inside this—alien craft—and it certainly looked alien, almost biometric—the Captain said they had recovered 50% of the craft and what appeared to be a cargo hold of a substance that they referred to as the 'black dot.' The term probably has some significance, and, they felt it was organic.

"I didn't know what to do with what I had. Was I being played? That was my first thought. But what if I wasn't? Just because I didn't believe in alien life, didn't mean it didn't exist. I decided to hold onto it for a week or so, while I tried to reach Cosmos. I couldn't reach him.

"Then I made the biggest mistake of my life. I told someone in the Martian government. After that video-call, the next day, everything in my life changed. My apartment was ransacked, they were looking for what I assumed was the video-file. I was flying a solo craft from the moon to Mars and another spacecraft tried to crash into me. A woman came forward and accused me of trying to abduct her because I thought she was a space alien. The Lunar police were after me. Then stories came out about these sick cow mutilations on Mars, and I was implicated. The Mars Police were after me. All these people came out of the woodwork, people I never saw or met before, accusing me of all types of weirdness and crimes. Then on Earth, an exposé was done on me saying that I didn't leave my show, but I was fired because I had a psychotic nervous breakdown. I was fired, but for drug addiction. I went into rehab and it took three years, 100 pounds, and one divorce to get clean. They doctored my employee files. They destroyed my life.

"However, I've built up a good network of friends and contacts over the years. They helped me stay ahead of them, but barely. Then I got the call. I was always expecting it. The voice told me that they wanted that video-file, and I could have my life back. I pretended to cooperate but instead did everything I could to find Cosmos. If they were willing to do this to me, what were they doing to him? What were they about to do to him?

"Nothing I did helped me find him, and I had to be careful, because I had two off-world police authorities looking for me. I found him, or I had a friend in the Martian science community find him. Cosmos had disappeared as did most of that Jupiter Outpost mining crew. But Cosmos was seen boarding a space freighter bound for Earth."

"The one arriving next week," I said.

"Yes, but it's worse than you can imagine."

"What is?"

"Besides the crew there are two civilians on that freighter that are not on the manifest—Cosmos and one other person. The problem isn't Cosmos. The problem is the other man, but I have no access to find out who he is. I think he was put on that freighter by the same people who framed me and destroyed my life. That space freighter has been dark ever since it passed Mars, and I believe that man is the cause."

"You said the freighter has gone dark?"

"No communications out and no response whatsoever to any hailing attempts—automated or human-generated."

"How can that be? A freighter not in communication with space authorities wouldn't be allowed to simply fly right to Earth."

"I don't know. But if Earth or off-world says they don't know about the freighter, who's on the freighter, and what might be on the freighter, they're lying. You know all that I know, Mr. Cruz."

"What you told me is a whole lot of nothing. There's no way for me to verify anything."

"You'll figure everything out. You're a detective, that's what you do." Merlin stood from his seat.

"When I figure everything out, then what?"

"I believe that all of this has to do, not with Cosmos, but this second man on the freighter. He's the key to it all, and if something has happened to Cosmos and the freighter's crew, I am convinced it is because of him. I am convinced that he was put on that freighter to seize control, silence Cosmos and the crew, and take possession of Cosmos's proof of extraterrestrial life, then ensure it lands on Earth."

"You're convinced of a lot without any proof yourself."

"The proof will be here soon enough. I have to be the martyr, so that you can have what you need. Mr. Cruz, it's time to part company."

"What? What are you about to do?"

"I'm about to jump out of my spaceship. Please take care of it. We've been through a lot together."

"You can't do a peri-terrestrial dive from this height."

"Yes, I can, Mr. Cruz. People have been sky-diving from as high as the exosphere for centuries. We're only in the mesosphere. Bye."

There was nothing for me to do. I was the one flying. Merlin disappeared down another trapdoor.

"Merlin! How do I land?"

He was already gone. I couldn't believe this. I stared at all the controls around me but stayed calm. "I should be fine," I said to myself and began my descent. "How do I turn off the cloak?" I flipped the switch and began my descent. An alarm screeched and I saw a tiny figure fly from the flying saucer—Merlin in a space diving suit on his way down too.

I let him get out of view and took a different landing vector. This whole situation was messed up, but a devilish smirk came over my face. When was I ever going to get this chance again in my lifetime?

CHAPTER 27

The Eye Candy Crew

I still remembered when I first showed up on the hovercar racing scene with my classic Ford Pony. An OG said if you drove a classic muscle vehicle you could drive, or fly, anything in the universe. He was right and I realized that I had no reason to have been nervous. Also, I didn't just drive a classic hovervehicle; I had built it as a kid. Nowadays, especially, everything that drove, sailed, or flew was "monkey-proof"—even a monkey could operate it.

Merlin's flying saucer was equipped with a computer voice with a sultry female Jamaican accent. "In three seconds, begin your descent vector," it said. Automatically, a holo-map appeared showing my craft in relation to every craft in the sky for a 100-mile radius. Really, I didn't need to do anything other than follow the computer prompts. Somewhat scary because it meant even Cruz, Jr. could sneak onto a modern spacecraft and literally fly to Mars if he wanted.

Well, I did want to see the wife and son. And I had my own flying saucer, at least temporarily, so I decided to just land it in the street like in those old alien invasion movies. All of the sky-traffic around my wife's job, Eye Candy, was frozen in mid-air, people gawking at my flying saucer spaceship as I landed. It was a smooth touch-down right on the street in front of the premiere beauty and image salon in Metropolis, Eye Candy in Paisley Parish.

Everyone in the salon was outside standing in front of the establishment. People didn't know what to do, whether to run, get a laser gun, what. The saucer's gangplank protruded and the door opened. Everyone was paralyzed watching. Then I came out trying not to burst out laughing, strolling to them. Everyone was standing there with their mouths hanging open. I walked up to Dot, holding Cruz Jr. in her arms. They were both frozen, with their mouths wide open.

I gave them a funny hand signal. "Take me to your leader."

I don't think anyone heard what I said; everyone was in shock. I don't know why. We had all seen Up-Top's flying saucers before. Cruz Jr. was staring at me wide-eyed, almost shaking. I did not want him to start crying. "Hey, little Cruz. It's okay. It's just a spaceship. Come on, smile. Take me to your leader. I was joking. You're the leader."

I never saw them. All of a sudden, I was tackled to the ground by over a dozen government guys in black. Cruz, Jr. started to bawl.

PART FIVE

I, Alien Hunter

CHAPTER 28

The Mick

People had asked me why I didn't keep the flying saucer. Hide it somewhere for my own personal use. The blissful ignorance of the public. Metropolis had more anti-aircraft heavy lasers than any other supercity on the planet. See unauthorized spacecraft in your airspace. Blow unauthorized spacecraft out of your airspace. I was not interested in being vaporized. The only option was hand it over. I wouldn't have even been able to sell in on the Net, though it would've been amusing to try.

I went back to Metro PD, but for the first time in my life it was involuntarily. Also for the first time in my life, I was booked by police and put in holding. No more games, it was real this time. It meant an arrest jacket, it meant I'd need a scummy defense attorney, it meant I'd be sitting in this holding cell for a day or three, until bail was determined, set, and Dot came to post it. All assuming they allowed me to have bail.

Two big police officers came to get me.

"Hello," I greeted. "I meant to ask where my buddies, Officers Break and Caps are?"

"Your buddies, huh? They're on vacation."

"Where?"

"Off-world to get away from you. Lunar colony, I think." They proceeded to put handcuffs and ankle cuffs on me.

"Is that really necessary?"

"Cruz, we have to do everything by the book today," one of them answered.

I was led to and seated in another interrogation room. This was not dirty and small, or white and large. It was an interrogation room I had never seen before. It reminded me of a board room.

A plainclothes detective came in and sat across the wooden table from me.

"Have you been read your rights, Mr. Cruz?"

"Yes."

"Do you wish to have an attorney present?"

"Um—yes." The detective smirked. "Don't look at me like that," I said. "That's what I was taught when I was a police intern. Even if you're innocent, at least have the attorney sit in the room next to you. But don't put me back in holding. My attorney is already waiting for me outside."

The detective stood and left the room. Thirty minutes later, the door opened, and a man entered. It was The Mick, Run-Time's third VP, who also happened to be an attorney. He was tall, brawny, blue-eyed, and now had a new Marine-style crew cut. He sat down next to me without saying a word. The detective entered and sat again.

"Have you been read your rights. Mr. Cruz?"

"Yes, I have."

He powered on his tablet and stared at the file. "How did you manage to get possession of a stolen spacecraft, Mr. Cruz?"

I waved a hand. "I don't have time for this. I can't allow you to keep me here forever. Have Chief Hub come in."

"Chief Hub doesn't work for you, Mr. Cruz. You have no standing in this interrogation. You are suspected of aiding a cop-shooter—"

"I don't aide cop-shooters and you know that."

"Yet, you were found with one and flying his stolen spacecraft."

"You're an idiot. He's not going anywhere. We have his spacecraft. This is so much bigger than you know. There's a Martian space freighter that will touch down on Earth next week on Friday. That space freighter is what you should be worried about. It has an alien organism aboard."

The detective just stared at me without blinking.

"And Up-Top knows it. They're going to use Earth as a laboratory for their alien xenomorphs." I pointed to my face. "I am not joking. You need to get your butt off that chair and inform Chief Hub, the Mayor, the City Council, the Metropolis National Guard, everyone. What are you waiting for?"

The detective turned off his tablet with his thumb, grabbed the device, and got up with a huff. He exited the room, slamming the door.

I turned to my "attorney." "Hi, Mr. Mick."

"The room's bugged," he said without looking at me.

"Hi, Mr. Mick."

He slowly turned to me. "Hello, Mr. Cruz."

I leaned back in my chair. "How on Earth did a simple missing persons case turn into this? Killer meteors, ET watchers, and possible real ETs. I need a vacation."

"The police can definitely help with that."

"The vacation I have in mind does not involve colored jump suits and caged accommodations."

The detective returned. The same two officers came in. "Stand up, Mr. Cruz." I did, and the officers unshackled the handcuffs and ankle cuffs.

"What. That's it?" I asked.

The Mick stood from his chair. "I want this arrest record expunged, the arrest file deleted, all arrest biometrics collected deleted."

"Already done," the detective answered.

"That's it?" I asked again. "I don't get to talk to the Chief?"

"As I said earlier, the Chief doesn't work for you, Cruz."

"I'm saying that not because I feel I'm his boss but as a citizen."

"Get out of here," he snapped.

"Mr. Cruz and I are leaving," The Mick said. "Mr. Cruz, let's collect your belongings, and you can exchange your jumpsuit for your civilian clothes."

He marched out of the room and didn't even check to see if I was following, but I was. It still took an hour for me to get out of there. When I walked out of the back entrance of Metro PD there was no one around. Mr. Mick was gone.

I pulled my fedora down, pulled my coat tighter, pushed my hands into my pockets and proceeded to walk to the closest hovertaxi stop in the rain.

CHAPTER 29

The Sidewalk Johnny Brigade

If Run-Time had sent Mr. Mick to help me out, but hadn't contacted me yet, there was a very good reason. He'd get in touch as soon as he could. I couldn't forget that politicians here on Earth and Up-Top were still trading insults, and megacorps everywhere were still holding their breath at the possibility of economic boycotts. I had to carry on.

When I first came up with the idea for the Sidewalk Johnny Brigade, it was supposed to be temporary. Phishy didn't know it, but it was really to expand what he already was doing—use the network of the supercity's street hustlers. They could find people, gather street intel, and do surveillance. The possibilities really were limitless, as long as it wasn't dangerous. I would not purposely put any of them in harm's way.

Centuries ago, government passed a law that created what was now called, Legacy Housing. Once a mortgage was paid off, it could be passed on to family and descendants forever. Housing for rich, poor, and everyone in-between was essentially free. Housing was mandatory for all residents, so for those without legacies there was Free City. But for sidewalk johnnies life was the streets—hanging around, watching for trouble, causing trouble, hustling, and looking for a hustle. Still, they were harmless, not the real street criminals.

I insisted that the sidewalk johnnies who made up my Sidewalk Johnny Brigade were presentable at all times—no booze, drugs, dirty or smelly clothes. I insisted on class. They did two things that annoyed me to no end—thanks to Phishy. They wore fedoras and Liquid Cool T-shirts!

Before I hired her, PJ hung around the sidewalk johnnies. She wasn't considered a sidewalk sally, just part of the crowd. That was back when PJ and I were frenemies, even though I was the one who saved her life (okay, I did have to cut off her arms to do it, but she did get cool bionic ones to replace them.)

I was back at Liquid Cool, and she watched them gathered in the Liquid Cool waiting area. PJ never liked the johnnies, but recognized their value. I finished my calls, opened the door of my private office and gestured the smiling bunch in.

"Go on in." I walked to PJ. "How many did Bugs find?"

"There were seven of them."

"That many?"

"He said you should sweep the offices twice a day."

"Why can't we have portable sweepers, so we can do it ourselves?"

"He said you'd ask that. He's going to have a pair of portable ones delivered tomorrow. We should have done it a long time ago."

"Yes, we should have. Basically, Bugs is telling us that after every time a client sets foot in our office, they could be leaving listening devices."

"*Exactement.*"

When she started speaking French it was time to leave. I left her at her desk to join my guests in my personal office.

"What's the job, Mr. Cruz?" one of them asked.

PJ popped in and started scanning us with some kind of flat rectangular device. The sidewalk johnnies chuckled, but let PJ do her thing.

"Can I start now?" I asked, as she walked back to her desk.

"You can continue," she replied.

"Thank you! I thought I was the boss," I said to the amusement of the johnnies. "I have another person-locate job, but—I want you to be smart and careful. The person is this fugitive the police are looking for."

I saw their faces change. "The cop-killer, Cruz?"

"The officer hasn't died yet, so he's a cop-shooter. However, there's a chance—a very small chance he didn't do it. I'm not going to get between him and the police, and neither are you, but if you can find him, and I can talk to him again, I'd like to. There's another case I'm working he may have info on."

The johnnies began nodding, more relaxed.

"The police are very good at tracking people down, very good. But this Up-Topper is clever. That flying saucer you saw me on the news come out of—well, it has cloaking tech. Up-Top keeps all the wonderful toys for themselves and they don't share with Earth."

"Cloaking tech, Cruz?"

"Yeah, and I know for a fact they have cloaking clothes."

"Cloaking clothes?"

"Yeah. I found out about it in my Blade Gunner case. But whether he does or doesn't you all have a better chance of finding him than the police. He'll be on the look-out for the police, but a sidewalk johnny is just one of the harmless folks on the street.

"All I want you to do is, if you see him, call me ASAP. That's it. No heroics. Don't follow him. Don't look at him. If he did shoot this officer, he's more than dangerous and can kill you. I'm not hiring any of you to get killed."

"We know you look out for us, Cruz."

I nodded. "Stay safe. Let's put that sidewalk johnny network to work."

"We'll do our best, Mr. Cruz."

"Okay, off you all go."

The men shuffled out of the office. Sidewalk johnnies didn't move fast, but I wasn't tasking them to run the 200-meter dash. They'd put the word out in the sidewalk johnny community and that was what moved at the speed of light. Before I knew it, their eyes would be watching all of Metropolis. I always paid for good information and that meant if anyone saw him, they'd make sure I knew right away. My Sidewalk Johnny Brigade had joined in the supercity's dragnet to find Merlin—who actually was not an Earther after all, but a spaceman, Moonie, or Martian.

"You are the Alien Hunter," PJ said from her desk.

"Don't remind me. This case is supposed to be a missing persons, then a chaperon job, and now it's this too. More trouble, but less money."

"What about the cow people reward money? Isn't that why you let him get away and why you have them looking out for him?"

"I bet the cow people already have dozens of real bounty hunters out looking for him, besides the police. No, if our brigade finds him, it will be sheer luck."

"You are made of luck, boss." The main phone rang, audio-only. "Liquid Cool Detective Agency," she answered. "Yes, he's right here. Oh, okay. Yeah, I'll make him go. He'll be there." She hung up.

"What is it you'll make me do?"

"He'll meet you at the curb."

CHAPTER 30

Run-Time and The Mick

In a supercity of over 50 million people, megaskyscrapers as tall as 300 stories, and hovercars flying in sky-traffic 20 to 50 feet high, "the curb" wasn't a common term at all. However, Run-Time and I still did. It was his way of telling me it was him. It was also his way of telling me that he didn't want to be seen going into my building or coming out. Who knew how many different people and parties were watching me.

I came out of the mega-tower's main entrance with something I never use—an umbrella. It was PJ's—hot pink and ridiculous, but that's why I had it open to cover my upper body. "There's no way Cruz would use a hot pink umbrella, it can't be him." At least, that's what I hoped any watchers would say.

At the curb, hovering inches from the ground was a yellow hovertaxi. I hopped in as I folded my umbrella. I didn't even need to look at the driver, because I knew who it would be.

"Where to?" I asked Flash.

"A secret location."

"We're like real spies on this case." Flash got a kick out what I said, smiling. "How's your boss?" I asked.

"Not happy."

"My talk to his business colleagues didn't help?"

"It did, but more things have happened."

"What things?"

"All I want to know is, will you keep your promise and be there with us at Metro Spaceport?"

"That's what I was hired to do, so that's what I'll do. What things?"

"Reports of UFOs all over the planet. I know what you're going to say, but this time it's our governments accusing Up-Top of these sightings."

"Sightings of what? What does UFO even mean anymore? I was flying a flying saucer yesterday. We all have UFOs, Earth and Up-Top. That means we're living in the End-Times?"

Flash laughed. "You're not taking any of this particularly serious."

"Why should I? When it gets serious, I'll get serious. Right now all I see is craziness and hysteria. Flash, I'm telling you, people will soon start reporting that they're seeing real space aliens running around. The media will hype everything, making everyone an ET watcher, then there will be more sightings, then more media. It could go on forever."

"This only gives the movement a bad name."

"I agree, but Free Earth allows everyone together in the same city—sane and crazy alike. That's the problem. As long as you keep doing that, all of you will continue to get the same bad name. If I had a crazy uncle, I wouldn't let him stay in my apartment. I'd send him down the street and stay in another apartment."

"Do you even have a crazy uncle, Cruz?"

"No, but I have crazy in-laws."

"Do they stay in another apartment down the street when they visit?"

"No, in my apartment."

"Case closed."

Police, fire, and taxis. Those were the three professions that knew the supercity better than any other. Most people only knew their own district and a handful of others. If there was a fourth group, it would be hovercar racers, a pastime which I had previously been a part of. I thought I knew every part of the city, so I'd know where to avoid, but this area was right in Downtown and I never knew it existed.

The elevator capsule wasn't going up, but down—far down. Flash had parked in a guarded parking bay with no signs or displays of any kind, guarded by hulking cyborgs in black uniforms with no markings or name tags.

When the elevator opened we were greeted by more cyborgs—bodies covered in flashing indicators. They let us through the doors across the elevators, and I found myself in what looked to be another cavern carved out of the Earth. In the dim light, we came to a wall and I realized I was at the top of a large man-made pit. The wall encircled the pit, which went down about two stories and in the center was a giant rock. Was it my killer meteor rock? It was surrounded by men in white coats. I felt someone nearing me and looked. It was Run-Time, The Mick at his side, and behind them were a group of business-suit types.

"My meteor?" I asked.

Run-Time nodded. We were whispering, but a man was yelling commands over the intercom. Thankfully, his yelling stopped, and we watched hoverrobots move to the meteor with the scientists.

We noticed the light of the door behind us opening. "Ladies and gentlemen," a voice said. We all walked out into the hallway to an awaiting scientist in a gray coat.

"We went over it again, and it's a fake," he said to Run-Time and the businesspeople.

"Why has it taken so long for you to finish your tests?" asked one businessman.

"We don't rush things, sir. We take our time and follow proper procedures. Initially, there was a concern about biotoxins, which is why our physical examination was delayed. It's a fake, but a very good one. Most of the rock is real, but it's not from space."

"Has the government been notified?" another businessman asked, impatiently.

"Before you arrived."

"You have to understand, sir," Run-Time began, "that this whole incident is damaging the Metropolis business community. It's also damaging the off-world business community. We've taken it upon ourselves to take a very proactive approach in clearing up this matter. We need to know more than it's fake—the who, how, and why. Then the public must be informed—hold a press conference at the earliest possible time."

"Those questions are being investigated but not by us. What I can tell you is that it was shot from some type of cannon to where it landed."

"What's being done then?" another businessman asked.

"You need to take that up with Metro PD. They're leading the investigation."

"The reason we're here is because the Metro PD is not going to do anything until after they apprehend an off-worlder who attempted to ambush and assassinate a police officer, everything is on the back-burner until then. But this matter must be dealt with before it escalates any further."

"Yes, we heard about the shooting. I sympathize with your predicament, but I'm just a city consultant on payroll. We were brought in to determine if it was real or not, radioactive or not, contained any biological contaminants or not. That is all."

"Do you have any recommendations for us then as the best way to move forward?" Run-Time asked. "The police have to do what they need to do, but the politicians may do what we don't want them to do, as far as this is concerned. Once the wrong thing is done, reversing it may be far more difficult."

"If you'd like, we can have staff stand with all of you at any press conference."

The businessmen and women smiled and nodded. "That would be very helpful," Run-Time responded.

The man gave a bow of the head and walked away, while we waited. I still didn't know what my purpose was at the meeting, and I noticed that some of the businesspeople were giving me dirty looks.

"What?" I asked.

"The man who made this worse with your words to the media," one of them said. "What did you say: the Up-Top was testing their new meteor death weapon on Earth? There are a lot of people, serious people on Earth and off-world, who took what you said as hard fact."

"I'm sorry."

"Do you know the devastation a boycott could cause the city?"

"I said I was sorry. Incidentally, I was the one who was almost killed by that meteor, not you. You were sitting comfy in your climate-controlled office."

Run-Time stepped in. "My friend and I are going to talk over here while we wait," he said to them. The Mick followed as Run-Time took me over to the side. He was smiling, so he wasn't mad.

"So I'm here for political damage control?"

"You are."

"Do you have any contacts on Mars?" The Mick asked me.

I immediately thought the question was odd. "No."

"You don't know any police on Mars."

"Why?"

He ignored me. "Do you know that whoever launched that meteor was aiming for you?" The Mick waited for my reaction.

"They were aiming for Free Earth."

"They were aiming for you."

"Leaving aside how you know that with the certainty you're saying it, why? I only happened to be there."

"They saw you were there and changed the trajectory to hit the building you were in. We intercepted their conversation."

"Who's 'we?'"

"A lot of the Alien Life community regularly monitors general transmissions to capture government or law enforcement chatter. They happened to capture these off-worlders."

"Why do you want to know if I know any Martian police?"

"It was Martians who launched that meteor aiming for you. Earth authorities won't be able to identify their voice recordings, but Mars would. We thought you'd want to know who tried to kill you. The rumor around is that you don't like people who try to kill you hanging around."

I turned to Run-Time. "Is this true?"

"All of it, Cruz."

"Why would Martians try to kill me? I haven't even taken the case—not the real case. All I'm doing is a chaperon job."

"How would they know that?" The Mick asked. "You were at Free Earth and meeting with their leaders. You have taken their case."

"The case is a missing brother who's not even on Earth."

"No, he's on a Martian freighter that will be on Earth next week. Martian scientist, Martian freighter, Martian meteor launchers. That's a lot of Martians, Mr. Cruz."

I found The Mick to be particularly annoying that day.

My theory had been that one of the Free Earthers, or someone associated with them, sent the meteor as a publicity stunt—the fact that I happened to be there was an added bonus. However, this Martian revelation changed everything. It meant that Martians were targeting the Free Earthers already. It meant Martians didn't want me investigating anything for them. I had to admit I didn't take anything related to this case seriously because I didn't take ET watchers or their movement seriously. This had been a mistake, and because of it I may have sent the detective I hired into harm's way needlessly, but—

When I listened to the audio tapes Run-Time and The Mick had, I expected to hear blood thirsty criminals plotting my demise and that of the Free Earth leadership. That's not what I heard.

"It's that detective from the news," one voice said.

"This is perfect! Launch it."

"But—"

"Launch it! We'll never get a platinum opportunity like this ever again."

It sounded like a bunch of bumbling doofuses who felt they had won the Super Lotto with my appearance at Free Earth. I didn't say anything but looked at The Mick and then Run-Time. These people had specifically targeted me with their meteor weapon, and they knew they could kill me, but they weren't trying to kill me. It wasn't about me. It was about Cruz the Private Detective.

For the first time, in this crazy case, I felt it wasn't crazy at all. There was something very serious behind it all. I just didn't know what. The motto was true: Just because you're paranoid, doesn't mean someone isn't after you.

CHAPTER 31

Officer Break

The Mick asked me if I knew any cops on Mars. Of course I did— ever since my Blade Gunner Case, but I was smart enough to know I couldn't reach out to him directly. But my police "buddies" Ebony and Ivory were on vacation on Lunar colony!

"Cruz! Why is your face on my vid-phone while I'm on vacation with my wife and kids? Why?"

Officer Break was a Black policeman who had been on the Force for over a dozen years. His partner, Officer Caps, was a White policeman, who never spoke much, at least whenever I was around. He joined the Metropolis Police Department a year later. They were senior officers who ironically worked the Rabbit City (where I lived) and Buzz Town (where I worked) beats, which was how we had all become "buddies." I called Break because Caps probably wouldn't have answered the vid-phone.

"Hi, Officer Break."

"Hi, Mr. Cruz. I got one of your T-shirts."

"Get out of here!"

"My kids."

"Your kids have great taste."

"They have awful taste. My wife and I don't know what's wrong with them."

"Officer, I need a favor."

"No, I'm on vacation."

"I'm calling in my favor on this one."

"Really? Are you sure?"

"I never like to owe people favors, and I don't like to have people owe me favors. It messes up the whole working relationship. This case I'm on is...weird, but I could have handled that. However, it may also be dangerous weird—very dangerous weird. I can't get a spaceflight to Mars, or call anyone there, myself, but I need someone I can trust to contact someone there, who may help or tell me to go space myself.

Break smiled. "Sounds like someone I'd like to talk to. Law enforcement?"

"Yeah. In fact, stay away from the news. You're an Earther vacationing Up-Top, you don't want to know what's going on."

"What did you do now?"

"Not me. Seriously, don't turn on the news. It'll ruin your entire vacation and I know you don't get many. Enjoy it with the family, besides vacations are never long enough anyway. When you get back, you'll thank me.

"Okay. Who do you want me to contact?"

CHAPTER 32

Martians

Inside, the layout of the place was a large, open cafe, all booths and barstools at the kitchen counter, with college-kid waiters and waitresses on hoverroller skates.

I sat in my favorite diner, the Wet Cabeza, with my silk coffee. I knew the owners and everyone who worked there. It attracted mostly a business crowd, people who worked; and besides being a diner and bar, they rented out meeting rooms on the upper floors. This was where Phishy delivered my weapons when I first started out as a detective.

The place had a large layout mostly of booth seating and barstools at the kitchen counter area. From my booth seat near the side windows, I saw steam billowing out from a descending hovercar. It was an indicator of a much-older hovercar model, when people wanted all that steam shooting to tell you a hovercar was coming down on your head. Nowadays, people didn't want that steam to mess up their hair or blow off their shades. Times were always changing.

A man in a crimson red jacket hopped out of the passenger seat wearing black shades. I never knew why Martians always had to wear red. Someone told me that they only did so off of Mars; on their planet they practically banned the color. He had already seen me. He entered the diner and walked past the waiters and waitresses serving customers on hoverroller skates. I leaned back in my seat.

"Mr. Cruz, your item." He threw what looked like a pebble on the table in front of me.

"Tell our mutual friend 'thank you' then."

"Our mutual friend says that you have the information, but unfortunately, others know that the information was downloaded and that you're the likely recipient of the information."

"How would they know that?

"Mr. Cruz, you're not the only person who knows you know our mutual friend. They can put two and two together also. We are smarter than Earthers after all." He said it with a smile, trying to get a rise out of me.

"When we Earthers insult Up-Toppers, we use stronger epithets than simply calling you dumb, but we can chat about that another time. Tell our mutual friend that I still owe him one since I'm sure he's still having nightmares from his encounter with my parents-in-law. If it makes him feel better, tell him I can't escape to another planet to get away from them."

"I'll tell him. Good luck, Mr. Cruz." He followed his steps back out of the diner and got back into the waiting hovercar. It disappeared with its billowing steam, rising into the sky.

I held the pebble in my hand—a data node that one accessed wirelessly. Up-Top loved its digital tech toys. I had the full crew name list of that approaching Martian space freighter. However, before I checked the data I had someplace to go. Less than thirty minutes earlier one of my Sidewalk Johnny Brigade members called me.

Incredibly, they had spotted Merlin the Martian. Now, I had to go play alien hunter.

CHAPTER 33

Chief Hub and Mr. Mariner

"Hello," I said. "Please connect with Chief Hub. My name's Cruz. He'll know who I am."

"Mr. Cruz, we all know who you are," the male officer said to me from my Pony's vid-phone, "flying Up-Top flying saucers and landing them in the middle of the damn street. You should be ashamed of yourself."

"Hey, I drive a classic Americas Ford Pony."

"Why should I connect you?"

"I know where the Martian cop-shooter is."

The play was over. "Connecting."

There was a delay of only ten seconds before his face appeared on my vehicle's dashboard display. I didn't wait for him to say anything. "Chief, I'm reporting where the cop-shooter is so you can send in your officers. All I ask is he's arrested and not turned into Swiss cheese. He may—and I'm not saying for certain—but he may have information that might be of Earth's interest in relation to this whole meteor death weapon thing with Up-Top."

"Why of interest? We know the meteor didn't come from space. It came from here on Earth. We believe they shot it out of some submarine from the Great Oceans."

"But the people who did the act may be from Up-Top too. Do what you want Chief, and I know you will, but it's better for all involved if he can breathe and actually answer questions in the future."

"Okay. Where is he?"

I gave the Chief the location and hung up my vid-phone, but dialed again. This time it was the face of that Martian cowboy on the display.

"Mr. Mariner, the Metro PD are picking up your cow-killer courtesy of yours truly. You'll be getting your tip call soon."

"I already have, Mr. Cruz."

"Then I've completed my tasks for the day."

"We can all sleep a little lot sounder, and I can fly back home to my beautiful red planet. Nice doing business with you, Mr. Cruz." He hung up on his end.

PART SIX

The Man On the Moon

CHAPTER 34

Shakespeare

Five days. That Martian space freighter was now only five days away.

Strangely, the Concrete Mama had never had a building party before. But it was having one now. I invited everyone! I had Hellspawn #1 (Dot's father) playing the music, blasting it through the hallway of our 150th floor. I had Hellspawn #2 (Dot's mother) as chief hostess. Cruz Jr. had his cool hat on and new hoverstroller. I had hired some college kids to make sure no one ever had an empty glass. My Ma and Pops had flew down and arrived an hour ago to join the festivities. Dot and I would never, ever have to buy diapers out of own pocket again— well, it was going to be our pocket, but that pocket had a massive inflow of new cash. We would never be Silicon Dunes or Opus Fields rich, or even Elysian Heights rich (where her parents lived), but rich enough for us. I had successfully hunted down my alien with a vid-call. I loved Martian cow people! I was already practicing my new lines: "I may not eat beef, but when I do—it's Martian beef!"

PJ lived in the Concrete Mama too, so she was there, of course, hanging out with Dot. They were teaching Cruz Jr. to dance. He was looking at them with confused eyes wondering what I would say as a baby: "What the heck is wrong with these big people, why are they trying to get me move like this?"

Everything couldn't be better. The space freighter would soon be here on Earth and then I was done with the ET watchers forever. I hadn't even looked at the data pebble yet. I had lost all interest—I got my big pay-day. All I wanted to do was relax and have fun.

I was already a hero to the Concrete Mama for dealing with our Rabbit City hoodlum problem. With this building party, I would achieve super celebrity status. I was moving through the smiling, laughing, dancing crowds, shaking hands (wearing my see-through surgical gloves, of course; it was, after all, hundreds of people!) I noticed that our doorman was talking to PJ. He knew she was my secretary. They were now looking at me. Oh no, I said to myself. What now?

PJ had come to the party with a new boyfriend. They were always shorter than her and spoke some other language—she only liked foreign men, she had told me. She moved to me with the boyfriend following her like a puppy.

"PJ, it's a party. There's no working at a party."

"You're the boss, and there's no break for the boss. Someone wants to talk to you in the lobby."

"PJ. It's my party. I'm not going down to the lobby."

"The man only wants five minutes."

"PJ."

"And he'll pay."

I was tempted, but I had already gotten a bunch of money, so I could pretend that I was above such monetary considerations. "Have him make an appointment to come to the office like everyone else. This is where we live. In fact, why is a client coming to our personal residence and not the office?"

"Mr. Cruz, I'd be happy to explain."

I turned, and there was a smiling android looking at me.

CHAPTER 35

Mr. Omni

If you worked or connected with Silver City, the center of Metropolis' robotic production, robots were the salvation of mankind. Otherwise, you viewed them as the corporatist malevolent force to steal people's jobs and turn us all into mindless "sheeple." Dot was co-founder of an anti-robot union for hair stylists, manicurists, pedicurists, skin techs, nutri-techs, tattoo artists, fashion consultants, and fashion stylists. There were many such anti-robot unions around.

However, all Earthers found metal-heads—androids—creepy, but Up-Top loved them. This android looked like it could hold its own in conversation and deed with any human. It's body looked like a human, it dressed like us, or like Up-Top with lots of white, light grays, and some silver. Its head was what purposely indicated it was a robot. The neck was a series of tubes that held its head, the skull looked like a white polymer, and its face was more like a mask. The slits for eyes and mouth each had a line of LED lights.

Shakespeare the android wanted to take me to the Moon, of all places, for a quick meeting. He was happy to compensate me for my time, but I insisted that I'd be remaining on Terra Firma. So he moved to his Plan B—we'd hold the meeting in virtual life, but then, I told him of my ordeal of being kidnapped and jacked into a virtual life world for the purposes of killing me. The android seemed genuinely empathetic. How many scientists did it take to design its facial muscles, I wondered?

It was on to Plan C. We'd do a holo-conference. Big room where I'd sit here on Earth. Big room on the Lunar Colony somewhere. We'd see each other and talk on giant view screens. Shakespeare escorted me to a waiting hoverlimo, nothing gaudy, but very classy. We arrived at the Zodiac Hotel, where the android had already reserved the meeting room. The room was massive, very nice, but was very basic, a chair in front of the viewscreen, that's it.

Shakespeare turned it on by tapping his wrist (more wireless stuff) and stood waiting. I leaned back in my chair. They had asked me if I wanted to have a drink, but I had enough to drink at the party. When the viewscreen activated on the other end, I was caught off guard by the sight of a middle-aged Caucasian man swimming in large pool sphere with *very* tight trunks and a gill device in his mouth. Oh, the life of the rich and privileged Up-Top. They called it zero swimming— swimming through the air in zero gravity. Actually, water wasn't needed; you were floating in the air. Another one of the many pastimes—like golf, cricket, or Canadian curling—that really didn't make any sense when you thought about it, but were popular nonetheless.

The man finished his laps and swam to the exit of the pool sphere. "I'll be right with you, Mr. Cruz. I thought you would have taken me up on my free trip to Cydonia colony to meet in person, so I kept my swimming routine on schedule."

"It's no problem at all, sir," I called out.

He disappeared off-screen. The man appeared literally seconds later sitting on a hoverlounge chair in a full suit and slip-on shoes. Like any man, I prided myself on being able to dress fast, but this was light-speed fast.

"Good day, Mr. Cruz. My name is Omni."

"Nice to meet you."

"I trust my over-bot has been satisfactory."

"If you ever do fire him, he can work for me." Omni gave a slight smile.

"Mr. Cruz, I know your time is as valuable as mine, so I will get to it. I understand that you were given a full crew and cargo manifest for a Martian commercial freighter that is nearing Earth's Metropolis Spaceport."

I wasn't going to waste his time with obfuscation. "I was, since you already know about it."

"Mr. Cruz, your name came to my attention in your case involving—what did you Earthers call him—the Blade Gunner. Strangely, your name has popped up a few times since then. There are a lot of people who really don't care for you, both here and on Earth, but I'm sure you're not too bothered by that."

"I'm not."

"For a man in my position, the only people I'm interested in are those who are not liked by the people I associate with—people at the very top of the financial, business, and political worlds. If they don't like you, then it means you are doing things of interest or import. If they do like you, then you are—nothing. I don't have time for the insignificant.

"I had Shakespeare dig a bit deeper on your background on Earth. Surprisingly, for a street detective, you have no criminal or blackmail-able entanglements. Your germophobic diagnosis as a child must have forced you to live a clean life in more ways than you realize. Family man. Self-starter. Liked by the masses.

"I probed further to get an answer to why the people I do associate with—and that is not the masses—consider you a troublemaker. It was as I suspected. It's because you get results without their help—or obstruction. In fact, you seem to be very good at that. You have even come to the attention of the Founders because of it. However, the area where I do agree with them is how you sometimes go about getting those results. That is the purpose of this meeting.

"I am not into obstruction, though many of my friends would say otherwise. I am a firm believer in allowing people to do whatever it is they are going to do. That way other people can do what they are going to do. Mr. Cruz, the manifest you have in your possession, and I don't care that it was illegally obtained—all I ask, is that you recognize it for the significance, and potential danger, it is."

"Mr. Omni, from my standpoint, this case of mine is practically over."

"Mr. Cruz, what I am telling you is that your case has not even begun. The case is not the late myth-buster named Merlin, nor the meteor that almost made landfall on top of you. It is the freighter, it always has been."

"Are you saying the freighter should not be allowed to land on Earth?"

"That freighter has already been cleared to land on Earth. I'm saying you should solve your case."

"I was told the principal of the case committed suicide by spacing."

"Do the family members believe that? I'm sure you told them. Do you?"

"I don't know either way."

"He didn't commit suicide, Mr. Cruz, but he may be dead all the same."

"Do you know something I should know?"

"You're the detective with the manifest. Detect."

"What is your interest in this?"

"I come from a long family line of astronomers and astrobiologists."

"You're an ET watcher."

Omni smiled. "Do you hear that, Shakespeare, the Earthers have a nickname for us?"

"We have Earth ET watchers, too. You all—what's the motto—Want to Believe."

"Yes, Mr. Cruz. I do. If there is even an off-chance that your client's brother found extraterrestrial life near Jupiter, I want to know. That freighter is the key to both of us. You want the man. I want what the man found."

"Why do you need me involved? If it's about the cargo for you, I'm sure you have ways to get access or possession of it—even if it's extraterrestrial."

"You're not a believer are you?"

"I'm an agnostic. I don't care either way."

"You don't recognize how all of life in the solar system will change if it is. Even you, Mr. Cruz, will be recorded as one of the discoverers whether you want to or not. We idolize our discoverers—statutes, holidays, streets, mega-towers, warships and spaceships named after you."

"Mr. Omni, I can't even handle T-shirts of me on the street. I surely don't want any of that. I'm not quite sure that people are ready for the discovery you're hoping for."

"I have to confess, Mr. Cruz, that I agree with you. I don't think humanity is ready, even now, with us having created human colonies beyond Earth. But I am satisfied as an agnostic, you will let the cards land where they will."

"That I will always do."

"When you do meet that freighter to locate Mr. Neil Cosmos, you'll already be there, so take a look at the cargo too. I do have considerable influence in the solar system, but not at the Metropolis Spaceport. There I am only a spaceman."

"Look at the cargo? That's all?"

"Nothing more. A layman's inspection of what he found is all I ask. Earth authorities can't seize the freighter without Martian permission, but Martian authorities cannot enter the terminal without Earth permission. You can bypass all of that as an independent agent doing legitimate work."

"Okay. Makes sense. I'll look at the cargo then."

"Very good, Mr. Cruz. Shakespeare will shuttle you back to your residence. Please do consider visiting Cydonia Colony one day. It is a beautiful and an exceptional place. And despite what your Earth ET watchers say, it is not the site of a secret government base controlled by space aliens."

"Thank you, Mr. Omni. I'll let the wife know and maybe we'll take you up on that."

Omni nodded, and his hoverchair flew away as the viewscreen shut off.

The "late" Mr. Merlin. That's what Omni said to me. They called those Freudian slips, and it told me I had to get to Merlin as fast as possible.

I sat in my vehicle staring off into space. I didn't even know who Merlin was. I didn't know what was true and what were lies. If there were a plot to get rid of Merlin, how would I stop it? I was just one guy. I was starting to wonder if Merlin actually allowed my Sidewalk Johnny Brigade to find him. He had eluded capture for 10 years, but was found by my people. They found him in all places right around City One in Downtown masqueraded as a sidewalk johnny himself. That was his great final play? I didn't think so. Merlin wanted it all to end. He did his information transfer with me and had had enough. But what exactly did I know?

I never did burst into Metro PD about my fears about Merlin's life being in danger. I went home instead and tried to put it all out of my mind. Then I woke up to the news: Merlin had been turned over to Up-Top police, and while in their custody had mysteriously died of unknown causes.

CHAPTER 36

Free Earthers

The Cosmos wanted a status update, so I was back at Free Earth. It seemed that the madness had subsided a bit. The crowds were not as large and insane, so it meant the novelty of it all was dying down. Soon the Free Earthers would be out there by themselves again.

They had me in the same meeting room, same communal board leaders, minus Mr. Conehead, but the same poor attitude.

"Yes, I believe Merlin, not you, but I can't prove anything, so it doesn't matter, especially now."

"What a thing to say! Everyone tells you he was a dark soul in the universe and I show you what he did to my arm, but you believe him and disregard everyone else." Ares was mad.

"Dark soul? My gut said he was telling the truth."

"Then I was lying to you? We're all lying?"

"I don't know. He's dead, so what does it matter? I did not come here for that. I want you to sit here and tell me what the plan is to get on the freighter."

"We're going to tell you that? How a plan stays secret is you don't tell anyone," Terra said to me.

"You don't worry about it," Mrs. Cosmos said. "We'll get you to the freighter and on it."

"I do worry, because I have no desire to get snatched up by Up-Top police."

"It's not so bad, Mr. Cruz," Mr. Cosmos said. "Up-Top prisons are better than any palace you have here on Earth." Did Mr. Cosmos really believe that would reassure me?

This was a suicide mission. Whether they got caught or not, shot or not, they were going to get to the freighter. That was unacceptable to me, but I was going to keep it to myself.

"Mr. Cruz, I don't know how to say this but, until the day the freighter arrives, we don't want to see you," Geo said. "Don't come by here or attempt to call us. Everything must go dark until then. We'll retrieve you."

These ET watchers liked the word *dark*. "What do you mean you'll retrieve me? I don't like how that sounds."

"Flash will pick you up."

"Why didn't you just say that? 'I'll retrieve you.' When an ET watcher says that to a person, who know what that could mean?"

Mr. Cosmos chuckled and Mrs. Cosmos punched him in the arm. With that they escorted me out of Free Earth. They were very serious; they didn't want to see me until it arrived.

That freighter was now only three days away from Earth.

CHAPTER 37

Run-Time and Company

Peacock Hills was one of the premiere business districts in Metropolis, with its monolith buildings extending like gargantuan fingers into the sky through the city's rain cloud cover. Each mega-tower was illuminated in the colors of white, light yellow, and blue. One tower was that of Run-Time's business empire, Let It Ride Enterprises, which took up all of its monolith tower on Electric Boulevard.

I came out of the elevator on the 250th penthouse level, and was greeted in unison, "Good morning, Mr. Cruz." Three women sat at the reception desk, evenly spaced apart from each other—three different colored outfits, three different ethnicities, three different accents.

"Are they waiting for me? I have the surprise coming up, but don't tell them." I was like a devious little kid, as I leaned on their receptionist wall.

When I came through the conference room door Run-Time immediately asked, "Cruz, why have my receptionists moved us to the

Floral Conference Room?" Behind him were his 3 VPs, and Bugs came in after me. I held up my hand.

Behind me came not one, but three gourmet cooks pushing a hovertrolley each. You could smell the delicious food underneath the metal covering on the top of each trolley. The conference room was spacious with an array of multi-colored flowers on the pastel wallpaper, its own working mini-waterfall on one side of the room and real potted bamboo trees on the other. The cooks set up against the wall near the waterfalls and opened the covers.

"Cruz, what is this?" Run-Time asked.

"This is my treat. Have a seat everyone, at the conference table."

The cooks each had a large plate in each hand and I directed.

"For Mrs. Phoenicia, you're being served the shish taouk marinated in lemon juice, garlic, paprika, tomato paste, and secret spices, and wrapped in pita bread." The cook placed the plate in front of her—her mouth open in shock. "For Mrs. Role, your favorite too: curry goat served with Jamaican rice and black peas." The second cook placed her plate in front of her. "Ah, Mr. Mick, for you we have black pudding served with sautéed scallops, poached eggs, and salad." When The Mick saw his plate, he looked up at me and covered his mouth so I couldn't see him smile. The cooks gave us all our chopsticks.

"Now for Bugs, where are you? Have a seat!" The first cook returned with a new plate. "This one is for you. We get Cajun with some Jambalaya." Bugs, wearing a purple suit, was laughing he was so surprised. He was a sweeper introduced to me by Run-Time and was the expert in office security: listening device detection, motion detection security, intrusion defense security, video surveillance, door and wall defense security, door and lock augmentation, trap door and panic rooms—always in high demand.

I looked at Run-Time. "Run-Time and I like to eat other people's food, so we're having samples of all of yours, except Mr. Mick's." They laughed, as both Run-Time and I took our seats at the table.

"What's the catch, Cruz?" Run-Time asked as his plate was placed in front of him. I was served my plate and the cooks returned to their stations to get large pitchers and glasses. They came back to our table and began pouring our drinks.

"No catch. I have some extra money and you're always treating me, so I'm giving back, so I can increase my karma points."

"Really, Cruz, what's the catch?"

I took a bite. "Notice that all of these have a meat theme?"

"Where is this meat from, Mr. Cruz?" Mrs. Role asked eating her curry.

"It's the best meat on the planet." I took another bite.

"Planet? Yet, you didn't say Earth?" Mrs. Phoenicia stopped eating. "Is this—Martian?"

I smiled. "Well, we're not on any other planets that we know about."

Bugs stopped eating immediately. "Martian meat? Cruz, I'm not eating no Martian mystery meat—"

"Bugs! Don't say that," I scolded. "The cooks are standing right there. You don't talk bad about food until after they give you all the food. We still have desserts. I don't want people spitting in my food. You know I'm a recovering germophobe."

Bugs looked at the three stone-faced cooks and forced a smile. He slowly began to put food in his mouth with his chopsticks, but he wasn't chewing.

"What happened to the excitement everyone? Authentic exotic cuisines with the best Martian meat in the universe. Come on, bring back the excitement."

They all looked down at their plates with the exact same expression I'd seen on Cruz Jr.'s face staring at a bowl of spinach soup Dot tried to feed him.

"Yummy," I said.

"Where did you get all this extra money to treat us so well?" Run-Time asked, who also had stopped eating.

"A group of clients. Come on everyone, it's Martians, simply humans who live on Mars, not mobsters. We're eating some good food!"

Personally, I loved the Martian meat. Actually, the Martian cow people gave me coupons to get it all at 95% off which made it affordable to a "rich" Earther like me.

Lunch was over, so it was time for business. In the pit of my stomach I had a bad feeling about that space freighter. It was less than 72 hours away. The Mick didn't protest like the others and had eaten his black pudding concoction, which was what I called it after reading, and abruptly stopping, what black pudding actually was. All three VPs were present with Run-Time across from me.

"Who is Omni?" I asked.

"Mr. Omni is the richest man off-world, outside of the Founders," Run-Time answered.

"I thought the Founders didn't let a non-Founders become as rich as them."

"Maybe they're getting softer and civilized as newer generations take over. They created and colonized all the off-world colonies. After a few centuries of simple governance all pioneers soften, even the most revolutionary."

"The richest man Up-Top? Why would he want Merlin dead?"

"Omni had Merlin killed?" The Mick asked.

"Don't listen to me. I'm just musing aloud. Why would the richest man on the moon want Merlin the myth-buster dead?"

"What myth was he trying to bust this time?" Run-Time asked.

"That's the question. Merlin was an anti-believer, but became a firm believer."

"Believer? What are we talking about?"

"Belief, not proof, of the existence of intelligent life."

Run-Time and all the VPs looked at me. "Make the call!" Run-Time yelled.

"Call! What call are they going to make?"

"I can't tell you," he said.

"Tell me."

"It's a legal thing."

"Then tell me what it entails."

"Buying stock."

I stood up, smiling.

"What?" Run-Time asked.

"Don't let me stop you."

"What's that look for? I've seen that look before, Cruz. What?"

"I don't know yet, but don't put all your money on whatever stocks you're going to buy."

"Cruz, this isn't a game."

"I know. That's what worries me. We may have people thinking it's a game while they're killing people and trying to kill people. Do what you have to do. I could be completely wrong, but I suspect as we get closer to that freighter landing more and more things are going to start happening."

CHAPTER 38

The Wans

When I woke up the next day, I couldn't move. I held my stomach in pain! I couldn't go into the office. I told Dot not to worry, so she'd go to work. She told me that her parents would be over to mind Cruz, Jr. I stayed in bed as long as possible, but I could hear the rapid-fire Chinese from the bedroom, even with the door closed. I had to save my son from the Hellspawn.

I could barely move in my pajamas, as I hobbled out to the kitchen and living room. It served me right for eating all that Martian mystery eat. I bet Martians couldn't eat Earth meat. I ate the equivalent of a small cow, and my Earth stomach was engaged in full-scale biological war.

"Help me!" I yelled. "I'm infested!"

The Hellspawn just stared at me shaking their heads, mumbling to each other in Chinese. Cruz Jr. was sitting in his high chair between them at the dinner table staring at me too.

"You got Martian food poisoning," Mr. Wan said, standing from his chair. "Good! That's what you get for eating food not of this world." He started to laugh, and so did his significant other.

"Very funny. Not of this Earth." My stomach did something, and I bent down in pain. "I need drugs!"

"You need a stomach transplant," Mrs. Wan said, laughing. "Good!" She called my son something. "Your father is a weak man," Mrs. Wan said, pointing at me. "Don't be like him!"

"What did you call my son at the beginning?"

"I called him by his true Chinese name."

"His name is Cruz."

"Cruz is name for the weak."

"Don't confuse my child."

Cruz Jr. then started yelling out the same word or phrase they were calling him and started to laugh. I stood doubled over.

"If you knew how to speak Chinese, you would know what he said," Mrs. Wan said. "He'll be able to speak English, Chinese, Spanish, Japanese, and French before he's three. You can barely speak one! Such a disgrace to your parents."

Mr. Wan was waving his hands in the air doing his impression of me crying. "I need drugs!" He liked impersonations.

Sick or not, I was outta there.

CHAPTER 39

Chief Hub and Company

I was still bothered by the whole dead Merlin thing. There was that voice within that said I could have intervened somehow. But there was also the other voice that said, "Intervene why—and how?" I didn't know if Merlin was telling me the truth; I only suspected that he was. He was also in police custody; what exactly was I going to do? Storm Metro One, burst through the doors, take charge of him away from the police? The fact was there was nothing for me to feel bad about. I did what I was supposed to—I turned him over to the authorities. My hands were clean. But—

I worked other cases, one-day, quick-solve jobs, but all that my mind was focused on was that freighter. It was like a giant monster floating its way to Earth, and I felt that no matter where I went or where I tried to hide, it was after me.

Late in the day, I was making calls from my personal office. I wrapped up no less than four cases in the morning—two domestics (also known as spousal "peeping tom" jobs), one straight surveillance job, and a municipal person-locate job. My plan was to head over to

Metro PD—again. I didn't trust the Free Earthers and their great secret plan to get to the Martian space freighter. If we were trespassing, we'd be arrested—period. Though expunged from all records, I had been arrested and I was not eager to repeat the "fun."

"Boss!" I heard PJ call out.

I hadn't made my next vid-call yet, so I stood and walked into main area. There they were—Chief Hub, a bunch of other police brass, including Captain Monitor, the Mayor, and the Mayor's chief deputy, Mr. Frame—everyone in their civilian clothes. I didn't know if I should be flattered, but I wasn't concerned. I frowned a bit.

"We're happy to see you too, Cruz," Hub said.

"You don't seem to be too concerned that we're here," a police exec officer said. "How do you know we're not here to bust you?"

"For one, I haven't done anything. Innocent people, like me, don't fear police. More importantly, other than the Chief, none of you jokers have arrested anybody this century. If the Chief was going to arrest me, it wouldn't be with any of you around, it would be with real street police."

"You little—" the police exec officer began.

The Chief stopped him. "We're not here to play. Cruz, in your office."

They all followed me in with PJ watching like a hawk. One of them closed the door. There weren't enough chairs for everyone, so I just sat on the edge of my desk as the rest of them arranged my chairs for the Mayor and his aide to sit; the rest stood.

"Is this room clear?" Mayor Likegate asked.

Three of the officers took wands out of their jackets and swept my entire office for listening devices. "Clear," one of them said, and all three returned to where they were standing.

"We meet again, Mr. Cruz," the Mayor said to me. "I hear you have a case that involves a certain Martian space freighter bound for Earth in two days."

"Before we start your meeting, I have to ask, since you're here. What happened to Merlin?"

The Mayor glanced at Hub. "We turned him over to Interpol, and that was that. Before they were to depart, we got word that Merlin had died in his holding cell—no further details were provided or offered."

"How is a Mr. Omni involved in this?"

The Mayor gave me a strange look. "Why would he be involved in this?"

"I had a virtual meeting with him, and he seemed to know that Merlin would die in Up-Top police custody before he actually did."

The Chief and the police brass looked at each other. "Do you think that information should have been shared with us?" the Chief asked.

"Why? What would you have done? Nothing. That's why I didn't call you. Remember, Chief, I was the one who reported him to you to arrest in the first place."

"Yes, yes."

"Mr. Cruz, what I'm about the tell you is extremely confidential and must not be shared with anyone, including your wife and new kid. We have been debating whether to bring you in, but it seems that we don't have a choice now, since you've remained in the middle of this and will continue to be so—to our great displeasure."

"Thanks for that, Mr. Mayor."

"You're welcome."

"These Free Earth cult members that hired you—"

"That is a bit unfair. I've dealt with cult members before and I wouldn't include them in that category. They're over-eager to see an ET, but that's all. They're not holding anyone against their will."

"But they are stockpiling weapons," a police brass said.

"There're a lot of people in Metropolis who do, and they're not in a cult."

"Mr. Cruz, do you have a classified crew and cargo manifest of that freighter in your possession?"

"No," I answered without a pause.

"Well, we know you do."

"You know I have the manifest. Omni knows I have the manifest. Are you all working together?"

"Certainly not," the Mayor said. "Omni knows about the manifest?"

"Mayor, let's stop playing games. What do you want? That freighter touches down on our planet in two days. I'm supposed to be there when it does. Should I be worried? Do you know the thing about kids, now that I have one myself? Kids say it to you straight. Adults try to be all clever with each other rather than being straight. They end up causing more problems for themselves than if they were to just play it straight. Okay, we're all smart, clever adults in this room, but let's move on. What do you know? As that freighter gets closer to Earth, I've been having a constant feeling of approaching doom. What do you know?"

The Mayor looked at one of the men, who nodded. "Mr. Brackets is with Metropolis's Space Threat Division."

"I could have used your help when that meteor tried to land on my head."

"As you already know, Mr. Cruz, that rock didn't come from space. But my story does involve another rock. We have reason to believe that two and a half years ago a Martian mining and salvage crew working the asteroid belt happened upon what they reported as an artifact buried in an asteroid the size of Texas. Our intel is spotty, but we can confirm that that salvage crew with the authorization of the Martian government detonated a micro-nuclear device on that asteroid."

I realized that play time was truly over. All Earthers got sick even at the mention of the word. "Nuclear? The Martians are detonating nukes?"

"They split that asteroid into five pieces," another man said.

"After that detonation," the space threat man continued, "more spacecraft arrived at the scene. We believe it was a terraforming outfit to create semi-habitable structures for the artifact and a larger salvage team. They're the only ones who can build such structures."

"Wait, wait, wait," I said. "You believe the ET artifact story?"

"That's what they believe. They hired your client's brother to head up the effort. Then everything went underground, figuratively speaking. All our informants who kept us abreast of things were suddenly unreachable, the entire area of space that could give us a good line of sight with our surveillance ships was restricted. We have had no information, no intel, nothing.

"Then about 18 months ago something happened in the Martian science authority. We don't know what exactly—some kind of scandal, people were removed from their positions, people suddenly retired, which means fired. That's when we first heard of this freighter, but was told it was a standard cargo freighter from Mars."

"The Free Earthers also said that freighter has been incommunicado ever since it left Martian space. Is that true?

"That's how my office got pulled into this," the Mayor said. "The off-worlders have cleared this freighter for landing, but it is expressly forbidden to allow any craft to land on Earth without steady and consistent communication with the crew. There has been none."

"There are other rumors," the Chief added. "A certain mutual acquaintance from Mars got a message to me that a military ship intercepted that freighter while it was in Martian space."

"Military? What did they see?"

"None of us can find out," the space threat man said. "What do your clients expect to find when that freighter lands?"

"There were Up-Top agents that spoke with me when I first got this case. It was right at Metro PD—a Mr. Weborg." Hub grimaced at the very mention of the man's name. "What?" I asked.

"What did he tell you?" Hub asked.

"That Neil Cosmos committed suicide by spacing."

"He was lying."

"I know that now. His name is on the freighter manifest. Merlin said something too."

"Why would you listen to anything that attempted cop-killer would say?"

"Well, we know he was telling the truth, don't we? He's dead. Merlin said the problem wasn't Cosmos. He said another civilian was on that freighter that was the problem."

"Where's the manifest, Cruz," Chief said.

"The only other civilian on the freighter besides Cosmos was a man named Orion."

I walked to my desk, opened the front drawer, and took out a print-out. I had already printed the names and memorized them, though it was useless since they were all off-worlders. There was no database I could access that would tell me who they were. I handed the Chief the manifest. "Maybe you can find out who they all are and what happened." I looked at the Mayor. "Are you really going to let this thing land? Can't you keep it in orbit?"

"Mr. Cruz," the Chief said.

I smiled and returned to my desk. I grabbed my bounty hunter badge, then handed it to him. "Does this mean we're space aliens too? We're able to read each other's thoughts without words." I turned my attention back to the Mayor.

"I have no authority, Mr. Cruz. Technically, Metro International Spaceport doesn't belong to Metropolis. It belongs to the world, and where the freighter is landing belongs to Mars."

"This isn't right. We all know it."

"Like the decision you made when it came to Mr. Merlin. Yes, but what is there for us to do about it?" the Chief asked.

None of us in the room were pleased. I realized that the list of crew names would be as useless to them as me, without Up-Top giving them access, which seemed unlikely.

"The freighter arrives in two days, and I'm going to be there with my clients. They're keeping a big secret from me as to how they're going to get access to the landing port for the freighter."

The police brass began to laugh. "It's no secret," one said. "They work there. They all do."

"Work there?"

"They're terminal security agents."

"Great, which means they plan to do a whole bunch of illegal things. Since I don't want to be arrested, can you get me a pass? I know you all sometimes give them out to civilians. I want to avoid being arrested."

"What do your clients expect to find when that freighter lands?" the space threat man asked again.

"I really don't know. They believe he's being held on the freighter against his will. They just want someone there to hold their hand when they board. I don't think they really know what they want or expect. They just want me there."

The Mayor looked at his aide. "Get Mr. Cruz an appointment with the Martian director of the Metro Spaceport." The Mayor looked at me. "He's a friend."

I thought it was going to be smooth sailing until the freighter got to Earth, but I was wrong. It was Dot who texted me while I was with them. I ran and turned on the news on the large wall screen in the waiting area of my office. We all gathered around.

"Ladies and gentlemen, we have breaking news, some are saying it is news beyond Biblical proportions—proof of extraterrestrial life has been found near Mars!"

Omni was right. This was all just beginning.

PART SEVEN

E.T. World

CHAPTER 40

La Familia

The Chief's face was pale. The Mayor looked like he was going to pass out. The police brass had deer-in-the-headlights expressions. It had nothing to do with whether an ET or ET craft was found. They didn't care. What they were panicking about was the potential reaction of the public to the prospect of real ETs. I was just as concerned.

The men couldn't get out of my offices fast enough. PJ sat at her desk, smiling. "We found aliens! I wonder if they speak French."

I marched back to my private office.

"What's wrong with you?" I heard her ask, as I went behind my desk and rolled my chair to in front of the wall screen with the news.

"I don't want to be disturbed."

"Why? You're not going home to celebrate the discovery of aliens?"

"There may be space alien life in the universe, PJ, but I highly doubt that this is it."

"Why do you say that?"

"Ha!" I jumped from my chair pointing. There was a man holding a press conference surrounded by other men in business suits and lab coats. "I knew it! PJ, get me info on a Mr. Giancarlo Vega."

"Hello, my name is Giancarlo Vega with the Darwin Space Project," he began.

I watched him talk, but I really wasn't listening. I was watching him with laser-beam focus. Everyone on the planet would soon be under their spell—except for me.

It was later than my usual when I strolled home through the front door. I instinctively reached for my weapon; there was a strange man walking out of my kitchen.

"Who are you?" I asked.

"I'm a guest."

"I live here."

"Oh, you're Cruz. Yeah, your wife said."

"My wife said, huh? There are so many places I could take this conversation, but I'm not in the mood."

The man paid me no more mind and continued walking into the living room. I stopped. There were all these people in my living room! All of them, eyes glued to the news. I noticed my Ma and Pops on one side of the couch against the wall opposite me. I could see the heads of the Hellspawn watching the main TV screen. Dot was sitting amongst others on the floor. My son was in his high chair, but there were other babies in strollers around him. Everyone was watching the TV like zombies. It was creepy. No one even noticed that I had arrived. Good! I left them all to go to bed. I had a busy day for me tomorrow.

I didn't go into work. I had called PJ, and she informed me that Liquid Cool was swarming with reporters. I thought being called Meteor Man was bad. Now I was the Metro P.I. involved in the Proof of Alien Life Case. Free Earth had so many people surrounding their city to get "insight" into talking to the aliens, that all of them, sane and insane, were barricaded inside.

"Cruz, why did you have me stay home today? I have to work."

"In this?"

The news switched from district to district. Eye Candy was under siege from media and onlookers too. I imagined the whole world were now ET believers.

"You have a point there." She looked at Cruz, Jr. who was lying on his back on our bed wiggling around. "He wants his hoverchair."

"Cruzie, you need to start walking."

"Cruz Jr., ignore him. I'll get your chair." She pulled his hoverchair to the bed. Personally, I didn't like hoverchairs for babies. It made them think they were adults since they were hovering at adult level. When they started walking, they'd think they were going backwards in life. "When I was 1 and 2, I was all the way up there, now I'm 3 and 4 and I'm down here on the ground with smelly feet and possible isopods."

She put him in the hoverchair and already he was smiling. "Why are we home, Cruz? Are we hiding?"

"All I want to be is a private detective, but it's like I'm a galactic secret agent. This whole case isn't just crawling with Martians, but government agents too, and I'm sure Up-Top megacorps operatives, and there's talk of military spaceships, ETs, ET artifacts. It's too much."

"It's too much? What do you mean? That's the case."

She was monitoring Cruz Jr. in his hoverchair. He flew right up to my face and he playfully touched the side of my head and then hovered away. "No, Dot. This is not the case. That's the problem. They're trying to keep me away from the real case, but I'm on to them. They want secret agents, we'll give them secret agents."

She looked at me with her hands on her hips. "What?"

"Pack your bag, Mrs. Cruz. You, me, and Cruz Jr. as of this instant are galactic superspies. We're going to break this whole case wide open. Let's get going. Mission one: get out of the Concrete Mama undetected by everyone."

"Superspies, Cruz?"

"I find myself being pulled further and further away from the kind of detective work I want to do. It's like the OGs when I was a hovercar restorer. Who were the happy ones? The ones who kept a low profile, had their own stable of classics that they could manage and wash by hand weekly without any robots. The unhappy ones had all the prestige and fame, had a big staff, ran major racing teams, and oversaw merchandising and marketing globally. They were miserable. They never saw their classic vehicles, never even got a chance to sit in one to breathe in that new minty smell. They were cut off from what they loved and why they got into the biz to begin with.

"I want to be a street detective—it may be small, but I want small. Look at all this. I got the Mayor and Chief in my office, I'm known by rich spacemen and Martians, and the Council of Corporations. I keep this up and I won't be in charge of my life anymore—all of them will. I don't want to be the PI to the uber-governments and megacorps of Earth and Up-Top. I am a Metro PI who has Average Joe and Jane clients, an occasional corporate, an occasional government. That's it. I can control that. This I can't control, no one can. I keep complaining about it. I'm taking back my persona.

"Dot, you could have taken your skills on the road and left Earth to pamper those Up-Toppers. Could have made tons more money but your life wouldn't be your own. You'd spend more time on shuttles bouncing from the space colonies to the lunar colonies to Mars and all over again. Who cares if you have the big money and big money friends, if you're a miserable wreck? If it's not you. Eye Candy is great because you're there and the Up-Toppers fly down to you! Yeah, I'm taking back my persona."

"Good for you, Cruz. But your vehicle is bright red and everyone knows what it looks like. How do you suppose you'll get us out of here undetected?"

"Ever wondered how I'm able to disappear so readily when you've had your people looking for me?"

"Umm?" She smiled. "Cruz, what are you playing at?"

"You have wondered. Let's go."

I said one bag only, but Dot still had three and that was not including the bag just with diapers and baby stuff. Cruz Jr. also had his small case of clothes. I had my suitcase. Amazingly, all the suitcases fit in the trunk of the Pony. Cruz had the whole backseat in his super baby-carrier while Dot and I were in the front seats. I traded my standard tan slicker for a black one, and my tan fedora for my "secret" black one. Dot was all in black, too, and we both wore blue shades. Dot bundled Cruz Jr. up in his hooded slicker, he looked like a girl, so I just let that be his disguise.

I started the vehicle up and we flew out of the parking bay. Dot was watching the madness of the hovercraft all around the Concrete Mama watching for us. I casually drove past everyone.

"No way!" Dot said. "How did that just happen? They didn't see us."

"They saw us, just not a red Ford Pony."

"What did you do? Do you have a Martian cloaking device on the Pony?" She leaned up as far as she could to look out the front windshield. "Cruz, your Pony is black! You sneaky devil. That's how you've been doing it. You have a changeling cloak on your vehicle. Isn't that illegal?"

"We're spies. You're going to see a lot of illegal things going forward to solve this case."

"What is the case? Your client's missing brother on that freighter?"

"No, Dot. That's not the case anymore. That's a side-issue, just like all this ET artifact madness. The case is murder."

"Murder? Who got murdered?"

"Merlin. People are going to go to jail or fry for it, and they don't even realize it yet, even the ones who think they're untouchable. Who killed Merlin and why, is the case. Up until them doing that—this was all a big game—not even a misdemeanor, but it's homicide in three different jurisdictions now. Murder is the case, and I have to solve it because the police can't."

CHAPTER 41

The Alien Evangelist

The idea for hoverhotels came from Up-Top. On Earth, where people were accustomed to buildings that were huge and imposing, it seemed like such a fad would never catch on. They didn't, except for a very loyal, often eccentric, tourist base that loved the idea of a residence floating through the sky in an endless loop around the supercity. There was also a class of the uber-rich that preferred to live no other way. Vega was such a person. He lived in a pink domed ten-story hoverhotel.

We had rented a room in a silver hoverhotel that wasn't especially close, but that's what telescopes were for. The only way I would involve the wife and kid, was if their safety was assured. They'd be on stake-out duty: take pictures of any and everyone seen with Vega whether on the balcony or within his residence. I'd set it up so that our recording telescope would never be seen and the curtains on our windows would always be drawn.

"This is called a crypto-wall, very secret, but government intelligence and the megacorps use it all the time. It creates a sonic and electromagnetic bubble around you so no one can see you and Cruz. Jr inside it. All these wealthy types have all kinds of devices looking out. You'll be invisible to them."

"Cruz, where did you get all this equipment? Can we afford all this?"

"All rentals."

"But what about this hotel room?"

"The Martian cow people money."

"Cruz, we already had that money set aside for stuff."

"I'm not spending all of it. I plan to make it all back with this case."

"Your case. Who's your client?"

"I'll have many clients. They just don't know they're clients yet."

"Exactly as I thought."

"You have the video surveillance monitors on the front door and anti-intrusion system. I also left a piece for you in the bag."

"Cruz, I'm not shooting anyone, pretend spy or not."

"Anyone meeting with Vega, listen in on their conversation, too, see if you pick up anything. You're good with deciphering conversations, and you speak every language."

"What's the story with you and this Vega?"

"Long story, but I'll tell you when I get back. I have to do my real detective stuff."

"While Cruz Jr. and I are stuck in a hotel room."

"The room is huge. Cruz Jr. has his toys and TV. You have your spy duties. I won't be that long. Surveillance is boring work, I won't lie, but in this case you have a very flamboyant target. You'll be entertained. But no images or sounds inappropriate for underage minors."

Dot laughed. "What is it you've gotten me into?"

I kissed the wife and kid, then I was off in my disguise black fedora and slicker outfit.

The media was going to make any client visits to Liquid Cool impossible, so I had PJ close the office and work out of her apartment. She'd route all calls to her mobile computer. Her job was to monitor the media, which she did anyway, but now it was important. Since we were all being watched by the media, of course, we'd all stay off the phones. I knew others would be watching—we didn't know who exactly, we could guess, but we'd never see them.

Phishy had his task too. He and his sidewalk johnny friends would take over Metro Spaceport. I didn't care how many men and women he needed, they were to blanket that spaceport so we'd know everyone coming and going.

PJ had a way to get priority messages to me—an old texting unit. Mine vibrated, and I looked at the display: 911M.

Merlin had been known as a crusader against scams and hoaxes related to extraterrestrial life. He was the superstar of the non-believing community. The public didn't know about his end-of-life conversion and never would.

On the other side of the ledger was the alien life believing scientific community. They had their own superstar: Giancarlo Vega. He called himself an Alien Evangelist. I never knew what the hell that meant other than to elevate the belief in space alien life to its own religion and Vega being the chief prophet. My NeuroDancer case left a very bad taste in my mouth in regard to "prophets." But Vega wasn't just a showman, he was a real scientist, lots of Masters and PhDs all having to do with space and the exploration of space, astrophysics, and much more. What had made him immune from the broad brush that Merlin and those like him waved at the entire Alien Life Movement was simple: kids. Vega was a TV teacher always surrounded by the little kiddies. He could spread his ET evangelism unimpeded, but I knew all about Vega. I had been one of those kids.

I never met Vega before, but I noticed that when I came into the room his eyes immediately zoomed in on me out of recognition. As a "famous" detective, I came across people who knew of me, but this seemed more than him simply seeing me on the news.

Giancarlo Vega as a scientist superstar was loved by the science community because he gave their profession great press with his good looks, infectious smile, ability to distill high scientific concepts into great stories and humor that the public could relate to, and he could raise lots of money for the community. It also didn't hurt that he was popular with the female population. The media had been in love with him for many years, decades; he was always a great feature. He looked like he was in his thirties, but he was about to touch the big 7-0, but that meant he had another three or four decades to be the premier science cheerleader that he was.

Vega stood in front of the throngs of reporters in front of Free Earth. "We are doing this not only with the cooperation of Lunar colony and Mars, but the Darwin Space Project of the Earth governments. This will truly be humankind on Earth and off-world coming together for the greatest project ever known. We have found, and it has been confirmed, that Jupiter deep space miners discovered an unknown artifact of extraterrestrial origin on an asteroid between the planets of Mars and Jupiter. We have dubbed the find the Neolith."

The media went wild. They loved new words and terms. There would be a million T-shirt designs and posters on the Net within ten seconds. Vega gestured, and a group of well-dressed men flanked him, all smiles and handshakes.

"People of Earth, we are bringing the Neolith to Earth." There were gasps. "My colleagues here, the best, brightest, and wealthiest businesses of their generation will be creating the exhibition site so that every man, woman, and child can see for themselves what we now know, beyond the shadow of any doubt: that we are not alone in the universe."

Vega's group was clapping and then every reporter and onlooker joined in. There must have been two hundred thousand people and more applauding the great alien evangelist.

The press conference event went on for four hours. That was how long the Q&A was, and Vega personally answered each question. He was in top form, able to answer scientific and silly questions alike. The media ate up the images of people in the crowd crying that they would be able to touch something constructed by an extraterrestrial life. It seemed that it would never end.

When Vega's handlers began to close down the event, the businessmen with him gave him another round of handshakes. Media were moved back to their waiting hovercars, limos, and vans. Rings of security surrounded Vega. One of the guards watched me, because I was standing right where I was, waiting.

A smiling woman came up to me. "Mr. Vega is not seeing anyone else, sir."

"He'll see me," I said. "Tell him it's Cruz, the detective."

I could see from the woman's expression that she now recognized me and knew who I was. She ran through the security to Vega. They talked a bit, and then Vega looked my way.

He casually strolled to me with the woman following. He shook my hand. "Mr. Cruz. It's an honor. I feel that I know you so well, even though we've never met in person."

"Quite a show."

"Ah, I can see from your tone and body language that you don't approve."

"An exhibit. 'Step right up and see the fake ETs for our discount price of nine hundred and ninety nine.'"

Vega smirked. "An alien life denier. I'm surprised, Mr. Cruz, that you would be one closed to the infinite possibilities of the universe."

"I remember you, Mr. Vega, from when I was a kid. 'The evidence is irrefutable that there exists no intelligent life in this universe, except for humankind. Believers of such are no different than those who believe in a divine creating deity or a fat man in red who flies around in a carriage propelled by flying deer.' Who said that, Mr. Vega? Oh, that was you 30 years ago. A little hair dye and little nip, a little tuck. You must be what—over 70, but with a new message."

"Mr. Cruz, part of life isn't merely getting older; it's getting wiser. The great ancient prophet Muhammad Ali once said: 'A man who views the world the same at 50 as he did at 20 has wasted 30 years of his life.' I'm 71 now."

"Yeah, that's one answer. Another is you figured out one scam to get money, that dried up, so you shifted to a new scam. I look at you, and I don't see a life student of the prophet Ali. I see a corner hustler with a PhD."

"That is a dirty accusation," his female aide said.

"Sir, you need to move on," said another aide.

"Vega, I'm not a 'alien denier' as you call it. I don't care if you believe in one god, ten, extraterrestrials, the Easter bunny. I don't care. If there are E.Ts, as long as they don't cause trouble, pay their taxes, don't scratch my vehicle, and don't bring any more nasty germs to this planet, I'm good.

"But I know you're up to something. Ask around. I'm OCD, so I simply transfer that unhealthy compulsion to my mark—you. I'll find out what you're up to. You can bet on it."

"I don't know what I did to upset you, Mr. Cruz. If I've wronged you somehow, I apologize. If you don't believe in the Neolith Exhibit, then you can simply stay home as all of Earth's people appear at its gates."

"Yeah, I don't like big crowds, so I will stay home."

"There is no scam, Mr. Cruz. There is only the beginning of a new era."

"Mr. Vega, there is nothing new under the sun. I've seen it all before, so I'll let you get back to your work. I have some murders to solve. Maybe the media will dub it the Neolith Murders."

The aides nervously looked at Vega. He glared at me, as I turned and left.

There was no way Vega would have remembered me. Someone like him must have met and spoken in front of millions of people. I hated him because he scratched a hovercar. It wasn't mine, it was my father's. It was back when I was learning to drive. Vega had some bimbo in his hoverspeedster, sideswiped my Pops, scratched his vehicle, and jumped out wanting to beat my father up. Knowing what I know now about my Pops, that would not have gone well for Mr. Vega, but my Pops smiled and apologized. I was so mad that my Pops apologized to him. I had received two driving lessons from my Pops then that stuck with me to this day. You never have any conversation in anger when you're driving, and if you ever get into an accident, it's by definition your fault—that is the defensive driver's code.

Basically, I had been harboring a childhood gripe against the Alien Evangelist all this time. However, that was unimportant. I remembered how Vega had noticed me when he first saw me in the crowd, and I paid close attention to his death look and the look of his aides when I said "the Neolith Murders." I'd suspected that their discovery was a hoax. I was convinced of it now. Hopefully, the wife would catch him doing something stupid to prove it when he returned to his hoverhotel residence.

CHAPTER 42

The Exobiologists

Metropolis had a million of them and probably would have a million more pop up now—space observatories with their own super-telescopes where amateur astronomer societies could also hold monthly meetings. However, this wasn't a random visit. I was looking for two specific proprietors.

"Hello," I said, walking down the aisle of the large auditorium with theater-style seating and the view of space from the Martian colonies holo-projected on its dome ceiling. The two men talking near the stage turned to me. "Hi, my name's Will Character, from the Metro Earth News." Now, they were interested in talking to me and stepped forward with smiles and handshakes.

"Hello. I'm Sagan and this is Mr. Vostok. We run the Redstone Observatory."

"You two must be quite busy these days."

They laughed. "That would be an understatement," Vostok said.

"I hope you don't mind me stopping by like this, but I have to get my stories."

"Not at all—"

"Will," I repeated. "Just call me Will. I was told that you two are xenobiologists."

"We prefer exobiologist or astrobiologist. You start using the xeno prefix and people look at you funny, certain you're only looking for little green humanoid aliens."

"May be more science than sci-fi, eh?"

"True, but we are people of science," Sagan said seriously, then his expression changed to glee. "But this is all so cool!"

I laughed as Vostok added, "I'm not as positive about the whole thing, as my good colleague. What if the extraterrestrials are evil or conquerors?"

"That's why I wanted to talk to you. I'm trying to get more diversity of opinions. Do you remember a college classmate, Neil Cosmos?"

The men nodded. "Oh yes, I actually sat next to him in class," Sagan said.

"Were you two friendly?"

"Yes, I'd say so. We all hung out together—laboratory to the local bars and back again. That's how it was. Long hours, so we all spent a lot of time together as a group."

I leaned forward and whispered, "Off-the-record, I have some sources telling me that he found the alien artifact."

The two scientists looked at each other. "I told you it was true," Vostok said to Sagan.

"You believe the background rumors?"

"Cosmos always stood out in the group—top of the class, determined to find proof, any proof, in his lifetime that we weren't alone in the universe. He was also a fanatical writer in the astro-sci journals."

"Everyone in the community knew him then?"

"Oh yes, everyone. Anyone within or who followed the Alien Life community would have known him. His family were the street activists, he stuck to the science, but when he wrote those articles he was every bit the activist that they were."

"Did he need to be an activist at his level?"

"In the scientific community, those who get the attention are the ones who get the management jobs. He was as quiet and unimposing as the rest of us in a group setting, but through those articles—watch out!"

"There's one thing I don't understand. How did an Earther get hired by Mars for a top science post?"

"Yes, he went straight to Mars rather than join the Darwin Space Project. We would have, too, but like you said, off-worlders don't hire Earthers to fill off-world jobs. Well, Cosmos, somehow got sponsored."

"By who?"

"We don't know," Vostok replied. "It probably would be hard to find out. Off-world they don't bother with things like transparency and the public record as we do Earth-side."

"Everyone was envious of him. Right out of the gate, he gets a plum job on Mars—an Earther. We were all jealous."

"Especially at that time," Vostok added.

"What is that?" I added.

"They'll deny it now, but they were going to close the program."

"Don't tell him that," Sagan said to his colleague. "He might publish that."

"Oh no," I said. "I'll keep it confidential. I never heard that. Close the program—the Darwin Space Project? When was this?"

"When we all graduated back then. It wasn't public knowledge at all, but you can't keep secrets like that within the scientific community. Someone leaked it to the grapevine. Everyone was secretly looking for another job, but when you're an astrobiologist, the only entities funding that work is the government. We were all stuck.

"That's how it is in government. Everything has its season. It was the governmental effort to resurrect the former SETI program, when it was private, generations ago, but was falling out of favor with governments."

"Fewer and fewer politicians supported the expense," Sagan said.

"You can't make money looking for extraterrestrials," Vostok said.

"There was a view that even the talk of searching for extraterrestrials was incompatible with the real human colonization of space, the moon, and Mars."

"I was told he didn't like Mars," I said.

"It turned out to be the same way there. They didn't want to spend government money searching for extraterrestrial life anymore. He ended up being stuck too, only on another planet. Then we heard about the new Jupiter Outpost. He was a shoe-in for that position."

"We're actually on Jupiter?"

The men smiled. "Oh no, Jupiter doesn't have a solid surface, it's a big ball of hydrogen and helium gas."

"And the gravity thing would be a problem."

"A big problem—two and a half times Earth. No, if humankind wanted to set up a colony that far away it would have to be one of the moons, maybe Europa, Ganymede or Callisto. However, the colonization community has moved away from the knee-jerk colonization of other planets simply because we can, to creating our own planets and advanced space stations wherever we want. But back to your point, no, the Jupiter Outpost is on the asteroids."

"An asteroid outpost."

"Yes, asteroid mining and exploration is something Mars is very interested in—very lucrative. Precious metals, and water too."

"Seems strange that the Martians would hire him, an Earther, to be a science director on their planet, then chief science director for a new outpost rather than a Martian."

"With Cosmos' literary and research reputation, or maybe a family connection, he must have made a friend with the right Martian, who got him the job."

"Speaking of which, Neil Cosmos is the one who found this alien artifact—a respected scientist rather than—"

"You can say it, we won't be offended," Sagan said, "a space alien groupie. I know there are dozens of much cruder names."

"And funny ones too."

"Are you trying to—suggest something?" Vostok asked me. "Neil more than anything else was a man of the highest integrity. He would never say he found proof of something when there wasn't. He was a hard science man. He only went where the science took him, no matter how much he wanted it to take him further. He would never be involved in any kind of fabricated evidence."

"Read his journal articles over the years," Sagan said. "More than one scientist got his full wrath if they dared publish shoddy research or made scientifically unsubstantiated claims."

"Oh no, you misunderstand me. I'm only saying how fortunate it was that he made the discovery and not someone else, because of his reputation among believers and unbelievers on Earth. If an off-worlder found an extraterrestrial, then everyone on Earth would say it's fake. If an Earther finds it, people believe it."

"I didn't think of that, but you're right. Cosmic luck then."

I didn't believe in cosmic luck, even when I was Cruz. Jr.'s age. I continued my conversation for about another five minutes, then said my thank yous and goodbyes.

This was the job. Covering all the bases, running down every lead. The two men were not the first of Cosmos' college-mates that I talked to, nor would they be the last. I'd talk to all of them because that's what you had to do to get the information you wanted or needed. Mr. and Mrs. Cosmos had only given me a very limited profile of Neil Cosmos. He didn't have a good reputation; he had an unimpeachable one. He was an Alien Life believer, but spent most of his time going after fellow Alien Life scientist hacks. If there was anyone on Earth or Up-Top whose word of the authenticity was the gold standard, it was Neil Cosmos. And now he was "missing" after he found proof of a real alien artifact. How convenient? Neil was the scientific version of Merlin the Martian Myth Buster—both men natural skeptics, both men believing in this "proof" and both men absent—the latter was dead, and the former missing. Now that I had been able to focus on being a detective, rather than nonsense, I was making progress. I would talk to everyone that could be talked to.

CHAPTER 43

The Fiancée

"Will Character with the Metro Women's Gazette."

"But you're a man," she said.

"Do you read Dainty Debbie in the Women's Health section?"

"I know of it."

"Three-hundred pound guy in Baja."

The fiancée was visibly of the upper-class set—hair, nails, clothes, nothing out of place, and everything perfect. I caught her as she came out of the elevator capsule in the hallway to the parking bay. We were in a residential mega-tower in the Neon Blues district—the "good part." A driver stood near a hoverlimo waiting for her and had been watching me.

"That, Mr. Character, is quite a disturbing factoid. What you're telling me is all my favorite female writers may be fat men in Baja."

"Yes, but all the good female writers write for the men's health and sports pages though," I said.

"I can feel my world crumbling around me. What can I do for you, Mr. Character?"

"Neil Cosmos."

She grinned. "What took you all so long? Is this to be a puff piece or hit piece on my former fiancé?"

"Personal interest story. The woman behind the man," I said.

"That title belongs to another. Neil traded up."

"For who?"

"Neil was living in the stars. It was always a possibility that I'd dump him for someone here, or he'd do the same for me for some Martian trollop. He found his Martian trollop. Didn't even have the decency to speak to me in person on the vid-phone. Left me a message that he'd found someone else and it'd all be for the best."

"You found out who she was, didn't you? You don't seem like a woman who is bested by the competition easily."

She grinned again. "Nice touch, flattering my ego. You're correct. She was the daughter to one of the wealthiest men off-world. I guess I couldn't blame my ex for dumping me for her. He traded up alright."

"This richest man off-world lives where?"

"On the moon, Mr. Character, but you wouldn't know him."

"Humor me. What's his name?"

"Omni is his name. You can look him up."

"Did your ex have a lot of friends, or a best friend?"

"I think a man by the name of Perseus was a close friend from early college days. I remember him, but no one else. All my ex's friends were space alien life scientists, of course."

"Who was going to be his best man at the wedding?"

"We never got that far in the planning, so I'm not sure. Most likely."

"Before his breaking off his marriage to you, was everything okay?"

"No, Mr. Character, it wasn't. I was here on Earth, he was a year away on Mars. Not a healthy arrangement, but the plan was that I would join him. But he got harder and harder to get a hold of and his messages to me, got less and less frequent."

"That's strange isn't it?"

"No, it's not, Mr. Character. Again, he was year away on another planet and he found his Martian trollop. Are you wanting to ask me something specific?"

I smiled. "Anything unusual or strange happen?"

"The dirt, Mr. Character? No behavioral issues, mental problems, sexual eccentricities, health concerns; the worse I could say about my ex was that he was the consummate workaholic. Despite that my parents despised him; and his, me."

"I know how that is," I said.

"Do you? Your spouse's parents despised you?"

"Threatened to either poison me or cut me if I didn't go away."

"I feel inadequate now, Mr. Character. My future parents-in-law didn't threaten me with any violence. I feel cheated. Well, no dirt on my ex. He was supposed to be a 'safe' marriage, and that was it. He was, however, very much on the fast track of his career. Everyone knew it."

"Not surprised that he found the alien artifact?"

"Why? If there was one to be found, he would find it. Can't say I'm a believer myself, but now I wish I had been. That Neolith Exhibition Park is going to make all involved, including my ex, very, very wealthy people."

CHAPTER 44

The Best Friend

"Who did you say you're with?"

Even with the grainy vid-phone connection, I saw how annoyed the man was. He'd be looking for any chance to hang up on me.

"My name's Will Character with the Metro Earth News. One of Neil Cosmos's friends gave me your name. We're doing a—I guess, I'd have to call it a tribute piece to the man who finally discovered proof of extraterrestrial life. There's a lot of interest in him and I want to write a great story featuring quotes from people like you who knew him."

"Oh, okay. What do you want to know?"

"Are you surprised he would find this alien artifact?"

"Not in the least. It was his life's ambition. That's why he took the Martian job."

"I heard that he was going to marry an Earth female tycoon, but called it off to marry this other woman."

"Yeah, Tess. I didn't like either of them personally, but it was his funeral."

"Why didn't you like the Earth woman?"

"Have you met her? Aloof, cold, bitchy, moody, I can go on. I've been divorced five times, so I'm an expert. He wouldn't listen to me, but then he called it off to go into bondage with the Moonie woman."

"The off-worlder woman on the Lunar colony."

"Yeah, what was wrong with her?"

"She was gorgeous, but there was no way she wanted to marry him for him."

"Why would you say that?"

"I tell it like it is. She wasn't with him for no love. I told you, I'm the marriage expert. I can spot a bad marriage connection from a hundred miles away."

"Except yourself." I couldn't help myself.

"Well, yeah, which is why I already instructed my attorney that if I ever try to marry number six that the prenup should say that she'd get everything, including my legacy, and I get nothing should we divorce. That would snap me out of psychosis instantly."

"Do you think it's strange that no one can find this off-world woman now?"

"The Moonie? Not really. What's strange is that Neil is nowhere to be found."

"Where do you think he is?"

"The rumor is that he's secretly on his way to Earth or may already be here. They'll trot him out when this alien artifact exhibit officially opens."

"When was the last time you spoke with him?"

"I—uh—"

"Come on Mr. Perseus. Don't hold out on me now. When did you speak with him? Recently?"

"No."

"When?"

"Two years ago. When he discovered the artifact."

"Wow! What did you do? What did he say?"

"It was the most amazing call I ever had in my life. We talked for hours. And I know I wasn't the only one he called. He couldn't contain himself."

"You knew then about the artifact?"

"A lot of people did, but he swore us to secrecy and we all knew the stakes, so we kept our mouths shut until the announcement. That was the plan. But it is strange that none of us have heard from him yet."

"I have to ask a question, but I don't want you to get angry at me."

I could see him face change. "What are about to ask me?"

"The piece I'm writing is a tribute piece, but we have other reporters out there who are always looking to take people down. I'm on your side."

"What are you going to ask?"

"Have you or your friends entered into any business dealings that would enrich yourselves as a result of the revelation of the alien artifact?"

"There it is. That's why you wanted to talk to me. I should hang up on you, but then you'd publish that I was running away or hiding from the questions. Yes, I did. We all did. So what! Why shouldn't I make any money off of this? No one wants to fund space exploration anymore, not the governments, not the megacorps, so we'll fund it ourselves. That isn't greed. That's the genuine pursuit of science. If there is one alien artifact out there, there must be more. Everyone who experiences the Neolith Exhibit will be contributing to humankind exploring the stars. Today, the artifact. Tomorrow, the creators of that artifact!"

CHAPTER 45

The Retiree

Some people loved retirement; others were the epitome of miserable. The man I had followed back to the lobby of his apartment mega-tower was the latter. He looked like a miserable sad-sack shuffling through life. To think he was a producer on one of the top-rated shows for a decade—*Merlin's Myth Busters*.

"Hello, sir," I said. The man turned. "My name's Will Character with the Metro Earth News."

"Yeah?"

"Can I talk with you briefly? It's for a story."

"I would think you'd be more interested in the alien artifact than me."

"I'm interested in Merlin, and why someone would attempt to character assassinate him."

The man stared at me. "Cruz. I knew you looked familiar. Come on up."

I wasn't a tea drinker, but that's all Mr. Starlights had, so I joined him. His apartment was practically empty. We sat in some chairs clustered around a small table near the balcony.

"People are wondering about possible bad space aliens from other galaxies, when we already got them here," he said. "Murdered Merlin right in police custody."

"I noticed that you were the only one not on record as to Merlin's nervous breakdown and psychotic behavior," I said.

"How did you find me?"

"I'm a detective. That's what I do."

"I like the disguise. Everyone knows you for that tan hat and coat. All you have to do is change up the colors and you're a new person. They did try to make me go along. They found me too."

"Who?"

"These men."

"Where? Here?"

"No, at the offices, when I was employed. These men came to the offices. They told me the circumstances of Merlin's departure from the show, and that's what I was to say. They 'forgot' a case of money in front of my desk, but I made sure they didn't 'forget' to take it, all of it, with them as they left. A week later I was fired. A month later, I realized that no one would ever hire me again, so I took early retirement."

"Were you surprised to see your friends making up the stories about Merlin?"

"No. I remember how much money it was. I happened to be in a bad mood that day or I would've taken it too, but I didn't. Then it was too late."

"What's this about, Mr. Cruz?"

"Why do this to Merlin?"

"You know why. The greatest space alien hoax revealer gets discredited and killed. Then the greatest space alien find is revealed to the solar system."

"But Merlin believed in the space artifact too."

"Did he? Did he get to inspect it himself? No, he didn't."

"You believe it's a hoax."

"I'm telling you it is, and you already know so too."

"Are you a believer, disbeliever or agnostic on the space alien thing?"

"A disbeliever. I know, I have no credibility, but it doesn't change the facts."

"Ever heard of a man named Neil Cosmos?"

"No. He's the one behind this?"

"No, not like you think, but maybe also manipulated."

"If I were you, I'd prove this is a hoax before that Exhibit opens."

"Why?"

"Do you know how much money they're going to make off this exhibit? Once it opens, they're untouchable. There's going to be too much money changing hands—government, politicians, unions, megacorps. Then they're not going to allow anyone to stop that."

"Maybe."

"You don't seem to worried."

"I've been in similar situations before."

"Yes, you have."

"Were you in touch with Merlin at all? Did he give you anything or is there someone he would given something to?"

"Never talked to him again after the show ended. All I did was keep up-to-date on what he was doing. He would never reach out to me. From his mindset, if everyone else turned on him, why not me. In fact, how do you know I'm not lying? I could have turned on him like the others."

"Because you're the only one not living the good life."

"Isn't that the truth, that is a big giveaway. Neolith Park. That's the name. Have you seen the site on the news yet? It's almost the size of Metropolis itself, and it's all built. How is something like that possible? All that construction, manpower, permits, and legal challenges to squash. How do you do all that so fast?"

"Seems like it has been in the works for quite some time."

"A long time, Mr. Cruz. Merlin never stood a chance against them."

CHAPTER 46

Thugs

The glaring hole in my investigation was my lack of direct access to anyone off-world. There was nothing I could do about it, so I had to be creative.

"Cruz!"

I was leaving the retiree's apartment complex through the main entrance, which was my first mistake. I didn't have my hands on my omega-gun in my pocket, which was second mistake. The way my name was called was what had frightened me, not that they knew it was me. I managed to dive but a blast hit the wall near me and I suddenly felt woozy. I hadn't been hit by laser-fire; the blast had missed me and shattered on the wall, but one of the fragments hit me in the cheek.

I fell to the ground on all fours and fought with all my might to pull myself back from the shock of the blast's stunning effect. I heard men running to me and had barely looked up. My body still couldn't move, so I couldn't run or take cover. I did the only thing I could do—I opened up with blinding gun-fire.

The men were still firing at me, but, as the saying goes, "my gun was bigger than theirs." In two seconds, there were three dead thugs on the ground, crowds of pedestrians ran in panic, and I slowly got to my feet to hobble away.

I was mentally kicking myself. They did what I would have done—not try to find me, but wait at all the places I might show up, and I did. People knew I was out there investigating, and they didn't like it.

CHAPTER 47

Visitors

I couldn't take any chances that I might unwittingly lead someone back to the hoverhotel. Three came after me, but that didn't mean there weren't more. I sat in my vehicle for almost three hours watching everything and everyone from my secluded parking lot. My location wasn't that far from the hoverhotel at all; in fact, the block of hotels was due to pass by overhead within the hour.

Was it a coincidence? I noticed Shakespeare the robot in the passenger seat of a jumbo hoverlimo coasting by the parking lot. The robot never turned its head from looking straight ahead. Maybe it was a coincidence. Maybe they wanted to see us Earthers in our natural habitats so they could laugh about us at their next cocktail party. I watched the hoverlimo disappear as it rose into the sky-traffic.

I also watched the scene of my shootout on my dashboard display. I had developed a taste for leaving listening devices around—but there were also remote video devices. I watched not the police, but a team of suits arrive in their hovercars, drag or pick up the bodies of the three men I shot and killed, dump them all in the trunk (well, that's kind of medieval), get in and fly away. All that was left was the blood, but the rain would wash that away within minutes.

At least I got the licenses of the hovercars—assuming they were real and the hovercars weren't stolen.

I was met at the hotel room door by Cruz Jr. who possibly had too much sugar in his system. He was enjoying flying through the air in his hoverchair a bit too much. If he didn't stop giggling, he'd pass out from lack of oxygen. Dot had given up trying to keep him still. When he was like this, you had to let him tire himself out completely so he'd sleep through the entire night.

Dot had done an excellent job! Vega had visitors all right—they had been coming and going all day and night. I had a personal project of trying to commit to memory as many of Metropolis's crime world figures as possible, but that left our corporate and government crooks. I didn't know which of the latter two categories these men and women belonged to, but they looked dirty to me. I took the pictures of every last one of them and created an ever-growing picture gallery of them. A few of them did look familiar, but it was vague. I really had no idea who any of them were in their expensive suits. I did recognize one person—or personoid—Shakespeare had visited. Apparently, when I saw him, he had just left.

I got a page from PJ.

"What is that?" Dot asked me when she saw me looking at the device.

"It's another high-tech device." A lie. The damn thing was older than our great-grandparents. I looked at the code: 911CC. "CC" meant Council of Corporations. Dot and I looked at the newsfeed on the rooms TV screen.

"What are they up to?" I asked, seeing the story that the Council of Corporations was going to hold a press conference within the hour.

"What does it mean?" Dot asked.

I looked at her. "It means I'm making people nervous. They're going to try to speed things along faster."

My posthumous mentor, Wilfred G., said that the street detective has to know when he's out of his depth. A misplaced ego had killed plenty of P.I.s in Metropolis and beyond. You should never be afraid to retreat or ask for help. More importantly, you had to be able to sense when you were in the weaker position. Even in a high-stakes game of cat-and-mouse, when the mouse is chasing the cat. The mouse is still the mouse.

The problem was that Dot and I couldn't call anyone from the room. We'd be traced for sure. Dot and I had a good three-day run as spies. Besides the successful surveillance job Dot did of Vega's place, she also redesigned my online storefront's entire look and expanded the Liquid Cool merchandise page, which made me want to puke. It meant that both wife and my secretary were in league to franchise me to the world.

Before we headed back I wanted us to check in first. We bundled up Cruz Jr., went out the back way to the secluded parking bay to the Pony (in secret mode, as I called it), and I flew out. I wanted to be as far away from the hoverhotel and any place even remotely close to Rabbit City, Paisley Parish, Downtown Metro, or any place we frequented.

I parked right in front a bank of empty public videophones, which meant they were grungy looking and nasty. Dot had some illegal wet wipes (read my earlier cases to find out about that) and wiped the two we used thoroughly. I would still need a supershower afterward but I would be able to cope for the moment.

I called PJ; Dot called her boss at Eye Candy.

"PJ," I greeted.

"*Mon Dieu*, Cruz. You have to get back—*tout de suite*," she said.

"What?"

"Metro PD, the office of the Council of Corporations, the FBI, Run-Time, people from the moon, people from Mars, the media—everybody is looking for you. They have the Concrete Mama surrounded, Eye Candy, your parent's place."

"My parents!"

"And Dot's parents. All of Buzz Town. They want you bad."

"Why?"

"Get back to the office, and I'll debrief you."

"Okay." I hung up.

"Cruz, what did you do?" Dot gave me a look. She was still on the videophone with Prima Donna.

"Hi Prima," I said smiling.

"Mr. Cruz, do you know how much business I've lost?"

"Lost? Eye Candy is even more famous than ever before."

"I was already famous and it's somewhat difficult to provide service to any client when 10 million people are blocking the way into your business establishment."

"Why are they bothering you?"

"Because your wife works here!"

"Why are they after me?"

"You're the guy working the Cosmos disappearance!"

"What?"

"The media is saying that."

"Yes."

"Who told them that?"

"Who cares? Everyone knows it now, and he's considered essential to being at the grand opening of this Neolith Exhibit. He discovered the alien artifact."

"Alien artifact, hooey."

"What did you just say?" Prima asked. "Oh no, I'm getting off this call right now. Mr. Cruz, do you have death wish? Two planets and all the spacepeople in our solar system says that a real, live space alien artifact is on its way to Neolith Park. You better not say anything opposite of that if you want to see your little boy reach his third birthday. Bye!"

The videophone disconnected.

"Cruz, I thought you said you were returning to simple private detection work—low key, safer—quiet," my wife scolded. "This sure doesn't seem like it. It sure seems like another 'save the galaxy' case to me, but instead of major movie actors trying to kill you, it'll be everyone in the galaxy." She stormed back to the Pony, and I reluctantly followed.

Dot opened the door and began yelling something in Chinese. "What? What are you saying to Cruz, Jr.? He can't speak Chinese yet. He can't even say Mommy or Daddy yet."

I peeked in and Cruz Jr. looked at me, frowning. "Mama good. Daddy bad."

"What the—"

I had no choice but to fly into Buzz Town to my Liquid Cool office, back in my red Pony, tan fedora and coat attire. Immediately, I was besieged by hovercars, hovervans, media jet-packers, hoverbikes, it was a damn obstacle course, but I made it to my parking bay spot. Already media reporters swarmed around my vehicle.

"Hey!" I yelled through my vehicle's intercom. "Step away from my vehicle so you don't scratch it." They ignored me. I flipped the switch. An electric shock wave threw them back six feet and on their backs. "I warned you!"

I ran—to the elevators, inside the first one that arrived, then out of it. People were chasing me down the hall. I flung my main office door open, slammed it on them, leaving about twenty of them yelling my name trying to get in, but it was locked. I caught my breath and turned.

There was PJ sitting at her receptionist area, all prim and proper, with a bunch of people around her, but I was only focused on her.

"I could have used your help," I said.

"You were doing well without me. Besides you need more exercise. You're starting to get pudgy."

"Pudgy? I have never been—"

In the waiting area were a bunch of people in shimmering business suits. I recognized the President of the Council of Corporations herself. After our last encounter, I couldn't help but to smile and I walked over.

"Madame President."

"Mr. Cruz."

I looked around and saw that the entire office was filled with people. I noticed Flash, the Cosmos, and the other Free Earthers in the corner. Standing near PJ's desk was Mr. Mick, but no Run-Time. I didn't recognize any of the other people. I turned back to the CC President.

"Would you like to step into my office?" I asked.

"That would be nice. It won't be a long meeting."

I lead her and her entourage of eleven into my personal office. I did a double-take noticing the hovercraft right outside my window. I walked to my desk, pressed a button, and the entire window went black.

"Have a seat," I said, gesturing, as I sat.

She did, as her people stood around her. Only two of them were real aides. The others were samurai corporate soldiers. I could tell by the sheath devices on the forearms of their suits.

"I understand, Mr. Cruz, that you're working the Neil Cosmos disappearance case."

"I can neither confirm nor deny such a case."

She smirked. "The Council of Corporations for obvious reasons is very interested in this case. Neil Cosmos must be found."

"I was told he committed suicide."

She watched me for a moment, waiting for me to say something else. "That is not funny."

"It wasn't meant to be. I suspect they told me that to make me go away, but now the truth, I'm sure other methods will be tried."

"Mr. Cruz, I have no interest in your life—delusions or otherwise. You say the things you're saying as if I know what you're talking about. Let me be simple. The Neolith Exhibit opens next week. It will be advantageous to all involved if the man who discovered the Neolith is there for the opening, that's all. If you can see that that happens, the Council of Corporations will remit a bonus of an undisclosed, but substantial, amount to your business account. That is all I have to say."

"Thank you. That is very generous."

"The last time we met, it wasn't the most positive situation. However, this time the interests of the City and the Council of Corporations are aligned."

"Yes, but one condition."

"Mr. Cruz, please."

"Have one of your flunkies here give me access to the Council of Corporation database on their mobile computer."

"Mr. Cruz, that is impossible."

I opened my desk drawer and showed her the picture of Weborg. "This is the man who told me that Neil Cosmos committed suicide by spacing. He happened to say this to me when I was inside the Metropolis Police Department. I want his file."

The CC President tried to maintain her poker face, but she was slipping. "I can't. The man is with Interpol."

"You know him them?"

"I do."

"I thought you said my interests and yours were the same. It seems that Mr. Weborg isn't with our program. Why protect him?"

"You have no idea the players that are involved."

"Actually, I do."

"If those players are out of my depth, then they are surely out of yours. Good day, Mr. Cruz."

She stood from the chair and led her entourage of eleven out of my office. When they were out of sight and I heard the front office door close, PJ appeared.

"Debrief?" I asked her.

"Not yet." She let Mr. Mick walk in.

He closed the door and walked to sit in the same chair the CC President had been in.

"Why am I always so popular?" I asked.

"You're not."

"How can I help Run-Time?"

"I have a hypothetical situation—"

I almost started to laugh because I knew what was coming. "Okay."

"Let's say that you heard of a stock that was poised to be the largest stock in the history of mankind. If you bought that stock, and it delivered as wildly as it was expected by all, you could increase your worth by a factor of ten, a hundred, or more."

"Mr. Mick, let me stop you. I don't know politics. I don't know finance, let alone stocks. I'm a simple man who thinks one syllable words are best and reads summaries rather than entire books. The Neolith Exhibit is a scam. I can't prove it, at least not now. If I could bet money on it being proved a scam down the road, I'd bet everything I own on it, including Cruz Jr.'s 18th birthday fund; and I don't bet. Does that answer your hypothetical?"

"It does." The Mick smiled and stood from the chair. "Oh, thanks for the black pudding."

"You actually liked it?"

"It was delicious." He opened the door and left.

"Someone has to eat that kind of stuff. It just won't be me," I said, but he was long gone.

Finally, PJ was able to fill me in. She came in and closed the door. It was more than madness. She repeated what I had already found out about Neolith Park—it was built in record time. It was as if the Up-Toppers set the entire structure down from space during the night. No one knew how they could build it so fast. The Neolith artifact was on its way to Earth on a new Martian space freighter that could get to Earth in half the time—six months. But as the anticipation built, tickets would go on sale starting next week. Governments around the world wouldn't allow them to sell tickets now, because they knew it would crash the Net. Techs were working around the clock to expand capacity for when tickets did go on sale.

I also had PJ researching Vega, Omni, and any and all business associates. PJ told me that she needed to bring in temp help. The list she compiled was at 500 people and she hadn't even scratched the surface. I approved the request, even though the information might not be needed, as the space freighter was only two days away.

The Council of Corporations knew that the Free Earthers and I were going to meet the freighter and wanted Neil Cosmos at the grand opening of their Neolith Event. But why couldn't they just get access to the freighter themselves? The Council of Corporations included Up-Top members, including Martians. Something was off about all of this, including her general apprehension about some Interpol agent. I wished that the freighter could arrive today, so that I could finally end this whole case, which I never wanted to begin with.

Mr. and Mrs. Cosmos, the Earth Free Earthers, the Up-Top Free Earthers, Flash—I had fifty people in my personal office.

"I'll make this quick. I know you guys are TSA. Guess how I found out?"

"The cops," Dawn said.

"Yes, they told me, which means they know what you're up to."

"But we have—"

"Let me finish. I'm speaking to the Director of the Martian sector of the Metro Spaceport tomorrow morning."

"The Red Zone?" one of asked.

"Do you really call it the Red Zone?" I asked.

"Yes, what else should it be called?" Mrs. Cosmos asked.

"I'll get us access, so we don't have to go sneaking around. I told you that I'm not getting arrested by Up-Top. They'll snatch you up and put you in a Zero-G cell. Not my idea of fun. Do you know how nasty that would be trying to go to the bathroom in Zero-G?"

Mr. Cosmos laughed. "Shut up, you!" Mrs. Cosmos yelled.

"You'd be trying to run away, or float away from your own waste. Nasty!"

"Mr. Cruz, I'm continuously amazed by how your mind works," Geo said. "You really do think of things like that."

"I do. I'm an Earther and a recovering germophobe. We like gravity. Gravity is good. You know where things are going. Anything else? Why are you all here? I thought you didn't want to see me until the retrieval."

"No one knew where you were," Terra answered.

"Actually we thought They got you," Mrs. Cosmos said.

"Yes, Them. Well Them didn't get me. This will be the longest 48 hours of my life. Anything else?" Everyone just watching me with blank stares and frowns. "Flash, you ride shotgun with me."

He smiled. "I'll be there."

"And bring a weapon, no more than two. This whole thing still makes me nervous."

My meetings were over! I had PJ get all those people out of my office, and I was going home. The media would never let me alone, so I ignored them.

"Mr. Cruz!" Holly Live caught me as I stood waiting for the elevator. The media were all around me, but they kept their distance, as I had a police-issue (which meant I had it illegally) stun-baton in my hand. By now, most of them heard I had zapped a bunch of them at the Pony. None of them wanted in on that fun. I looked at her with a half-smile.

"So the great Metropolis P.I. is on the side of the Alien Life Movement?"

"I'm on the side of the people and my clients," I said.

"Will you be at the Neolith Exhibit Grand Opening, Mr. Cruz?" I was about to answer. "Or will it be Will Character?"

"I have no idea what you just said."

"Mr. Cruz, do you think you're the first private detective in this supercity to impersonate a reporter or a police officer to interrogate people?"

"I have never impersonated any of this supercity's great police officers, and impersonating a reporter is not a crime, Ms. Holly Live. You do so every day. Bye."

All I heard was boos, as I got on the elevator and waved my stun-baton around so that none of them could get on with me.

CHAPTER 48

Shakespeare

When I heard the doorbell ring, I was just about to walk into my home office at the apartment. Dot and the Hellspawn were still preparing dinner. I was getting a bit irritated that Mr. and Mrs. Wan were seemingly spending more time in our apartment than theirs.

"I'll get it!" I yelled.

One of our neighbors was an amateur hovercar restorer like I had been and was teaching his ten-year old the trade, so from time to time I lent him various tools. He had already called us to tell us that he'd stop by before dinner time.

As soon as I saw Omni's robot standing there, I immediately drew my weapon. It was an Up-Top gun against an Up-Top robot—the robot was better. It blocked my shot, lunged at me, slapped my omega-gun out of my hand, and pushed me back on my left side so I couldn't engage my pop-gun.

Suddenly the wall near the robot rippled, as Mr. Wan shot a semi-automatic pistol at it. The robot ducked and weaved, dodging every last one. All the wallpaper in that area was destroyed. Mrs. Wan threw a cleaver at the robot's head, but it caught it in the air like magic, dropped it to ground, and did something that looked like it was both back-flipping and flying out of the door and around the corner.

I must admit, for a split second had I thought, "What the hell are my in-laws doing with automatic weapons in my apartment while babysitting my newborn son?" That's what I thought as a responsible parent. Now, I needed them to kill that killer robot in my place.

Mr. Wan gestured to his wife, and she ran. I got up and picked up my omega-gun from the floor. Dot had Cruz. Jr in her arms was running for the bedroom, just as Mrs. Wan appeared with a machine gun. The Cruz family residence was under siege.

"Mr. Cruz," I heard the robot's calm voice call.

"What are you doing at my home, Shakespeare?" I yelled.

"I simply came to speak with you, sir, on behalf of my owner. There seems to be a gross misunderstanding here."

"This family doesn't like robots!"

"Yes, I can see that now. I do apologize, Mr. Cruz. I am not programmed for anything other than defensive action. May we speak, perhaps in the lobby, Mr. Cruz? It won't be long. I'll stand in the center of the lobby in full view."

"Okay! Go down and I'll be there."

"Thank you, Mr. Cruz. Again, I apologize for any misunderstanding. As an off-worlder, we do not always know the proper etiquette when interacting with Earthers."

"Don't come to people's homes announced!"

"Yes, I will add that to my memory as a primary rule when dealing with Earthers in the future. Thank you, Mr. Cruz. I will wait for you in the lobby."

I was rattled. My family and parents-in-law were rattled. If that Up-Top was programmed for offensive purposes, would we have been able to stop it? Dot didn't want me to go to the lobby. The Wans wanted to call the police. I told them I'd go down, talk to it, and send it off on its way. All I wanted was dinner, a shower, and sleep.

I got off on the second floor which had a set of steps down to the lobby. I peeked around the corner when I first came out of the elevator and then when I reached the railing at the top of the steps, I could see the robot in the center of the lobby.

"Is everything okay, Mr. Cruz?" It was the night watchmen who came on when our regular doorman got off shift.

"Everything's fine, Jax." The man gave the robot another look and then stepped back. I came down the steps and the robot approached. I had my omega-gun in hand, but knew it was probably useless. The night watchman kept an eye on me. "What do you want?" I asked the robot.

"Again, apologies, Mr. Cruz. Mr. Omni wanted to know your intentions."

"Intentions?"

"Your behavior has been erratic lately and I did see you today near the residence of Mr. Omni's colleague, Mr. Vega." So the robot had seen me. "Mr. Omni is very concerned, based on your past behavior, that you may try to sabotage the opening of the Neolith Exhibit with baseless claims to the media."

"Tell Mr. Omni, I don't care about any Neolith Exhibit. I have a case which involves determining the status of a missing person and that's it. Once that's done, I'm gone."

"Mr. Omni will be very pleased to hear that. We understand that you are meeting with the Director of the Metro Spaceport—Martian Sector tomorrow morning. Please be assured that the meeting will go as desired."

"Really now."

"Yes, Mr. Cruz. If you experience any further difficulties in wrapping up your case with Neil Cosmos, do not hesitate to contact us."

"Well, thank Mr. Omni, and thank you."

"You are very welcome, Mr. Cruz."

"Shakespeare, can I ask a personal question?"

"Of course, Mr. Cruz."

"If you were an offensive robot, would we have stood any chance in stopping you?"

"None at all, Mr. Cruz. You would never have seen me, and I estimate that I would have killed all five persons in the residence within 1.8 seconds. However, again, I am only a defensive model. Such robots are strictly prohibited by Earth, Mars, and all off-world directives. You were never in any danger."

"Good to know, Shakespeare. Have a good night."

"Have a good night, too, Mr. Cruz, and to your family as well."

The robot turned and walked out of the lobby, as we watched.

Yeah, this was cat-and-mouse, and I was definitely the mouse—a very, very tiny pathetic mouse.

CHAPTER 49

The Martian Metro Spaceport Man

I had been to the Metropolis International Spaceport twice before. The first time I was in a shoot-out with gangsters while riding a hoverboard. The second time was when I took Dot to the Space Station colony for the same Blade Gunner case. Hopefully, there would be no shootouts and I had no intentions of leaving Earth ever again.

Metro Spaceport was so large that it really made no sense to ever look at a map of it. There were the public terminals but that was only the tip of the iceberg. With cargo tunnels, staff offices, security centers, maintenance, waste management, garbage disposal, on-site hotels, energy facilities, there was no end to it. It wasn't its own supercity, it was its own planet.

I was in the Red Zone. The section controlled by the Martian Authority for flights departing and arriving from Mars. The Space Station and Lunar Colonies didn't mind Earthers in charge of flights to their destinations—but not the Martians. They had to be in charge of everything.

I sat in the Director's office. When I arrived at the director's office, I was brought in promptly. Based on what Omni's robot told me, I assumed that I was going to get rubber-stamp approval for me and my crew of Free Earthers. Instead, Mr. Deimos was not pleased to see me at all though he didn't make me wait. He was like a bureaucratic lifer who was told to do something by his bosses but didn't want to do it, and would look for any excuse not to. I quickly realized that I still had to convince him, which was fine since that's what I had prepared to do before my Omni over-bot encounter.

"They're the Rope-A-Dope Squad," I said, seated in front of his strange desk, possibly carved out of real Martian rock, or that's what it was supposed to be.

"Never heard that term," he said.

"Let's say the police want to bust a teenager hovercar speed racing crew and get them off the streets. They get one undercover cop to infiltrate the scene, then later sponsor a race himself, he might even drive a hovercar himself. The crew illegally races in this race, police snatch them all up. Law enforcement does that all the time."

"Entrapment, Mr. Cruz—"

"Mr. Deimos, it's still an illegal act they're doing. I like entrapment, and the people like entrapment when it comes to getting criminals and pests off the street. The police have a division called PsyOps— Psychological Operations. The military had them, so did law enforcement. Some civilians called them the "James Bond Division." They were the human gremlins who set out to make the lives of criminals a living hell through mischief—pranks, misdirection, scams, brute force, blow up your favorite hovercar just to rattle you or make you think your rivals did it."

"All sounds borderline illegal."

"Maybe. With them legal is a flexible concept, but the public's fine with it. It's always against the worst criminals—sick, twisted, terrifying criminals—so every tool conceivable to use against them is allowable. These MIB guys, they're PsyOps. They've lied to Free Earth, and done other things, to make them do something stupid or illegal to round them all up."

"Mr. Cruz, I cannot comment on any of that."

"Mr. Deimos, these people are my clients. The only thing they want is to have one of their own safely off that freighter. This is all Earth versus Off-World politics. We don't want any part of it. I'm helping my client get her little brother and then I'm out. You know what they're planning. I can make sure it's orderly, quick, and you have no headaches at all."

"You know I can fire the lot of them. They're TSA agents conspiring to illegally board an arriving space freighter."

"Mr. Deimos, is it really worth it? The publicity, the trials, the protests, the media stories—"

"Okay, okay."

"You'll let us on the freighter."

"Will you go away, if I authorize it?"

"Yes. Believe me when I say I want this all over."

"I'll authorize it. Tour the freighter, inspect it and be done with it. And don't ever make up stuff like that again to the media. There are enough tensions between Earth and off-world. We don't need any bit players adding to it."

"It wasn't personal."

"Yes, whatever. Our business is concluded then, Mr. Cruz."

CHAPTER 50

The Free Earthers

I had to see it for myself—ET World. That's what I called it. I expected the Neolith Exhibition to look like an amusement park, but it was much more—a mega-city. The closest one could come to the site was fifty miles away; security was already in place via an armada of encircling hoverbots. Metro Traffic Control also piped in warnings over your vehicle's audio that you were in restricted airspace, as if approaching an active military base.

I had to do what everyone else was doing—watch the newsfeed. Media reporters were getting the red carpet treatment with their access. They were allowed to walk the grounds, fly over the facility, interview staff—all while broadcasting the images to billions.

Giancarlo Vega was giving another press conference—he never seemed to tire of them, but this time he brought a scientist from Mars. When he was introduced as Mars's chief astrobiologist, I perked up in my seat in the Pony. Neil Cosmos had left the post for Jupiter Outpost; this was the man who replaced him. The presentation was billed as

Breaking News, and I could see why a few minutes in, as the man spoke.

"In archaeological science, we classify civilizations on an ascending scale," Vega said. "It all starts with an intelligent life form's historical period, as opposed to its prehistorical period, meaning its ability to record its own past and current events through the written word in whatever form.

"The scale progresses from Stone Age, Iron Age, Agricultural Age, Industrial Age, Information Age, Energy Age, and what many call our Space Colonization and Exploration Age. Yet all that progress of humankind still makes us an infant in the universe. We are really still in the first phase: the ability to harness the energy of our own planet, and nothing more.

"We have done preliminary examinations of the artifact, and a theory among the majority of us is starting to take shape. We believe that not only is the artifact proof of extraterrestrial life in the universe, but was made by a race of beings that have mastered the second civilization progress principle: the ability to harness the energy of a star."

Yeah, yeah, I said to myself. And the third progress principle is harnessing the power of the galaxy, then the power from other dimensions. I remembered the book from when I was a kid.

"We are a race of beings standing at the rim of the Great Oceans and we have only stuck our toe in," Vega continued. "But we have so far to go. They, in contrast, are able to swim the very expanses of the Great Oceans. Yes, they are far more advanced than we are."

I turned off my dashboard display. This was the insane hype and hysteria that I was going to have to deal with for the rest of my life if ETs were in fact found. The recklessness of it all too. What if they were bad ETs? What if they brought some space virus to the solar system harmful to all organic life? They didn't want people to ask those questions because they wanted the money from their pockets.

My body was vibrating. I realized I still had the old pager on me. Why was PJ still paging me? *911LC* was what I read in the device's display. We were all probably still under surveillance, but I still would have to take the pager away from her. She was enjoying the retro-tech a bit too much.

I parked the Pony in the secure rental parking bays belonging to Let It Ride. Until this case was over, I wanted to try to keep as low as a profile as possible, so the Pony would remain in storage and I would be traveling by hovertaxi only. My driver was someone who I had used before and he knew what I did for a living, so he wasn't alarmed that I sat in the backseat with my gun in hand resting on my lap.

"Expecting trouble, Mr. Cruz?"

"These days, I always expect it."

"No problem with me. The cab is bulletproof and laser-proof."

"As long as you know how to drive super-fast to get away from any trouble."

The media still had the office mega-tower where my Liquid Cool office was, staked out. That meant I'd have to fight through a packed hallway to get to my own office. I let out a heavy sigh.

When we pulled into the parking bay, I immediately spotted PJ near the elevators. "Hover in front of the elevators there," I said to the driver. He coasted the hovertaxi to a stop and rolled down the passenger window facing her. She saw me and started gesturing to me to come out, then she pointed to other vehicles and started to walk to them. I guess I was meant to follow.

"I guess I'm changing vehicles."

"Give me a call as soon as you need me again."

"Thanks." I hopped out of the hovertaxi. He waited, as I dashed to where I had seen PJ go. I didn't see her. A large hovervan flew up and the passenger window rolled down. It was PJ.

"Get in."

"PJ, what's going on? Am I playing secret agent again?"

"No, you're not playing. Get in."

The side door slid open, and a man reached out to pull me in. I recognized him, but couldn't place the face yet. In the back was like a real secret command post with display monitors, flashing lights, controls, star charts, planet charts. I was so busy noticing all of the shiny objects I didn't notice the people.

"Cruz, you have to do something!" Dawn's near-hysterical utterance snapped me out of it.

With her was Geo, Terra, and Ares. It wasn't just Dawn. They all looked terrified and near panic.

"Where's the Cosmos?" I asked.

"Mrs. Cosmos is in the hospital. She collapsed when she heard. Mr. Cosmos is with her."

"Heard what?"

"The Martians tried to blast the freighter out of space."

"What?"

"Cruz, it's war. The Martians are attacking each other now. It's war, and it's only a matter of time before Earth is dragged into it."

I wasn't amused by their hyperbole. But now things were starting to make sense. As an Earther, I naturally viewed Up-Top as monolithic, but they had factions there just like Earth. I had wondered why Up-Top wanted me, as an Earther, get access to the Up-Top section of Metro Spaceport all this time. It was because other Up-Top factions didn't want them to. I let the Free Earthers rant and rave for a few minutes without saying a word. They eventually got the hint and quieted down.

"That is exactly the kind of statement that makes people think you're crazy. War of the Worlds? Really? Tell me what happened. I want facts, not commentary. Again, I am a street detective, I am not an intergalactic superhero. I'm supposed to be working a missing persons case for you, remember? Mars Attacks? What am I supposed to do with that?"

"Mr. Cruz, we'll show them. We are not crazy people," Ares said.

They all gathered around the largest display. We sat in our hoverchairs; Ares stood, one hand gripping a hold on the top of the inside of the hovervan.

"At 2 a.m. our time, a Martian military small frigate intercepted the *Nostradamus*, firing multiple missiles." I was familiar with these type of satellite photos, down to the time stamps and ID stamps in the corners. What they were showing me was real and I moved closer to the display screen. "Their attack failed, but there was some damage to the freighter. Two Martian standard military spacecraft arrived and fired lasers at the frigate. After a short period of encrypted communication chatter, the small frigate opened fire at the two spacecraft and attempted to destroy the *Nostradamus* again. One of the two Martian military ships used its craft to shield the *Nostradamus* from the missiles, the other opened up a full volley on the small frigate and destroyed it."

They all looked at me. I sat there, stunned. I had no words.

"Boss, Martians blowing up other Martians in Earth space? That is *War of the Worlds* stuff," I heard PJ say.

"Is any of this on the newsfeed?" I asked Ares.

"Nothing," Geo said. "All transmissions from off-world to Earth are being jammed. The governments are trying to cover this up."

"Put all that footage on a disk for me—right now." I sat thinking for a moment. "Is the freighter still on its way?"

"It'll be here in 26 hours," Ares replied.

"If the Martians don't try to blow it out of space again," Terra snapped.

"Calm down," I said. "I know what we can do. I need that freighter to land so I can be done with this Case from Another World for good."

"Yes, we love you too," Terra said with a snarl.

CHAPTER 51

Holly Live

When I arrived at the Wet Cabeza, my favorite diner hang-out, from the moment I walked in there was a buzz. People smiling and whispering as they watched me. I had been coming here for over a decade, but if people were going to act crazy like I was some kind of movie star, I'd have to find someplace else.

My party arrived in all her glory. Holly Live sat down across from me at my booth. Normally, I would have been served by now, but the wait staff were too busy giggling like teenagers and afraid to approach me.

"Mr. Cruz."

"Ms. Live."

"Are you going to grant me another exclusive interview?" she said. "This time without hiding your identity?"

"What's going on with Metro PD?"

"What do you mean?"

"I know you have contacts everywhere, and I know you're working on the story."

"What story? The only story there is is the Neolith Exhibit. There's no other story on the planet."

"This is extremely serious, and I need to know what you know," I said. "In my hand is a disk."

"Disk of what?"

"You give me the information I need and I'll give you the disk of satellite images."

"Cruz, I don't know what you think I know."

"Oh, okay. Then someone else will get the story." I stood from the booth and walked to the entrance. I got out the door and figured my hunch was wrong.

"Cruz, wait!" Holly Live came running after me. "You have to tell me what's on the disk first."

"In the short years you've known me, have I ever not delivered?"

"What do you want to know?"

"What's going on between Earth PD and Up-Top PD?"

"Cruz, I can't tell you that. My exclusive will break tomorrow."

I waved the disk near her face. "We sacrifice the small story tomorrow for the ginormous story tomorrow."

"Metro PD brass is in full revolt against Up-Top. They've expelled all Up-Top law enforcement and intelligence from Metropolis. The Up-Top have done the same for the moon, and the Martians are threatening to do the same."

I handed her the disk. "Don't wait for tomorrow. Watch it and break this story today."

"What story?"

That was it. Because the nano-second after she spoke that sentence, it was like someone flipped an off-switch on both of us. First, the world was normal with rain, and I was living life, the next moment I was frozen in a black void all around me. I remembered being conscious, but I wasn't anymore. I remembered seeing dark shapes closing in as my view faded away. There was no pain. There was nothing. But I was not afraid. I wasn't dead. I had been shot with some non-lethal incapacitating "toy" by those damn Up-Top cops!

PART EIGHT

It Was Always About the Freighter

CHAPTER 52

Seraff

When I awoke, I was sitting in a metal chair at a metal table in a metal room. Next to me in another chair was Holly Live, slumped over with her head almost touching the table. I tried to stand but my entire lower half felt like it was fused to the chair. More Up-Top law enforcement gremlin-tech, as I called it—tech meant for no other purpose than to mess with you.

Holly began to wake up herself. She saw me, made a face, then looked around the room.

"You're remarkably calm about all this. Have you been kidnapped before?"

"Cruz, you are a menace to society!"

"You can actually get that T-shirt from my online storefront."

"This is not funny. This is the off-world police. They could hold us at Praetoria Space Station if they want to and there isn't anything Earth could do about it."

The Spaceman came in soon enough. He sat and looked at Holly. "You were going to broadcast information related to ultra-secret classified satellite photos. You an Earth citizen, not a terrorist or criminal, a member of the press, so there is nothing I can say or do to threaten you. However, if you cooperate and voluntarily sign a legal non-disclosure statement, I would—owe you one."

"What's your title, your rank?" she asked.

"I'm Mr. Seraff of Interpol."

"Yeah, I can work with that. I'll sign whatever you want to let me out of here. Keep him, but let me go. Am I surgically attached to this chair? This is a new dress I'm wearing."

"Give it a moment."

Holly Live finally was able to stand. She couldn't get out of the metal room fast enough and left me with the Spaceman. I realized that I could now move my butt in the chair.

"Mr. Seraff, we meet again."

"I can't say that I'm surprised."

"Why did you shoot us?"

"We needed to get you in custody as quickly as possible."

"You may have the disk, but you can't cover this up forever. Martians blowing up Martians in Earth space. Are you all doing drugs up there? It will come out. If anything can knock this 24-7 Neolith Exhibit news off the news, it's this."

"Mr. Cruz, that's exactly why we had to bring you in. I had told my superiors to do so at the beginning, but they insisted you'd never get this close. But here we are. This, Mr. Cruz, is far more serious than you can imagine."

"All I want to do is meet the *Nostradamus* at Metro Spaceport, look for Neil Cosmos, he'll either be there alive or not, and then I'm off this miserable case. I'm out."

"You're not out, and Mr. Cosmos is on that freighter, along with 28 persons."

"Who's Orion? And it's 29 persons."

"Good God." I heard the voice come over the room's audio. "How could he possibly know?"

"I told you," Seraff said, looking up at the ceiling. He stood from his chair. "Follow me, Mr. Cruz."

We came out of the metal room, and I found myself in a maze of glass hallways—people in uniforms (silver, black or red) were in motion everywhere. I looked up; I couldn't tell how many stories it was, but it was more than ten, it kept going.

"Where are we?"

"We're in Interpol's Earth HQ. Our secret headquarters underneath the supercity of Metropolis."

"There are spacemen and Martians living underground? I don't how I feel about that. I'm not thrilled with you living above me in space. Now I learn you're under my feet too. This might push me over the edge."

The most I got out of spaceman was a slight grin, as he led me to a glass room, where a human-looking robot was waiting.

"Not another android," I said under my breath.

We entered the room, the door swung closed. "Have a seat Mr. Cruz." Seraff sat at the same table. The android handed him a folder. Seraff placed it on the table and opened it.

"I thought Up-Top was a digital society."

"Yes, but we're on Earth." He laid out the forms in front of me. The android startled me a bit when its hand appeared in front of my face with a pen.

"I'm signing?"

"Yes, Mr. Cruz. You're signing your life away. The first form is granting you access to off-world classified information of the highest levels of secrecy. The next two forms are legal non-disclosure forms with heavy penalties for breaching, including fines and lengthy prison time. You are not to disclose the presence of this headquarters to any

Earther—the Mayor, the Chief of Police, your wife, your secretary, your son, the usual suspects. You are not to disclose the contents of the briefing you will receive from the Founders—"

"The Founders?" I looked around. "Was that the voice I heard?"

"Yes, Mr. Cruz. After the briefing, you will receive the following licenses: licensed to carry any off-world manufactured weapon. I see that you have already managed to illegally acquire one of your own already."

"I want my omega-gun back."

"Yes, an off-world weapon used by off-world gangsters. Cute. You will also get a provisional use off-world bounty hunter license."

"Again? Bounty hunter? I'm a private detective."

"And bounty hunter."

"Who am I hunting?"

"An alien."

I stared at him awhile to see if he was going to say that he was joking, but he was deadly serious.

"Who's this off-world Agent Weborg?"

"There is no Agent Weborg, Mr. Cruz. Agent Weborg is an over-bot named Shakespeare who you are already familiar with."

My mouth was hanging open again. "You all *can* make androids look and act like humans?"

"That's old news, Mr. Cruz."

"Not for the people of Earth."

"Your own governments can too—not as good as ours though."

"Agent Weborg the Android was in the middle of Metro PD. How did it get past their security?"

"It's nothing amazing. Authorized personnel with a legitimate badge are never scanned by security."

"I don't care what legal documents I'm signing, but I'm going to go straight to the Chief to have that practice changed immediately."

"If it makes you feel better."

"Who's Orion?"

"So Agent Carter did get you the manifest. Sign all the forms and we'll start the briefing."

I picked up my pen and finished signing. I looked up at him. "Is there a war happening off-world?"

"Seraff! How does this Earther know these things?" the same male voice shouted.

"Sir, Mr. Cruz is very adept at guessing."

I finished signing the documents. "I'm very adept at figuring things out too, without guessing."

"Yes, you did build an advanced hovercraft in your parent's residence at the age of 15. That would classify you at the lower end of the genius scale."

"I'm a genius!" I smiled.

The android collected the forms, Seraff handed it the folder. The Spaceman stood again.

"I know. Follow you."

"No, Mr. Cruz. Take these shades and put them on."

CHAPTER 53

The Founders

Another virtual reality meeting—but unlike the VR gamers and VL-ers, who escaped from the real world into their computer-created fantasy simulations, this was a normal meeting in a gigantic conference room with a bay window facing the moon. Seraff sat next to me, also in a chair. Across from both of us was a silver-haired man in the center, a younger black-haired man, and a woman at the other end.

I imagined that they were none too happy that they had to bring an Earther into their confidence, a lowly Rabbit-City-dweller, street detective.

"You look smaller in person," the center man said. "What do you know about the Founders?"

"You're descendants of the people who made the space colonies possible—space stations, lunar colonies, and Mars."

"Earth didn't want them to succeed no matter the lies they teach in your schools. Our forefathers had to claw their way from Earth's clutches to create what you Earthers call Up-Top. When their governments failed to enslave us, organized crime tried. It didn't go well. We spaced a lot of people back in those days. Then the megacorps came. They were the worst, but we defeated them too. We created our paradise and we're not ever going to let anyone take it away."

"Even off-worlders," I said.

The center man said nothing, as he kept his death gaze on me. I suspected he was the leader of the trio. It was either him or the woman.

"Do you believe in space aliens, Mr. Cruz?" the woman asked.

"Honestly, I don't care," I answered. "I'm agnostic on the subject. I don't care either way. I have a business to run, a family to provide for, and a son to raise. That's what I care about."

They were satisfied with my answer, and the center man looked at Seraff and nodded.

Seraff stood and a large viewscreen appeared. It displayed that killer meteor flying through the Earth's atmosphere falling towards Free Earth. The image reversed and then stopped to show that the meteor was launched not by a submarine in the Great Oceans, but a flying saucer above the Great Oceans.

"The spacecraft was illegally in Earth airspace. Clearly, it was sent to incite fear within the Free Earth community."

"Mr. Seraff, the killer meteor was not meant for the Free Earthers, it was meant for me."

Seraff gave me a confused look. "What gives you that notion?"

"It's not a notion. We intercepted their communications. We heard them dance with glee in their seats and launch the meteor because they knew I was there. Mr. Seraff, how can you be briefing me when I know more than you?"

"I assure you, you don't know more than us," Seraff said back.

"Where's the detective I hired who was snatched up by Up-Top police?"

"You do know that's an offensive term," the black-haired man finally spoke.

"Mr. Crux was not 'snatched up' by us," Seraff answered.

"Then who?"

"Martian Police."

"Mr. Seraff, doesn't Mars work for Interpol? I mean, they report to you."

"Things have changed somewhat after our last encounter."

"What does that mean?" I realized that everything might be far more serious than I had originally thought. "Where's Agent Carter? You know he gave me the manifest. Where is he?"

"Agent Carter is unavailable."

"Stop it, Seraff. What is going on? Get Agent Carter on the line or have him join us here in your virtual reality room."

"That will be impossible."

"Why?"

"The Martians authorities have cut off all communications with Space Command."

"Space Command? When has there ever been a Space Command?

"There is now."

"What!" I said. "What's going on? The Martians tried to blow up the freighter. You stopped them by blowing up their spaceship. The crazy Free Earthers were right. You all are at war."

"Let's save the dramatics, Mr. Cruz," the man in the center said. "It is a misunderstanding that will be cleared up shortly."

"Why don't the Martians want that freighter to land on Earth?"

"Again, there has been a miscommunication, but that will all be cleared up shortly," Seraff replied.

"Miscommunication? You blew their ship out of space."

Seraff didn't answer me; none of them did.

"Why do you want the freighter to land?"

"Why wouldn't we?" Seraff answered.

"It's a Martian Freighter."

"Actually the freighter is jointly-owned by Lunar Colony."

"What is on that freighter that you want to be on Earth?"

"Proof," the man in the center said. "Proof that Omni and all the others are running the biggest hoax of all time."

"This is about you and Omni, isn't it?" I said. "You want Omni and Vega's Neolith Exhibit to fail."

"I thought you said you don't care either way. Besides it's none of your business."

"You're all gangsters. Your gang is in charge and his gang is coming for you. He succeeds; he can finance your downfall."

"Bravo, Mr. Cruz," the woman said. "Seraff, he isn't the typical dumb Earther."

"I know gangsters."

"Who else could have created Paradise, Mr. Cruz?" she said.

I nodded. "You're right. You had to be gangsters, because the government, megacorps, and criminal gangsters would have killed all of you and spaced you. I get it. I agree with you. I would have done the same, if it were me. However, I am not interested in getting in the middle of your gang war, because now we get to the heart of this whole thing—Founder versus wannabe Founders. Spacemen versus Martians. Are you all crazy? I have a wife, a kid, a vehicle and a cool hat. I'm smart enough to know when I'm out of my league. I'm out of my league. I don't even know why you're talking to me."

"Because you can talk to the Martians, Mr. Cruz," Seraff answered. "And you can get to the freighter, and we can't in the current climate."

"We know you already got full access to it," the center man said. "The proof is on-board."

"But you said it's hoax. Orion is aboard. The proof is a man?"

"He's not a man."

"Do you remember a man by the name of Ichi Jumper, Mr. Cruz?" the woman asked.

I swallowed. "I should. He tried to kick me to death."

"Imagine if there were a secret organization of...fixers. Men who were conditioned to be a higher-level of human. Men who were seemingly indestructible. Imagine 50 of those men, all individually ranked. The late Ichi Jumper. Congratulations on that, by the way, because he would have killed you eventually. Imagine Mr. Jumper as number 20 on that list, with 1 being the most powerful and most dangerous. Mr. Orion is number one."

For a moment I didn't speak. "Why is he on the freighter? Why are you letting him land on my planet?"

"So that we have the proof," the center man said.

"You keep saying that. What proof?"

"He's an alien hybrid."

I looked at them.

"He thinks he's an alien hybrid," the black-haired man said.

"Unfortunately, the Martians believe he really is. That's why they tried to destroy it," Seraff added.

"We'll give you the weapons to stop him," the center man said. "Stop him cold. Once in custody, we'll publicly expose the deception and Omni's complicity in the hoax. By that time, the Martians will be back on our side. We'll bring down Omni and his cabal."

"If the Martians are not talking to you, how do you know they'll believe the space alien hoax?"

"Did you hear that the Martians found the site for the artifact and used nukes to ply it out of the asteroid it was buried in?"

"Yes, the Free Earthers told me, and I'm realizing that they are a better source of intel than most, Earth or Up-Top law enforcement."

"The Martians didn't use the nukes for that," the black-haired man said. "The Martians were trying to obliterate the entire site with a nuke."

"Why would they do that?"

"They thought it was ground zero for a possible alien virus contagion."

I closed my eyes hard and clenched my teeth.

"Mr. Cruz, are you all right?" Seraff asked.

"Didn't you read his file?" the woman said. "He's fighting off one of his mysophobic attacks."

"Are you saying that this case involves possible space alien germs?" I said, slowly opening my eyes.

"It's a hoax," the center man yelled. "You said so yourself."

"We believe it's a hoax, but we can't prove it yet," I snapped. "Our gut instinct isn't proof. The other side actually could be right. Stranger things have happened in this universe. You've never bet on a sure-thing in your life, and it turned out bust?"

"This is different," he said.

"Yes, it is different. I'm the one who's going to be meeting that space freighter, while you all will be up in space sitting nice, secure and comfy. Maybe you're willing to risk Earth's biosphere in your quest to stop a rival, but I'm not!"

"Calm down, Mr. Cruz," the center man said.

"It's my planet, and it's the planet of your ancestors! Are we really going to risk it?"

"The problem is Mr. Orion, not any alien germs. There are no alien germs."

"How do you know?"

"You're friends with the Martians; ask them."

"There's also a war within Martian Authority, isn't there?"

"Yes," the center man answered. "Omni isn't a Founder, but he has Founder allies under his thumb. There are Martians who tried to destroy that freighter and there Martians who will do everything they can do to make sure it lands."

"Because they're working with Omni."

"Orion is part of their plan. We're just trying to stop it, so you can put your mind at rest, Mr. Cruz. No germs, but there is a super-human coming."

"Are Neil Cosmos and the crew alive?" Seraff and the Founders were all quiet. "Is someone going to answer me?"

"We don't know," Seraff answered. "It's unlikely though."

I had never met Neil Cosmos, but the possibility of his murder made me mad. "What weapons are you going to give me to be your alien hunter?"

"Mr. Seraff will see to it."

"I want my omega-gun back, too."

"Omega-gun?" the woman asked. "Do you know that's a woman's gun?"

"Don't say that! It is not a woman's gun. It's my gun. It's a cool gun. I won't tolerate that kind of talk about my gun—and I want it back— now."

The woman held up her hands to give the universal sign for surrender. "Okay, it's a unisex gun."

CHAPTER 54

Carter

The freighter was 13 hours away from landing on Earth. There was no way I was going near the Metro Spaceport without talking to Agent Carter. Seraff was my spaceman contact; Carter was my Martian contact. I wasn't sure how much I trusted them. They would always put the interests of their people above Earth, but they weren't bad or evil men. They were policemen looking out for their own people. As long as our interests coincided, there was no problem.

One always had to use the resources available to them. If I had needed to find Agent Carter in Metropolis, I could have put my Sidewalk Johnny Brigade on the job. However, there were no sidewalk johnnies on Mars, at least I didn't think so. And if there were, they wouldn't be involved with me. I did have something as good—the Free Earthers. Their network did extend to Mars.

The Free Earthers had moved their base because of all the attention. It was another underground facility, which made me wonder if everyone affiliated with space had some kind of biological or psychological need to be under the Earth, instead on top of it, like a normal person.

The Free Earthers had me sitting in a huge meeting room of thousands and all of them were on their mobile video-phones calling fellow Aliens on Mars—on Mars they were called Free Mars. There was so much noise, because of all the talking, but they were doing what I asked. They called their Martian contacts and then those contacts were calling Mars Police demanding to speak with Agent Carter.

One of them jumped up from their table and yelled out to everyone that he had Carter's aide and the aide was patching him through to Carter.

"This is Carter. What is the vital information that you wanted to report?"

The Free Earther handed the video phone to me and everyone in the auditorium was quiet, watching.

"Carter!" I greeted with a big smile.

"This is an unsecure line, Cruz."

"Then let's talk on a secure one, but we have to talk. I'm meeting that freighter in less than 13 hours."

"That would be very unwise."

"Why is that?"

"This is an unsecure line."

"Are you going to help me or not? The spacemen already gave me the classified clearance, and I have an Interpol bounty hunter badge."

"Those fools! Cruz, stay away from that freighter; you have no idea what you're getting yourself into."

"Are you going to help me? I'm the one going to meet it. You *off-worlders* will be sitting up in space all nice and comfy. Are you going to help me?"

Carter did not want to help me, but he was going to. I barely got out of the Free Earth underground meeting room—they all wanted to see what an Up-Top bounty hunter badge looked like.

Geo pulled me aside. "Is Neil still alive?"

"I will be there to meet the space freighter like I said. Have Flash be ready to get me, as soon as I find out where I'll be."

I waited above ground; we were near Wharf Way, which also held bad memories for me from previous cases. What came to pick me up wasn't a hovertaxi or hoverlimo. When I saw the flying saucer that Carter sent to pick me up, I hesitated. I had already been seen landing and exiting one. If I was caught anywhere near another Martian flying saucer that would be at least an all-day news story. It was so stupid that the Martians ever built "flying saucers." Some engineer's idea of a joke long before my Pops or I was born. Now, it was serious and Martians loved their flying saucers.

I looked all around—no media. I bolted for the flying saucer as the door raised open. Just as I hopped on, a hovercraft zipped by above and I glanced up. There was a damn reporter filming me jump into the flying saucer. He was smiling; I was cursing. I slammed the door closed.

"Don't slam my craft door!" the driver yelled at me.

I looked at him, as the craft ascended. It was a very plush and roomy craft. There were two crew members. "Keep your eyes on the sky," I snapped back. They ignored at me. "Sorry, I shouldn't have slammed the door. I know better. Those reporters are like pests."

"Got you on camera again." The drivers were laughing.

"It's not funny." I felt my mobile ringing. "Oh, here we go! The film is already on the news and this is the wife calling to rip me a new one." I answered. "Hi honey." I had a wide smile, as I looked at her image on my tiny vid-phone screen."

"Don't honey me, Cruz. You knew it was me calling. Do you remember that nice conversation we had in your vehicle? How you had your own epiphany about how you were going to let these big, crazy cases go to someone else. I was so proud of you. I thought all this would be behind us. Then I'm cutting Mrs. Fancy's hair at the salon and what do I see on the news? My husband not walking, but running onto another Martian space saucer! Cruz, were you and the Martians late for an appointment to take over the Earth?"

I looked up and the two Martian drivers were laughing so hard that I questioned whether they were flying properly.

"It's not what you think."

"It never is, Cruz."

"I can prove it. Look at these two." I turned the mobile to the drivers so she could see the laughing duo. "Say hello, you two."

"Hi Mrs. Cruz," they said, waving. "The three of us will have the entire world under our dominion by lunchtime."

I turned the mobile back to me. "This is what I have to deal with."

"You are not out of hot water yet," Dot scolded. "I will be monitoring the news about you. Loves." She hung up.

"Why couldn't you two pick me up in a hoverlimo or hovercar like normal people? You could have even sent a taxi. Did you hear her? The footage is already on the news! Cruz in a Martian flying saucer—again!"

I was dropped off at some tower nearby, then I was again taking an elevator capsule down. So it wasn't just the spacemen who liked working underground in the dirt—Martians too. The elevator door opened and there were a half dozen Martian police waiting for me in their red uniforms.

"What is with you spacemen and Martians and underground?" I asked. "Do you all hide from the surface like normal people because the rain will make you melt like in those sci-fi movies?"

"No, Mr. Cruz, because it's safer."

"You're right. It is safer. No chance of an Up-Top death laser being fired from space and blowing you up."

They were not amused—maybe because, in truth, the Up-Toppers did have lasers that could blow up things on the surface of Earth from space.

"Agent Carter is waiting for you," one of the Martians said.

"Mr. Cruz," the one female Martian police officer added as she handed me a tablet. "This is actually a very serious meeting."

I had taken the tablet from her without even seeing the image on it first. I stared at it. Play time had been violently ended. I was staring at a dead Neil Cosmos floating in zero gravity in a corridor of what had to be the freighter. A freighter that was eight hours from Earth.

Surprise! I was given another pair of shades and I was in another holo-meeting. Carter was seated at his desk wherever he really was on Mars.

"Hi Carter."

"Cruz."

"The family says hello."

Carter looked like he'd been up for days with the weight of the world on his shoulders. He managed a small smile. "Tell them hello."

Carter visited Earth and met me with Seraff on my Blade Gunner case. Then he ran into my parents-in-law (actually I called Dot and she told them) and his nightmare began with everyone wanting to take pictures with a Martian. It was a funny thing. Earth people didn't like the Martian government, but everyone wanted to take a picture with a Martian—it was a cultural thing.

"Carter, what's going on? Why aren't you talking to Seraff?"

"You met with him?"

"Of course, I met with him. He's here on Earth about this thing. Why aren't you talking to him?"

"His government and mine have differing opinions on this space freighter."

"It depends on which Martian and which spaceman you actually speak to. What's going on? Your agent has already answered one question for me—Neil Cosmos, who my clients hired me to find out about, is dead."

"Cruz, the only reason I'm speaking with you is because you have access to the freighter when it lands. We'll hire you to act on our behalf."

"Carter! The zone where the space freighter is landing is controlled by the Martian Authority. Why do you need me, the Earther, to get access to it? You're a Martian policeman!"

"There are members of the Space, Lunar and Martian Authorities who have differing views than those of us who view this space freighter as a serious threat to mankind."

"Your faction tried to blow up the freighter in space?"

"We did."

"Your faction tried to nuke the artifact site two years ago."

"Seraff told you. Does that mean they already hired you to work on his faction's behalf?"

"Carter, I'm working for my client's faction. Seraff and the Founders he's working with, are convinced this space alien thing is a hoax. You and the Founders you're working with, are convinced it's real."

"What do you believe?"

"Whatever part that involves Omni and Vega is a hoax. I felt that from the beginning, but when I found out that the meteor was launched not at the Free Earther town, but for me specifically, that was all the proof I needed. But two opposites things can be true at the same time."

"Part of it is a hoax, but part of it is real."

"I don't believe in any space aliens, but I'm agnostic. I don't care either way, but I want to have confidence that the part I'm involved with is the hoax part, not any real extraterrestrial stuff with nasty space alien germs."

Carter chuckled. "It's about the germs with you then?"

"Why do believe this is real? You obviously want me to help you with the freighter. Tell me what you know, and you won't be breaching any confidentiality. Seraff and his Founders gave me the necessary secret clearances."

"Unbelievable. If the Founders Consortium found out that they did that, heads would roll."

"Not our heads and if everything is resolved satisfactorily, no one will care."

"Not if a bunch of those Founders are in on the hoax."

"Not if those Founders are arrested by Space Command and Martian Police on multiple counts of murder."

Carter nodded.

Carter was desperate. That's why I was there. They all wanted access to that freighter but couldn't, so they wanted to next best thing—someone who could and do their bidding. That was me.

"Unlike Earth, off-world has strict population density laws. We don't allow dense populations as is the norm on Earth—it's strictly prohibited. As a result, our terraforming divisions were never mothballed when our main colonies were created by the Founders. We always knew that in a generation or two we'd have to look to expand.

"We have constant recon crews out there—95% of them are unmanned—either remote controlled or autonomous robot recon-probes. It was over five years ago that one of those robot probes, working the Main Asteroid Belt, photographed an object on an asteroid that was believed not to be of natural origin. We've had mining posts based on Ceres and Vesta for years, so they took charge. A year later after multiple probes, it was concluded that not only was the object buried deep within the asteroid not natural, but was of extraterrestrial origin.

"You can imagine the scandal at the time within the intelligence and deep-space community. Off-worlders ironically are more skeptical of the notion of extraterrestrials than Earthers. Space myths were legion, from the Earth to the moon to Mars. I remember the stories of UFO hunters before the space station and lunar colonies. Giant crash landings of alien spaceships. We still bear the brunt of Earth's Alien Life cults' conspiracy claims. Secret bases on Cydonia colony, that we're actually space aliens ourselves, that we're controlled by space aliens from the Andromeda galaxy. On and on it goes, so regardless of what the four mining colonies said, we didn't believe their findings.

"Mars Authority tasked two separate bodies to take charge of the investigation themselves. One was headed by Neil Cosmos, who had been newly appointed as chief scientist on Jupiter Outpost. Based on his longstanding reputation as a by-the-book scientist without ever letting his own personal beliefs get in the way, he seemed the perfect choice. The other group was run by scientists from Lunar Colony.

"I wasn't involved yet, but knew of the situation. For some reason, communications to the investigation team were infrequent at best. The project was also classified to a level above most of the Mars Authority, including me, which was unprecedented. There also seemed to be two sets of stories coming out of Mars Authority. No one knew what was going on.

"About two years ago, there was a nuclear blast on the asteroid that was supposed to be the site of the space alien artifact discovery. Terraformers had even constructed semi-permanent domes for the science investigation team to work. Mars Authority incredibly said that there was no such nuclear blast and that statements to the fact were a hoax. The problem was many people saw the blast, including me.

"Later we learned that scientists reported that they had also found an organic substance not of Earth, Mars or human origin. A containment accident happened. Someone thought the proper response was to nuke the site to ensure nothing was left. Words like 'parasite' and 'contagion' began to be used. Apparently, the blast had the unanticipated result of exposing an even larger structure.

"The Neolith," I said.

"That's what they said. They excavated the entire structure and more organic material was found. The organic material was secretly loaded onto one space freighter."

"The *Nostradamus*."

"Yes. Not even its crew knew the cargo they were carrying due to security concerns. Neil Cosmos came on as a civilian under an alias, but another civilian came aboard too."

"A man name Orion."

"Yes."

"Seraff and company described him as a super-human."

"He's a soldier, but the problem is no one knows who brought him on the scene, how he got authorization to board the freighter, or who, if any, he's working for. He simply showed up as a civilian passenger.

"The freighter departed Jupiter Outpost, made the stop on Mars, where Orion got aboard, and then the craft departed. Soon after all communications stopped.

"Thirteen months away from Earth, a Martian military recon, rescue and salvage craft intercepted the *Nostradamus*. Standard military crew that also included an onboard psychologist. It was feared that Pandorum Syndrome might be at play since every escape pod had been launched from the freighter, though the entire crew was still aboard. All the freighter's cambots were inactive, all on-board cams were off, all comms dead."

"That syndrome is—?"

"Emotional distress, extreme paranoia, hysteria—all due to exposure to living in space. Often the subject has an uncontrollable urge to get off their spacecraft, even if it means self-spacing. In extreme cases they might try to space everyone on the craft, including themselves. It used to be believed that long-term living in space was the trigger for some, but we now know that is not the case. Some people can't be at sea, some people can't be underground, some people can't be in space.

"The captain of the Bradbury sent in its recon team to the *Nostradamus*. He and the navigator remained aboard, standard procedure. However, they also lost contact with the team initially. When the team appeared, they were outside of the *Nostradamus* returning to their craft. But they were in such a state of panic, performing an illegal spacewalk to get back to their craft, that had they missed any of the spacewalk holds, they would have been floating into the void of space, possibly to their death.

"The team said they saw the dead bodies of the crew, some apparently gutted, some covered in a luminescent goo. More importantly, they said they saw it—a humanoid space alien creature with tentacles flailing from its arms and head. They said it 'dematerialized' from one part of the freighter to another."

I couldn't believe what I was hearing.

"These are not Alien Life crazies, Cruz. These are military men and women—lifers, a few of them I know personally. The captain is a friend. If they say they saw an extraterrestrial, then they did, and it killed the *Nostradamus* crew."

"You believe this, but are allowing it to come to my planet."

"Cruz, we're the ones who tried to destroy it in space."

"Why would Mars Authority ignore you?"

"We've been overruled."

"Overruled? What does that even mean? We have bio-con laws on the books for a reason. Does this not fall under the category of 'possible xenomorph'?"

"We were overruled."

"What is it you expect me to do?"

"Get on the freighter, find it, and vaporize it."

"Vaporize? You want me to hunt down and kill a space alien."

"We want you to defend your life and deadly force is authorized."

"Is 'vaporize' the word you off-worlders use? The spacemen gave me weapons already."

"Martians have better toys."

"What? Wait, you mean literally vaporize it?"

"Not it, Cruz—him. We don't believe Orion got aboard and released the space alien. We believe that Orion is the space alien. Man and extraterrestrial have merged."

"You can't be serious."

"That's what we believe."

"Then what do you want me to vaporize him with? Carter, this is too dangerous. There will just be me and one other person to watch my back."

"That's all you'll need. My officers will equip you."

"Equip me?"

"Yes, Cruz. You'll get to carry a Martian vaporizer gun."

This was supposed to be a deadly serious situation—life and death, but I was biting my lip to contain my exuberance.

I had called Flash first, to confirm that he was going to pick me up. I returned to the Concrete Mama and was running around the apartment. The Hellspawn were minding Cruz Jr., and I know they were talking about me in Chinese.

"What is wrong with you?" Mr. Wan yelled at me. "You've been flying around in fancy Martian flying saucers so much its killed the few brain cells you had left."

I wanted to shoot that Martian vaporizer gun so bad, but I couldn't. I was fighting the compulsion with all my might. I was now running faster around the apartment.

Well, I didn't need to find ways to distract myself anymore. The news was on. There is an urban myth that bad things happened in threes. When I began my career as a detective, all of Metropolis could have fallen to the criminal gangs. It was the Mayor, City Hall and Up-Top versus the entire 500,000 Metro police force and the people. It was the gangs that could have taken over. That was my Police Watch Conspiracy Case.

Then there was my last Electric Sheep Massacre case where a psycho had figured out a way to actually kill people in virtual life. It showed that even though not everyone played virtual reality games or lived in virtual worlds, everyone was touched by it. Actually, I was the one who ended up shooting the psycho dead.

Once again I was in the center of another supercity panic: an epidemic of space alien sightings in the streets, seeing strange alien craft in the skies, and people claiming space aliens tried to abduct them from their apartments, offices and hovercars. On one hand, it could all be viewed as funny, but I knew it was a matter of time until someone was killed for real.

A ten-year old boy and his friends decided to dress up as space aliens and ran after an elderly couple to scare them. He did and the elderly man shot the boy in the head dead. I had forgotten that sightings of space aliens and ET spaceships in the sky all over Earth were still pouring in. For law enforcement, the first news of extraterrestrial proof was only a prelude to this. Some kid lying dead on the pavement with his brains all over the place. I didn't need to run around the apartment anymore. The joking around was permanently over for me until the case was done.

CHAPTER 55

Vega

The madness had to end and I was going to end it before someone else got killed. The only way to knock a media frenzy off the news was to replace it with another. Holly Live was there, as I knew she would be. Metropolis had a million reporters, but she was my go-to person, and I wanted to make sure that she'd still take my call in the future. Run-Time always told me I was a businessman now and not just a detective. He said, "The only time it's okay to burn bridges in business is when the person is dead and has no living friends, family, or relatives. That means you never do it." I had promised Ms. Live a story, but the spacemen took that away, and since she was in custody she lost out on the story she was already working on.

We were on the steps of City Hall this time, and no rain was going to spoil Vega's press conference marathon. No dead kid was going to spoil it for him either. He was all smiles, flanked again by business types and aides; this time both the Council of Corporation's President and the Mayor were there. The throng of media reporters were in front of them, police were managing the crowds of onlookers as best they could. Even Holly Live, who typically had the best spot, was fighting to get through to the front, along with everyone else.

I walked up to her and touched her shoulder. She turned around. "Stay close," I said.

As I walked up the stairs, reporters noticed me. I was after all the "famous" PI involved in humankind's proof of extraterrestrial life case. I was like Moses parting the Red Sea, for the smiling reporters let me pass through, as I climbed up the stairs to Vega. The Alien Evangelist was busy smiling and talking to his entourage, for the benefit of the cameras, but the Mayor and the CC President stared at me with looks of terror, beads of sweat rolling down their foreheads.

I arrived. Vega saw me and turned. "Congratulations," I said and shook his hand. Vega was surprised and, rare for him, didn't know what to say or do.

Holly Live joined us. "Mr. Cruz, the Metropolis P.I. of Liquid Cool, since you're a frequent flyer of flying saucers of late, are you a believer after all?"

"I've always said whether there are real ETs out there or not, I don't know and don't care. What I do care about is our friend here, Mr. Vega, and all his business buddies of the Earth, Lunar, and Martian persuasion.

"I imagine it all started with the Darwin Space Project. The politicians were about to shut it all down because in all these centuries no 'aliens' were ever found. You can only play the 'this planet could support life' card for so long and nobody cares about microbes or water molecules on another distant planet. If you don't got a real ET, you got nothing. So, the Darwin Space Project suddenly did it—they found ET's spaceship. The first phase of their plan."

Holly Live jumped in. "Mr. Cruz, Are you're saying the Neolith is a hoax?"

I ignored her as I leaned in to whisper to Vega. "Normally, I would say your going down for murder. But I wanted you to know that Merlin set you up. He let you catch him. His last words to me was 'I have to be the martyr, so you can have what you need.' I didn't realize it until it happened. He knew you and your friends were going to kill him. He did give me what I needed, and I bet those men on the freighter are dead too, but you don't care about any of that. But I know what you do care about."

"Mr. Cruz," Holly yelled, "are you saying that the Neolith Exhibit is a fake?"

I turned to her. "I'm sorry. I'm really sorry, but it is. I know how many people out there really do want to believe. They've been working on this scam for many years. The government threatened to cut back or eliminate their Darwin Space Project. If your entire life is searching for ETs in the universe and the only place that can employ you says we're getting out the search-for-ETs business, what do you do? Megacorps are interested in consumer space travel and mining. Organized crime would laugh in your face, if they didn't shoot you first for wasting their time. You come up with the greatest ET scam of all time. Sorry folks, you've been had. Vega and company almost succeeded in the greatest, and most lucrative, hoax in all of human history!"

I had that feeling of falling into a void again, but I wasn't shot by any Up-Top weapon this time. It was Vega. He had his hands around my neck and was quite successfully choking me to death. To their credit, Holly, the reporters, and the Mayor were trying to pry his hands off my neck and the businesspeople were trying to pull him away. His grip was so powerful that I was positive that he had bionic hands.

When I blasted him with my pop-gun, he flew back and plopped on the ground. People were screaming, media were filming, Vega was dead, and one of his aides was tackled before she could shoot me. I stood there rubbing my neck, swallowing and catching my breath. The wife and I wanted me back working the gritty, street scene of private investigation. Well, that's what I was doing.

PART NINE

I, Alien Hunter (The Real Deal)

CHAPTER 56

Flash

It was something that Carter had said about the discovery of the alien "artifact." He said there were so many different stories coming from Martian Authority that no one knew what was going on. I thought this was a battle between Earth and Up-Top. Then it was Space Authority versus Mars, then the Lunar Colony Founder versus the Mars Founders, then the pro-Omni Founders versus the anti-Omni Founders. The reason that this was all a mess was that there were so many factions at work with their own agendas, that everyone was getting in each other's way. It was further complicated by the fact that some people truly believed this was about real ETs.

Then there was the freighter. It was always about the freighter. Not Neil Cosmos, but everything on the freighter, especially the mercenary named Orion. I didn't know which faction Orion was in, and no else did either, that was the problem. If he was part of the hoax, he'd try to kill me for exposing it. I actually preferred that scenario, because I would know where I stood. If however Orion bought into the hoax and believed he was transporting or guarding a real ET for use by his bosses, then there would be no telling how this would go. People who believed a lie often will do anything to preserve the integrity of that lie. No truth was going to get in the way of their belief in the lie.

The Free Earthers had insisted on going with me. Mrs. Cosmos had yelled at me for almost half an hour, but I wouldn't budge. I didn't tell them all that I knew from Seraff and Carter, and there was no reason to. This was an extremely dangerous mission and I had long decided that the only person who would accompany me would be Flash—that's all I would risk. Also, I didn't want to spook this Orion. If he saw a lot of people, who knows how that would look to him. However, two men would be okay—even if we were armed to the hilt. I also didn't want to use my Martian vaporizer on a person, if I could avoid it—my gun glee had been buried. No more bodies.

Flash picked me up in a borrowed hovertaxi. It looked like work was still being done on the exterior, but it flew fine. All we needed was to get there. Flash was in full body-armor. He looked like Metro PD, except for their visored helmet. I was dressed as normal—well, I had my body-armor underneath. I was packing my pop-gun, omega-gun with the deadliest rounds I could load it with, and, of course, the Martian vaporizer gun.

The general public, thankfully, still had no idea about the *Nostradamus*. If they had found out, there weren't have been enough police on the planet to have kept them away from Metro International Spaceport. Flash parked and we walked that long walk to the main entrance of the Red Zone terminal.

The spaceport terminal looked like any other part of Metro International, only bigger. Multi-dome design, massive, moving walkways everywhere, hovercart kiosks, overhead displays showing not only arriving and departing space flights, but all domestic and international planetary flights. Beyond that were the eateries and stores. Again, Metro International both planetary and space terminals were their own city.

We came through the doors, and there was only silence. There was not a person in sight. No civilians, no domies (terminal sidewalk johnnies), no staff, nothing. Flash and I looked at each other. The Red Zone had been officially evacuated.

"Actually, this is better," I said to reassure Flash, though I didn't believe it myself.

The walk through the massive structure was spooky. It was quiet and devoid of all life except for two people. We didn't even need the pass that Mr. Deimos had given me because all gates, barriers, and doors opened automatically for us. What was even spookier was the only arriving flight on all the display boards was the *Nostradamus*. The Martians were not even allowing anything else to land.

"Flash, are we sure about continuing with this?"

"No, but a promise is a promise."

I had never seen a spacecraft of any kind land from space up-close. The one time I boarded one, it was from the comfort of a boarding tube. Flash and I waited at the closest observation bay windows near the direct departure corridor. This whole area would normally be restricted until the craft had landed, and gone through all its customs, biological and radioactivity contamination checks.

"Don't we need some kind of protection—?" I began to ask aloud.

"Cruz." Flash was pointing. We hadn't seen them before with the dim light but there were two bio-suits neatly folded on the ground and respirator masks on top of them. "Cruz, this is creepy. Are they watching us?"

"Assume that a lot of people are. We wanted to go on the freighter. They're allowing us to go on the freighter."

"You said that the space alien discovery was a hoax."

"It was. They tried to kill me."

"Yeah, but what if not all of it was a hoax."

"Are you backing out, Flash?"

"Cruz, I've never been so scared in my life. I've taken on real-life gangsters, you've seen me, but real space aliens."

"There are no space aliens on the freighter."

"How do you know?"

"The Martians told me."

Flash was not satisfied with my answer, and what I said wasn't exactly the truth, but I had to calm him down, both of us down. He was on the edge. If a little mouse jumped out from the corner and yelled "Boo!" Flash would have been a streak of dust out of the Spaceport on foot.

I hadn't told any of them about what I already knew about the death of Neil Cosmos and the *Nostradamus* crew. Again, there was no reason to. I needed Flash to take charge of those bodies, while I dealt with Orion. That was the plan, Flash just didn't know it yet. He was stressed out enough at the moment.

We were in our thin body suits and wearing the respirators, which weren't the full helmet—only to cover the eyes, nose and mouth. Flash pointed to our ears and I wish he hadn't. We both had seen enough bad sci-fi movies where the alien organism crawls down someone's ear canals.

"Why did you put that image in my mind?" I yelled.

"Sorry."

"There is no alien, but now I have an uncontrollable urge to cover my ears with something."

"Sorry."

The automatic voice began the countdown. We looked up and so the *Nostradamus* high in the sky. The rain was only a misty drizzle as the space freighter grew larger in its descent. I was always amazed that something so huge seemingly floated down without a sound. It touched down on its landing pad, and the automatic grapplers locked on its landing struts, the automatic corridor connected to its airlock exit, and robotic arms extended from the ground to begin their scans and maintenance.

After ten minutes, we were given the "all clear," and the corridor lights changed from red to green. We could now leave the observation bay area for the corridors. We gave each other a final look. I opened the door and went first.

"What's that?" he asked.

I knew Flash wouldn't miss seeing my Martian vaporizer in my hand.

"Nothing." I placed it in the outside pocket of my coat. It was a good reminder. If I wanted to end this situation with bringing Orion alive without a shot, it probably would be a good idea for him not to see my Martian death ray gun in my hand.

From the beginning of the corridor to the *Nostradamus* airlock entrance was not far at all, but I seemed as if we were marching to Outer Mongolia. We may not have been thinking about space aliens burying into our eardrums anymore, but there was something very ominous about the *Nostradamus* when we reached it. I had never believed in inanimate objects having the stench of death, but that's what I felt. Even I had a difficult time moving forward, but I did.

Sometimes automation can be demonic. The door automatically opened and both Flash and I almost had heartaches. Our delicate minds thought "the alien" opened it from inside and not the automatic programming of the craft.

"I can't take much more of this," Flash said.

We collected ourselves and began the walk forward. I took a deep breath and found some bravery within, because I knew what we might be seeing very soon—Flash didn't.

The craft's bridge was where we were going. We reached it and everything was on as normal but there wasn't a soul around. Flash was a very good mechanic and I, of course, had been the hovercar restorer so we both could figure out the controls on any spacecraft—even Martian. We both thought the same thing and walked to the communication stations.

"Cruz, what's that?"

The captain's comm panel and the separate communications post were covered in amber gel. The controls looked like they were corroded.

"Forget it. We need to find the people." I was already exiting the bridge when I noticed I was alone. I turned around. "Flash, what are you doing?"

"There's acid spit on the comms."

"That isn't acid spit. Don't let your imagination control you."

"What is it then? It's burned out the circuits."

"There is no such thing as alien acid spit. Flash, pull yourself together. We're the only two on-board."

"Cruz, maybe you were right—"

"No Flash, you're not backing out now. We're here now."

We continued down a corridor with me in the lead. As a freighter, the *Nostradamus* wasn't only a huge craft, but there were so many places to hide; there was no way only two people could do a proper search.

"We're going back," I said to Flash.

"Why?"

"We're going to secure the bridge and let robots do the searching for us. We don't need the comms because we have our mobiles."

For the first time, I saw the real Flash. He smiled. "Good plan, Cruz."

We returned to the bridge, and I walked to the captain's station. First, I secured all the doors, including the airlock. No one else could get on or off the craft.

"Robots or cams?" I asked.

"Robots," Flash answered.

Flash tried to find any robots on the craft that we could activate. I tried to do the same with the craft's cameras. We found them listed in the *Nostradamus's* equipment directory, but none could be activated.

"Do you hear something?" Flash asked.

We listened for a while and it was clear there were voices coming from somewhere in the freighter. Flash had a deer-in-the-headlights look.

"We have no choice, Flash."

"No! I'm not leaving this room. It's a trap."

"Whether it is or isn't, we're going. You're armed, and I'm armed."

"But can we spit acid?"

"Stop that. There's no such thing. You're going to give me and you a heart attack. We're men! We're strong! We're brave!"

Flash wasn't happy. He wanted to run again—and I wanted to follow.

We slowly moved down the corridor again. Flash pointed his mini-machine-gun. I had my Martian vaporizer in hand—my very sweaty hands.

"I'm supposed to be a street detective," I said, "not a military soldier."

"I'm a hovertaxi driver," Flash said. "That's not a soldier either. Why are we here?!"

The hallway we had been moving down was along the starboard side of the *Nostradamus's* main cargo holds. Once we got close, we realized that the voices were hearing were not live; it was the news.

I peeked into the window of a door. There was a TV inside on, lying on the ground flat. It was the broadcast of me! I turned, and Flash was watching me.

"I'm going in—slow."

"Do you see anyone?"

"No."

"I'm telling you, it's a trap. Turn the TV on to bring the stupid detective and taxidriver to the cargo hold to kill them."

"Flash, all I'm going to do is open the door, look in and see what I see."

"Make sure to look up, too."

I was about to reach for the door when it began to open. Flash yelled as he started shooting. I had to dive for cover.

"Flash! Stop shooting!"

Flash let his finger off the trigger. I had been on my stomach and turned over to look at him. I checked myself and I wasn't shot anywhere.

"Sorry."

"Flash! Lower that machine-gun, and don't fire it again!"

"Sorry. The door opened."

"What if it was a member of the crew? What if it was Neil?"

"Oh no! I could have killed them."

"Yes, you could have." I stood and walked to the door. It automatically opened again. "I could have been killed because of an automatic door opener!"

I had originally thought the cargo hold was empty. The *Nostradamus* had three dozen of them on the craft, but this one wasn't the largest. I entered, and there was the TV on the floor, but in the far corner was a large object under a tarp tied to the floor. What protruded from underneath the tarp looked like rock.

"Is that meteor rock?" Flash was standing next to me.

"I don't know." I had almost forgotten what had piqued my interest in the first place about the TV broadcast. I walked to it.

There I was on TV blowing the entire Neolith scam, then Vega trying to strangle me (wife not happy), me blowing Vega away (wife happy), and some after-incident commentary. The reporters were interviewing me:

"This scam was not Vega alone," I had said. "Regrettably, it also involved the business tycoon, Mr. Omni, of Lunar Colony, and involves many others in the business and governments of Earth, Lunar Colony, and Mars. The Neolith, the alien artifact, is a fake and has been part of a long series of manufactured events to get us to culmination of the scam—the Neolith Exhibit Park. Now we know how they were able to build the park structure so fast."

Flash slowly tapped my shoulder, but I'd already seen him. At the very end of the cargo hold, in the dim light, was a man, standing. He was too far away to make him out clearly but I was almost positive it was Orion.

"Omni!" he yelled.

"Omni?" I asked. "Are you crew or one of the passengers?"

"Omni!" he yelled louder.

"Sir, we don't understand. Have you seen the other crew and passengers?"

"They're dead!" At that moment, Flash and I both glanced at the door. "Omni will die too."

I looked at him. "Why does Omni have to die? Where are the other crew and passengers?"

The man crouched down to the ground. As we stared at him, his body seemed to grow smaller and smaller. There was nothing but a mark on the ground.

"I'm done, Cruz! I'm out of here right now!"

"Don't run that way!" I ran to the spot and stopped.

"Cruz, what is that?" Flash was next to me again pointing to the spot with his mini-machine-gun. "That's alien spit! He spit on the floor and crawled through. That man is an alien!"

Flash was more right that he knew. Carter was right; Orion was the alien.

"Oh my God!" I yelled. "We can't let him off this craft."

"He's off the craft! He spit his way through."

"Flash, call the police! All of them! Metro, then get them to call the Up-Top ones!

I ran to the object in the corner. It was something I shouldn't have done, but I yanked the tarp off the object. I found the crew and Neil Cosmos.

"No!" Flash was dialing the police when he dropped his mobile to the ground and ran to the object, but I held him back. Honestly, I couldn't explain what it was—a giant clear cylindrical chamber filled with solutions and the floating dead bodies of the *Nostradamus* crew and Neil Cosmos—in something that looked it was supposed to be a spaceship buried in a flaky red giant meteor. I didn't know what the hell it was supposed to be. However, I did know what it was—a sick killer's grave for his victims.

"Flash, do you want me to get him?"

Flash angry and crying. "Yes!"

"Then you have to hold the fort until the police get here. They're probably already storming the Spaceport. I have to get away before they get here. I know where he's going.

"Go!"

I couldn't take the chance that I'd run out of the freighter into the hands of the police. Eleven seconds later, an army of Metro heavy police troopers burst into the cargo hold. But I had already escaped the exact same way that Orion got out.

CHAPTER 57

Alien Man

I had never taken my Sidewalk Johnny Brigade network off the streets. All I did was expand the people they were looking for. Mr. Omni said he never set foot on Earth. I had met many a crook that said one thing to your face, when you knew it was only a mind-fake. If they said they didn't carry a gun, it meant they carried three. I had the johnnies looking for Omni and they never saw him, but had spotted his robot. I also found out that one of Omni's hundreds of companies owned the hoverhotel Vega lived in.

I stood there in the hallway of the penthouse floor of the hoverhotel. Shakespeare the robot had been ripped to shreds and pieces of him were strewn everywhere. If a mouse came across the cat, now dead, that could have killed him, did that mouse really think it had any chance against the thing that killed the cat? I stood there for what seemed to be an eternity. I looked at my Martian vaporizer gun in hand. Time to go to work.

The main door had been knocked off its hinges, and that door was as thick as a bank vault. I stepped inside.

Orion casually sat on the living room couch, his clothes wet, his arms stretched out across the couch, like he was watching the game on TV, but the TV wasn't on. What was unnerving was that it looked like someone threw up black vomit all over his body, but as I stared at him I realized they were actually black worm-like tentacles coming out of his arms, neck, and who knows where else. They were just hanging around him, and he seemed as comfortable as a slug in a shell.

"Where's Omni?" I asked.

Orion watched me. I had put my Martian gun in pocket, so he didn't see it, and I put my hands on the sides of my hips.

"He's here," he replied. "I'm resting."

With his mess of tentacles, I could see why. "Where you from soldier?"

Life seemed to come to his dead eyes.

Earth had cyborgs, Up-Top had genetically modified humans. Here I stood, calmly, with a tentacled human.

"I—I'm from planet—Paragon."

"How do you like Earth?"

"I want to go home."

"Home? Where's your mom and dad? They were born on Earth."

He began to cry. "You're trying to confuse me. I am from the Planet Paragon, and I was sent here to conquer the planet to prepare it for my brethren."

"What about your Earth mom and dad, soldier? They'll get killed."

"Stop talking," he cried.

"We can't let anyone hurt your Earth mom and dad. I can't let you hurt them either."

I revealed my gun. He flashed a smile. "You can't kill me, Earthman."

"Lots of people have said that to me. Super-cyborgs. Shadow megacorps. Your friend Ichi Jumper said that too. He's a crispy critter deader than dead in a grave. But let's just stop all the killing. I'm tired of it. I got to get home to the wife and son for dinner. Why don't you stop it, too."

"Omni lied to me. He is not from Planet Paragon at all. He is human. He is the great liar. You all are."

"I bet your Earth mom and dad would want to see you," I said. "I bet they haven't seen you in ages. Don't you want to see them too?"

He began crying again. "Stop talking. I can't think. I—I can't." He held his head.

"We're going to help you, Orion. Everyone wants to help you. I'm putting away my gun because I think we can end this without any more killing." I put my omega-gun in my pocket. "You get to go home and so do I."

His face went blank. "You shouldn't have done that. You Earthlings are so weak. It's why Paragon will conquer this planet as easily as it has so many others."

He moved so fast, charging me with his tentacles whipping around. I remember what Carter said about the military crew. They said he "dematerialized" from one place to another. Did I believe it? Was such a thing remotely possible? There was no way I was going to be unarmed with this guy. My other hand behind my back never let go of my Martian vaporizer on loan. The only decision I had to make was to kill him or almost kill him, but he was getting shot. There was no two ways about it. I remembered what he did to Neil Cosmos, the *Nostradamus* crew, what he did to Shakespeare the Robot. No more games.

The Martian gun did what its name said it would do: Orion was vaporized. There was no kick to the weapon. It just turned him to dust.

I held it firm as I walked to the vid-phone and called the police, then quietly waited.

CHAPTER 58

Omni

Another series of events that lead to murder and mayhem by people only obsessed with money and power. The crooks always tried to dress up their scams and crimes in new clothes, but it was always the same. Back before history there were the caveman detectives after them, and here I was in the future dealing with them.

"They volunteered for the mission." Omni was now staring at me on the TV viewscreen. "They all volunteered—the crew, that is. Their families and their offspring in perpetuity would become adopted members of the Founders."

The silence of Vega's apartment had been broken by the TV turning on itself and there he was.

"Did Neil Cosmos volunteer? Did Merlin volunteer?" I asked.

"Two people. Two homicides is all you have. This is a solar system of tens of billions and you talk to me about two people."

"Orion?"

"He was insane—the perfect soldier for our purposes. Yet, he was also a volunteer."

"What now Mr. Omni?"

"You have ruined a mission that took twenty years to assemble."

"Oh, that long. Can't say that I'll lose any sleep over ruining your scam, because with all your money, supposed power, and false superiority, you're just a little scummy crook like the ones on the streets of Metropolis."

"I'm going to kill you, Mr. Cruz."

"How? Shakespeare, your robot is dead in a million pieces in the hallway."

"You must know by now that I own the hoverhotel you're standing on. What if I was to switch off the hoverengines?"

"I don't know."

"I'll give you a chance to run to save your life. Let's see how lucky a detective you really are."

"Really?"

"I'll count to ten."

"Okay, you do that. Where are you right now by the way?"

"I am in place off-world that neither you nor the authorities will ever find me."

"Or you're hiding in this apartment somewhere. I'll wait for the police right here, but feel free to flip that switch to send me crashing to the surface dead, if you like."

"Ten-nine-eight—"

"Keep counting. I bet I even know where you're hiding, but I'll wait for the police."

"Seven-six-five-four-three-two-one. Time to die, Mr. Cruz."

The screen went black.

"Yeah, that's what I figured," I said.

CHAPTER 59

Crux

I learned that when I snuck out the *Nostradamus,* that the Metro PD were so disturbed by the scene and a possible real space alien running around in the supercity that Flash and every last police trooper on the scene was put in full quarantine at a secret CDC site. Immediately, there was an all-points put out on me and Orion, and Metro PD deputized every fireperson, EMT, first-responder, retired law enforcement, and anyone else they could grab to find us. It was truly the largest dragnet in Earth history.

My call to police allowed the supercity to breathe a sigh of relief. The hoverhotel was quarantined, and so were all the tenants, and me. However, I was the only one who knew all the CDC personnel by sight and on a first name basis. As a recovering germophobe I had taken the liberty to use their site many times. They were not happy to see me.

"I get a full decon like normal, but this time it's courtesy of the Metro PD," I told the CDC guys with a smile.

I also told Metro PD that I knew somewhere in the apartment Mr. Omni was hiding; Orion didn't go there for no reason. I put two and two together: Orion was wet—and I don't think it was perspiration from tangling with Shakespeare—and Mr. Orion liked swimming in those showing-too-much trunks of his. The police found him. The apartment had a large aquarium tank in the walls visible from the master bedroom. Orion was wet because he had been trying to reach through the pipes to get Omni—the man who turned him into an alien. They found Omni at the bottom of the tank hiding, wearing a cloaking costume to be virtually invisible in the water. Omni was trying to scare me out of the hoverhotel because it was also a working spacecraft, and he planned to use it to fly it into space to escape.

I spent a week in quarantine until all the powers-that-be confirmed that it was all a hoax and not real-life extraterrestrials. The Neolith Exhibit Park was gone as quickly as it appeared, and many scientists, businessmen, and politicians decided to leave Earth to live off-world for an indefinite period of time. I knew everyone was involved, knowingly or unknowingly, in the scandal, but only Vega and Omni would take the fall.

Later, I learned how Vega already knew me, and it wasn't because he remembered me as a kid when he scratched my Pop's hovercar. He was the one who had set the psycho Ichi Jumper after me in my last Electric Sheep Massacre Case. Vega was the buyer for The Geek and Mad Scientist's "Free Energy" module, on behalf of Omni. I read Omni's past writings and plans thanks to PJ who found them through her Net research. Omni had big legitimate plans. He wanted to create New Jupiter—a space station planet larger than Earth itself. Mars was never going to fund such a project, so he needed the money and energy sources. I ended up taking away both from him with two cases. With his power, I expected Omni to be charged but never serve any time; though, there was justice—he too died in custody from "natural causes" on the way back to Lunar Colony. I imagined there would be a lot of accidents and suicides to come. Earth organized crime could never compete with those Up-Top Founders.

I had planned to attend Neil Cosmos's funeral, but it happened while I was in quarantine. I did send my condolences anyway. I never heard back from the Free Earthers, but Flash told me they all appreciated the gesture and did thank me for sticking on the case to the end.

Apparently, Run-Time was the only Metropolis businessman who did *not* invest heavily in the Neolith Project and as such would not be going bankrupt or bought out by other competitors. Run-Time also signed the deal to expand Let It Ride Up-Top. As a thank you, Dot and I became Let It Ride's first lifetime Andromeda members—any and all services for free for the rest of our lives.

I was back at Metro Spaceport waiting. The shuttle had landed, and there was only one passenger departing. It was Crux, the detective. I had never forgotten him and made sure that in all the madness he was fine. He was being held by the pro-Omni Space Authority; now that they were being demoted, fired, resigning or disappearing; he was found in the Up-Top prison system and released. I told his wife that I'd personally pick him up and deliver him home.

We sat in the Pony coasting in the sky-traffic. He wasn't too talkative and visibly he had lost a lot of weight.

"Do you know I changed my name to Crux so people looking for you in the detective directory might mistake me for you," he said.

"I know. That's how I found you. There was a guy named C-R-U-Y but I didn't know how to pronounce that, so I skipped him and went to you."

Crux laughed. "My rotten luck."

It wasn't my fault, but I felt bad. Crux was a different man, a damaged man. I didn't know what they did to him in custody, all the way up there off the planet. I felt bad.

"I'll never go into space ever again," he said. "Being in a Z-gravity cell, all day and night, no privacy ever, is not any kind of picnic. You're never touching the ground. You float around and it never stops. Going to the bathroom in Z-gravity is an endless joke on the comedy shows, but not so when it's real and it's you. You can never crawl away into a corner. I would have said anything, signed anything for a corner. It's funny the simple things you take for granted—being able to crawl into a corner for comfort. The Up-Toppers can keep space. I'm never going up there again. I don't know what I would have done, if you hadn't gotten me out of there." He was wiping the tears streaming down his face.

"What are your plans now? Besides no more investigating meteors from space."

I made him smile again. "I had a lot of time to think. I'm too borderline criminal to do this detective stuff anymore. They may have illegally held me, but they picked me up on a legitimate thing—illegally trying to hack into someone's file. It's time to listen to the wife. Something nice and quiet. Maybe I'll become a detective thriller writer, so I get to stay home. With all the dirt I know in this city, they'll pay me money not to write books. I'll do that."

"Just don't make any of the characters a composite of me," I said. "I'm franchised enough."

"You never know."

We got to his apartment complex. There waiting on the massive steps in the rain was his wife, surrounded by his nine kids. His eyes were tearing up again.

"I appreciate the ride, Cruz." He shook my hand.

"Any time."

He hopped out and his children ran to him. He hugged them all, reached his wife and gave her a big kiss, then a hug. Mrs. Crux gave me a wave. A happy ending to an unhappy case—not too bad. Now it was my turn to get back home to my family, until the next case.

Thank you for reading!

Dear Reader,

I hope you enjoyed my **Liquid Cool** cyberpunk detective novel, *I, Alien Hunter*.

Can You Write Me a Review?

If you enjoyed *I, Alien Hunter (Liquid Cool, Book 5)*, I'd greatly appreciate an honest review on one or more of the following sites:

Reviews are the best way for readers to discover good books. My writer's motto is simple: "Readers Rule!" Thanks so much.

Always writing,

Austin Dragon

CONTINUE THE ADVENTURE

Get Your Next *Liquid Cool* Books!

- ***These Mean Streets, Darkly*** *(Liquid Cool Prequel Short)*
- ***Liquid Cool*** *(Liquid Cool: The Cyberpunk Detective Series, Book 1)*
- ***Blade Gunner*** *(Liquid Cool, Book 2)*
- ***NeuroDancer*** *(Liquid Cool, Book 3)*
- ***The Electric Sheep Massacre*** *(Liquid Cool, Book 4)*
- ***I, Alien Hunter*** *(Liquid Cool, Book 5)*
- ***A.I. Confidential*** *(Liquid Cool, Book 6)*

- ***Liquid Cool Box Set*** *(Liquid Cool Prequel and Books 1-3)*
- ***Liquid Cool Box Set 2*** *(Liquid Cool: Books 4-6)*

Also by Austin Dragon

See all my books in science fiction, horror, and fantasy at: http://www.austindragon.com/books

ABOUT THE AUTHOR

Austin Dragon is the author of the ***After Eden Series***, including the mini-series, ***After Eden: Tek-Fall***, the classic ***Sleepy Hollow Horrors***, the new epic fantasy adventure ***Fabled Quest Chronicles***, and the cyberpunk detective series, ***Liquid Cool***. He is a native New Yorker, but has called Los Angeles, California home for the last twenty years. Words to describe him, in no particular order: U.S. Army, English teacher, one-time resident of Paris, political junkie, movie buff, Fortune 500 corporate recruiter, renaissance man, dreamer.

He is currently working on new books and series in science fiction, fantasy, and classic horror!

Connect with Austin on social media at:

Website and blog: http://www.austindragon.com

Twitter: https://twitter.com/Austin_Dragon

Pinterest: http://www.pinterest.com/austindragon

Google+: https://google.com/+AustinDragonAuthor

Goodreads: https://www.goodreads.com/ADragon

Other books by Austin:
See all my books at: **http://www.austindragon.com/books**